THE PIRLIE PIG

Matt and Lily Barclay live in the Fife village of Pennyglen, with their children Janet, Meg, Ellen and Willie, whilst the local 'big house', Pitlady, is home to Mr and Mrs Grierson and their son Colin. Before her marriage Lily had been lady's maid to Mrs Grierson's sister Lucille, who now lived in America. As the children grow older, Colin and Willie become friends, and the lives of the two families become linked once again. The Barclay girls are beginning to spread their wings and look for employment, when Meg overhears something which changes her life...

THE PIRLIE PIG

The Pirlie Pig

by

Anne Forsyth

Magna Large Print Books
Long Preston, North Yorkshire,
BD23 4ND, England.

British Library Cataloguing in Publication Data.

Forsyth, Anne
    The pirlie pig.

    A catalogue record of this book is
    available from the British Library

    ISBN   0-7505-2376-X

First published in Great Britain by D. C. Thomson

Published in Large Print 2005 by arrangement with
Dorian Literary Agency

Magna Large Print is an imprint of Library Magna Books Ltd.

Printed and bound in Great Britain by
T.J. (International) Ltd., Cornwall, PL28 8RW

Chapter One

'That's me finished with school for ever!' Janet Barclay said joyfully. She danced a few steps as the girls made their way home along the lane that led from Pennyglen's school.

'What *are* you doing?' Her younger sister, Meg, watched in astonishment as Janet paused at the low bridge that crossed the burn.

'I'm done with these! I've left school. I'm grown up now!' Janet crowed, as she tore up her school jotters.

She scattered the bits into the water like confetti. Pages of copperplate handwriting floated away. A geometry theorem she'd never been able to prove got stuck among the weeds.

The hard cover of her grammar book became lodged under a stone, and there it stayed until it was chewed by a passing water rat.

'How *could* you?' Meg was rather shocked.

'No more Miss Macintosh. No more old Soutar and his tawse. No more reading and composition. No more geometry!'

Janet picked a willow twig and flicked at the wayside grasses.

'But leaving school, going to work in the mill, day after day. It'll be so dreary,' Meg protested.

'I'll be grown up,' Janet said. 'I'll be bringing in a wage. First money I'll save, I'm going to buy one of those blouses in shantung silk. Or maybe a sunshade – I saw them in one of the shops in Cupar, only three and eleven.'

Janet loved clothes – she was quick to learn and, even at fourteen, could use the Singer sewing machine that belonged to Lily, the girls' mother.

She enjoyed reading about fashion, and pored over the descriptions of social events reported in the local paper.

Meg leaned over the parapet of the bridge, her eyes thoughtful.

'Well, it wouldn't suit me, working in the mill. I want something better than that.'

'Oh, you'll go into the mill like the rest of us,' Janet said.

'No, I won't.' Meg was quietly determined. 'I don't know what I'm going to do yet. I might be a business lady. I might go to Skerry's and learn to type. I want to be rich,' she added.

Janet laughed.

'You and your fancy ideas,' she said, tearing up another page of sums.

'Wait for me, oh wait for me!' Ellen, the youngest of the sisters, caught up with them, her round face rosy with the heat of the day.

At nine years old, Ellen was everyone's favourite. Gentle, sunny-tempered, with a passion for animals, Ellen would often bring home a stray kitten or a puppy, and it was she who made certain the birds were fed in winter.

Now, she skipped along the road beside her sisters. But the two elder girls didn't pay much attention to her chatter.

Janet was thinking about Monday, when she would start work in the flax mill in the village.

Meg was miles and years away – grown up, beautifully dressed, running a shop maybe, or a business, always assured, always elegant. A very different Meg from the twelve-year-old in her serge skirt and sensible boots.

At home, the girls' mother, Lily, put down the heavy flat iron and wiped her hand across her brow. It was hot for the end of June, even in the big, airy kitchen.

As she waited for the iron to heat on the range, her glance fell on the money box on the mantelpiece.

'There you are,' Lily's mother had told her when she'd left home to go into service all those years ago. 'That's a pirlie pig.'

Lily had smiled – she'd never heard the term before.

'A pirlie pig!' she'd echoed.

'It's for your spare pennies,' her mother

9

had said. 'It'll give you a bit of independence.

'Get into the habit of putting spare coins in the pig – they'll soon mount up, and then you'll always have something to spend on extras, or to help you out when you need it most...'

Lily had smiled at the time, but often, during her years in service, she'd been thankful for her mother's gift. Thanks to the pirlie pig, there was always money to buy a special present, or to spend on a new ribbon.

Now, she remembered the pretty teapot she'd seen in Pirie's on her last trip to St Andrews.

She reached up and shook the pig. Yes, it rattled in a very satisfactory way. There would be plenty there to buy the teapot.

Then she stopped. Janet was leaving school – she should have a new dress for church on Sundays. Lily had seen a pretty blue sprigged cotton – it would suit Janet, with her fair curls and fresh complexion. The teapot could wait.

She lifted the iron and smoothed out the bolster pillow slips.

But would it be fair to buy the material for Janet's dress? It was important to treat all the girls the same, not favouring one above the other.

They were all so different, she thought.

Well, Meg *was* different.

Hastily, she pushed the thought away. She's the same as the rest, she told herself sternly. Don't you ever go thinking that way...

Janet was easy-going, even-tempered and very practical. And Ellen – Lily's face softened as she thought of Ellen.

'She's still such a bairn,' she murmured fondly.

But Meg – sometimes she had to stop herself being impatient with Meg. She was such an impulsive, generous girl, but now and then her temper would flare up. She could be sharp, too...

Lily tossed a shirt into the mending basket. 'Out at the elbow – what does he do with them?' She tutted. Willie was a real boy, no doubt about that.

She smiled, thinking of her son. He was out all the time – usually up at the Big House to see the horses. Well, he'd come to no harm at Pitlady.

She heard footsteps outside, and then the girls were at the kitchen door.

'I'm starving!' Janet put her piece box down on the draining board.

'You'll get your tea when your father comes in.' Lily was a good cook, and the girls sniffed appreciatively as they smelled the rabbit stew bubbling on the hob.

'You can have a glass of milk while you

wait,' she said.

Janet dipped a glass into the milk pitcher in the pantry, set high on a shelf to keep it out of the way of the family cat. She replaced the gauze cover and drained the glass.

'Can I help?' she asked, noticing that her mother looked hot and a little tired.

Lily smiled. She hung the newly ironed garments on the pulley and turned to her daughter.

'You'll be at work soon enough. Out you go and enjoy the sunshine while you can.

'And mind your wee brother or he'll be hanging on the back of the baker's cart again! If I've told him once, I've told him fifty times.'

Outdoors in the sunshine, the girls sat down on the steps that led from the street to their front door.

They liked to sit there and watch the people and the carts that passed along Pennyglen's Main Street. And it was fun to slide down the iron hand rail at one side of the steps. Not that Janet would do that any more – not now she was grown up.

'There he is!'

Willie, their brother, was paddling in the drain that ran down the middle of the street.

'Mother'll skelp him,' Janet said, making no effort to restrain him.

'Come back here!' Meg called. But Willie

just put out his tongue and ran away.

'Oh, leave him alone!' Janet said dreamily. Nothing could spoil today.

Janet and Meg knew everyone in the little village of Pennyglen, which was set among the rolling farmlands of the Howe of Fife. They knew the mill girls who came along the road, laughing and singing, when the whistle went for stopping time; they knew the old women who sat enjoying a gossip on their doorsteps; they knew – at a distance – the folk who lived in Pitlady, the Big House.

'Oh, look!' Meg said suddenly, pointing.

A figure on a bicycle swerved from one side of the road to the other. He missed the hens clucking in front of the old cottage at the end of the road, and flew past old Annie, who was filling a bucket at the pump.

Meg couldn't see who the cyclist was – he wore goggles and his cap was turned back to front. But as he reached the girls, he took one hand off the handlebars and waved at them.

'It's Colin!' Willie stopped throwing chuckie stones and ran across the road.

The cyclist braked and took off his goggles. 'Hello,' Meg said, a little shyly. She recognised him now – she'd often seen Colin Grierson, the son of the Big House, around the village.

He grinned at Meg and Janet.

'You've not been up to the stables for a

13

day or two,' he greeted Willie.

'How's Bess and Prince?' Willie asked eagerly.

'They're all right.' Colin, from the height of his fifteen years, looked down on ten-year-old Willie, but he spoke to him as if they were the same age.

'He's got a way with horses, this brother of yours,' Colin told the girls. 'It's the way he talks to them.'

Suddenly Meg felt a little envious of Willie – though she wouldn't admit to the feeling. Here was her wee brother allowed into the Pitlady stables whenever he liked, while she would have loved the chance, but had never been given the opportunity.

She'd heard there were hothouses with grapes and peaches at the Big House, and rose gardens. She longed to see the gardens, and the house, too – the fine furniture and the pictures, and the library. Oh, how Meg wished she could look at all those books!

'I'm very fond of horses myself,' she said casually.

'No, you're not. You're terrified of them.' Janet was astonished. Meg always gave the milkman's horse a wide berth – she was scared of its huge mouth and enormous teeth.

Meg kicked her sister on the shin.

'Ouch! You didn't need to do that.' Janet glared at her.

Colin grinned.

'Well, you come, too – next time Willie's up at the stables.'

'Any day,' Meg said eagerly. 'I'm finished with the school – for the summer anyway – so I've plenty of time.'

'We'll see you then.' Colin adjusted the goggles and began weaving his way a little unsteadily back up the street.

'I wish I had a bicycle,' Willie said.

'They're very expensive,' Janet told him. 'The cheapest's about six or seven pounds.'

'Well, maybe I'll save up.' Willie was always optimistic.

Meg said nothing. She *would* go to the Big House, she promised herself. She was afraid of horses – Janet had been right – but if the way into the Big House lay through the stables, then she would have to steel herself.

'Your father's back,' Lily called.

The three girls and Willie went into the house, where their father, Matt, was taking off his boots and settling with a sigh into the rocking chair by the fireside.

'Now sit in.' Lily ladled out the stew and brought the vegetables to the table.

'I don't like rabbit stew very much.' Meg sniffed.

'Then you'll have to do without.' Lily was used to Meg's finicky ways and took no notice.

Meg said no more, but Lily noticed with

amusement that she cleared her plate, as did the others.

'What's for pudding?' Willie asked.

'Rhubarb, out of the garden,' Lily said proudly. Matt was no gardener, but she loved working in her flower and vegetable patch. Every summer the little garden was a riot of annuals.

Lily was proud of her vegetables, too, and soon it would be time to lift the first shaw of new potatoes. She might just put an entry into the Cupar Flower Show this year, she thought – by mid-August the dahlias and phlox would be at their best.

Janet talked happily about her day, about the excitement of starting work on Monday.

Matt, who'd worked in the mill ever since he and Lily settled in Pennyglen, exchanged glances with his wife. Both knew the work was hard; you were among the stour all day and the noise of the frames was deafening.

The hours were long. Oh, there was a wage at the end of the week, but even so, a girl didn't earn that much. Matt couldn't help feeling that Janet would be less enthusiastic after a week or two.

Lily sighed. If only there was more work for a girl as skilled with her hands as Janet. But the mill was steady work, and Lily's family had always worked there.

Anyway, Janet would have a fine new dress for the kirk on Sundays – and maybe one day there would be a young man.

There was time enough for that, Lily chided herself. Janet was only fourteen.

She rose and shook the pirlie pig.

'There's enough here for a new dress. I'll buy the material and make it up as a present for you,' she told Janet.

Janet's face glowed.

'Oh, Mother, thank you.' She beamed.

'What about me?' Meg put down her spoon.

'You'll get something, too,' her mother said. 'But Janet's just left the school. It's a special treat for her.'

'It's always all for her. I've worked hard, too. Why can't I have a new dress?' Meg asked petulantly.

'Your time will come.' Lily was firm. 'Just for now it's Janet's turn.'

Meg stood up.

'You're always spoiling her. I don't matter!' She rushed out, slamming the door behind her.

'Maybe,' Janet suggested, 'there would be enough for us both to have a dress.'

'No.' Lily's hand was trembling as she filled the kettle and set it on the range.

Later, when the children had all gone outdoors, she settled in a chair with her knitting. As Matt filled his pipe, she looked across at him.

'She'll come round,' he said calmly, as if

17

he knew what Lily was thinking.

'What are we going to do about her?'

'Treat her just the same as the rest,' Matt said robustly.

'I don't like rows in the family,' Lily murmured. 'I wonder where she's gone?' She stared into the fire and sighed. Her thoughts were far away – many years away.

Next day, Meg was her usual cheerful, happy self. She said nothing about her outburst, and Lily, grown wise over the years, didn't mention it.

Uppermost in Meg's mind was the visit to the Big House. When she was small, she'd always tried to persuade Lily to walk that way.

'Lift me up, Mother! I want to see over the wall,' she'd demand.

She never noticed that Lily was oddly reluctant, that she made excuses not to go near Pitlady. Meg loved to peer through the great iron gates at the sweep of the drive and, beyond, the Big House itself.

If only I could live somewhere like that, she used to think. As she grew older, she imagined herself in the Big House. She could see herself in the conservatory, among the ferns and palms and camellias, in a beautiful silk gown.

Meg had never owned anything made of silk, but she could imagine how it felt on your skin ... and how delicious everything would smell. The rich fragrance of the men's cigars ... the heady scent of flowering jasmine in the conservatory...

She never told anyone of these dreams, but sometimes at night, in the big feather bed she shared with Janet, she allowed herself the luxury of imagining...

Sometimes in the morning, when she awoke, before she jumped out of bed on to the cold linoleum, she would imagine the maid carrying in a tray of tea, set with such dainty china; running a bath, the water scented with verbena.

Meg read everything she could. She knew just how the rich people lived, and one day she would be one of them, too.

'I'm coming up to the Big House with you today,' she told her brother. 'To see the horses.'

'We don't want girls...'

'Oh, yes, you do. Colin said I could come. He invited me.'

'All right,' Willie agreed. 'You can come with me this afternoon.'

'Come on, Meg!' Willie was impatient.

'Just coming!' Meg called downstairs. She glanced at her reflection in the mirror. Her dark hair was long and straight, though Mother sometimes put in curl papers for Sundays or for a special occasion.

Meg often wished she had lovely natural curls, like Janet. She wasn't pretty, but when she was excited, as she was now, her dark eyes glowed, and the pale cheeks were flushed.

She ran downstairs to join Willie, who was swinging on the hand rail outside the house.

Lily looked up from her sewing and smiled. Meg was such a tomboy. She and Willie were great friends and together they roamed the countryside, looking for the blackbirds' nests down by the school, picking the first primroses to bring home, gathering brambles in autumn.

Lily remembered her own girlhood in the Howe of Firth, the pleasure of being out in the countryside, playing games, scrambling through hedges, wandering for miles.

She was thankful she and Matt had come home to Pennyglen. They'd settled here so happily.

At first it had been difficult for Matt, but now he was one of the community, no longer an incomer.

'Don't be late for your tea!' she warned them with a smile. If she knew Willie, they'd be back promptly with appetites sharpened by the fresh air.

'They've all gone out then?' Matt asked a little later.

'Yes.' Lily broke off a length of thread and smiled at her husband. 'Would you like a cup of tea?'

'That would be grand.' It was Saturday, half day, and Matt had been busy in the shed he called his workshop.

'Where have they gone?' He sat down at the table.

'Janet and Ellen have gone for a walk, and Meg's gone up with Willie to the Big House. Colin's promised to show them the horses. I hope Meg doesn't get into any bother.'

'You worry too much about her.'

Lily smiled at him. He was still the same Matt she'd met when she was in service to Miss Lucille. It had been June, 1892 – she remembered it as if it were yesterday...

'I want you to come to London with me,' Lucille had said all those years ago.

'London? Oh, no, I couldn't.' Lily had never been further than a day trip to Dundee.

'Yes, I insist.' Lucille usually got her own way. 'It's my season. I'm to be presented at Court and I must have a lady's maid.

'I don't want anyone who's terribly proud and stuck up, and frightfully efficient... Oh, dear–' she broke off. 'I've said the wrong thing. I'm always doing that.'

'I'm certainly not frightfully efficient,' Lily said in her gentle voice. 'But I couldn't go to London.'

'You'd love it, Lily. You'd see Buckingham

Palace and Hyde Park, and you could go rowing on the Serpentine or take a pleasure steamer down the Thames. And there are theatres and concerts, and oh, the shops! You should see the fashions!'

That had done it. Lily longed to see the wonderful shops and the fashionable ladies.

'Yes, I'll come,' she agreed.

London was everything Lucille had promised. Not that Lily saw all that much of Lucille. There were balls every night and Lily would wait up till Lucille came home, cheeks glowing, eyes sparkling and longing to tell about everything that had happened.

During the day Lucille slept late, then went out shopping. Lily was alone a good deal, but she wasn't lonely. A handsome young coachman had asked, very politely, if he might walk with her in the park.

The longer Lily knew this young man with the slow smile and shock of fair hair, the more she liked him. You could feel safe with Matt, she told herself.

The pirlie pig that Lily's mother had given her stood on the chest of drawers in her small attic bedroom. Now and then she would pick it up and shake the coins.

She'd already saved a fair amount – perhaps enough for a wedding bonnet, she found herself thinking.

Now, as she rose and filled the teapot setting out the cups and a plate of scones she'd made that morning, Lily remembered those days. At first she'd hardly liked to talk about Matt to Lucille.

'I wish you could find someone, too, Miss Lucille,' she'd said at last.

'Me? Oh, no. I'm having much too good a time to settle down.' Lucille had laughed at her, but she was kind hearted.

She was thrilled about Lily and Matt's romance; she was there at the wedding, throwing rice at the couple. She'd helped them find their little home, admired the curtains that Lily made on the new sewing machine, and brought gifts of china for the mantelpiece.

'Don't you ever want to go back to Scotland?' Lily asked her once.

Lucille shook her head.

'Not me. I'm a London girl.' Her family had a Mayfair house; it was more of a home to Lucille than the grey stone house in Fife.

Lily was wistful. She loved Matt and would go anywhere to be with him, but sometimes, walking the city pavements, sitting in the park feeding the pigeons, she longed for the rolling farmlands of Fife, and the woods and paths she knew so well.

But then there was little Janet. Both Lily and Matt were thrilled with their first-born.

'Funny, isn't it,' Matt said, leaning over the cradle, 'to think she'll be growing up in the twentieth century. I wonder what exciting times she'll live through.'

Lily touched the baby's soft cheek.

'I hope they're peaceful times,' she murmured.

Lucille was one of the baby's first visitors, bringing an exquisite lace-trimmed christening gown. And from then on, she was a regular visitor at the little house.

Lily admired her greatly – Miss Lucille was always so elegant, from the fashionable buttoned boots, to the grey kid gloves, to her feather-trimmed hat.

Lucille watched, smiling, as Lily sang old Scots songs and rhymes to her baby – 'Kitty Bairdie had a coo', and 'Wee chookie birdie'.

Lily caught her smiling, and said rather defensively, 'My baby's going to grow up knowing her own language.'

'You miss your home,' Lucille said.

'A little,' Lily admitted. It was strange how they were friends now, not mistress and servant. Lily would never have admitted to Matt that she was homesick, but she could tell Lucille.

Nowadays Lucille's talk was not so much of balls and theatres and shopping. She was quieter somehow. And then it all came out. She'd met a soldier – he was different from the rest. Lucille had fallen in love.

'But that's wonderful.' Lily was thrilled for her friend.

'He's going away, with his regiment. I'll

never see him again.' Lucille wiped her eyes.

'You will.' Lily was optimistic.

One day, Lucille went to wave goodbye to her soldier. After that, she was even quieter, for a very long time, and she didn't visit the little house quite so often.

It was a distraught, dishevelled Lucille who burst into Lily's kitchen one sunny afternoon.

'I have to talk to you,' she said urgently. For once, she ignored little Janet, now a happy-natured two-year-old.

'It's awful.' She twisted her hands together. 'I don't know how to tell you, Lily. I'm ... I'm going to have a child.'

Lily rose and put her arms comfortingly round her friend.

'We're going to be married, just as soon as he gets leave.'

But poor Lucille had been denied her happy ending...

'You were very good,' Lily said to Matt, bringing her thoughts back to the present. 'You know, when Miss Lucille told us...'

'What's brought this up now?' Matt was puzzled.

'I don't know.' Lily stared into her cup as if she could see the future. But she could only see the past, many years ago.

'When Miss Lucille's soldier was killed,' she said, 'and the baby was born...'

She recalled Lucille's white face.

'Will you take her, Lily? Bring her up for me? I can't give her a home. It's a lot to ask, I know, but it's for her, not for me. The old selfish Lucille, she's gone...' Her voice had shaken.

'I'll have to talk it over with Matt.'

'Of course.'

'You didn't hesitate,' Lily said now. 'Right away, you said, "We'll take her".'

'She was a fine wee girl,' Matt said. 'And Miss Lucille wasn't one to bring up a child.'

'She's changed,' Lily put in, trying to be fair. 'You know how kind and generous she is. Always sending gifts, keeping in touch.' She paused for a moment.

'Most days,' she said thoughtfully, 'I forget that Meg's not like the others.'

'You've got to make allowances,' Matt reasoned as he refilled his pipe.

'We knew that when we adopted her...' Lily's voice trailed off.

There was a pause. Matt looked up.

'What was that noise? Is there someone at the door?'

'I didn't hear anything.' Lily shook her head.

'It'll never make any difference,' Matt said warmly. 'She's one of the family, just like all the rest.'

Meg skipped along the road beside Willie,

excited at the thought of visiting the Big House.

Somehow, the house had taken on for her the magic of a palace in a fairytale. She could picture the smooth lawns, the east and west turrets – you could almost imagine a princess leaning from a turret window, waving goodbye to her betrothed.

'We go round the back way.' Willie's voice broke in on her thoughts. He was whistling cheerfully.

Sometimes, Meg found Willie's whistling a bit exasperating, but today, his easy-going approach was reassuring. She was – to tell the truth – a little nervous of visiting the Big House.

That was silly, she told herself. After all, they were only going to the stables.

A dim hope rose in her – would Colin take them into the house itself, into the conservatory, maybe into the drawing-room? She shook herself. Now she was being ridiculous!

'Hello!' Willie shouted, as they opened the gate in the wall that led into the stable yard.

'Hello!' Colin, smiling, came out of the stables.

Meg hung back. Now that they were actually here, she couldn't admit that she was scared of horses. She stood uncertainly by the stable door while Colin and Willie went from one stall to the other.

'Here's Prince. He's restless today.' Willie stroked the large grey horse, talking gently to him. 'There, Prince – you're a fine one...'

'You've got a real way with horses.' Colin was full of admiration.

'I want to work on a farm,' Willie told him. 'I'd like to be a ploughman.' He looked up, his face flushed with excitement.

'We went to a ploughing match, a few months back. My father took me. He knows a lot about horses.'

'Wish I'd been there.' Colin was quite envious. 'I was away at school.' He turned and saw Meg standing at the stable door.

'Come on, Meg. They won't hurt you.'

'Oh, I'm not nervous at all,' Meg said airily.

Colin wasn't the least bit deceived by this.

'Tell you what,' he said. 'Mother promised there would be lemonade and biscuits for us – why don't you go in and ask Mrs Mackay?'

'Yes, of course.' Anything to get away from the horses, Meg thought.

'It's through that door.' Colin pointed across the yard.

Meg pushed open the door and found herself in a small scullery. She looked round at the waterproof capes hanging from the pegs, the boots and fishing rods.

The scullery led into a large kitchen, which seemed to be empty, though a pan was simmering on the hob. A black cat lay curled on the window sill, beside a bright red geranium. In the centre of the kitchen was a large table, scrubbed white.

Meg stroked the black cat, who purred sleepily, and looked around her. There was no jug of lemonade, no plate of biscuits. She decided she would just sit down and wait.

And then she had an idea. Surely no-one would mind if she took a peep into the rest of the house?

'You'd better not,' her wise, sensible self cautioned.

'You'll never get a better chance!' the impetuous Meg retorted.

The impetuous Meg won. She pushed open the kitchen door and found herself in a narrow passage which led to the entrance hall.

Still no-one appeared, so Meg was able to look about her at the chandelier, the rich furnishings, the deep pile carpets. On the far side of the hall was an open door.

'Hello,' Meg called softly, but there was no answering sound. She crossed the hall and peeped through the open door.

To her twelve-year-old gaze, the room was like something out of a story book. It was panelled in oak, and a large desk stood in the centre. Dark red damask curtains hung at the windows which looked out over the green lawns.

But Meg had no time for the view. She

stood amazed at the shelves of books – surely there couldn't be so many books in all the world?

Her eyes widened. There was a little flight of steps leading to a gallery with yet more books, row upon row.

She glanced at the beautiful, leather-bound books and sniffed. There was a rich scent she'd never encountered before – a whiff of leather, of linseed oil and polish.

By the window was a table which held a splendid globe. Greatly daring, Meg spun the globe round with a touch of her finger. There was Britain, coloured red, and all the continents and seas and oceans.

She was so lost in thought that she didn't hear the footsteps behind her. 'And what are you doing here?'

Meg spun round. She flushed with shame and her voice trembled.

'I'm … sorry.'

'I should think so.' The dark-haired woman in the grey striped taffeta dress looked at her sternly. 'And who may you be?'

Even in her distress, Meg couldn't help noticing how elegant the woman looked. The grey dress was beautifully cut, with a row of tucks on the front of the bodice, and a jet brooch pinned to the neckline.

She stored away these details to pass on to Janet.

'Who are you?' the woman asked again.

'I'm Meg – Meg Barclay.'

'Ah, Lily's daughter. And what are you doing here, Meg?'

'I came for the lemonade – I'm with my brother...' The story poured out.

'I thought you were an intruder,' the woman said, but she didn't sound quite as angry as she had done at first.

'I wasn't going to steal anything,' Meg protested. 'I just wanted to look at the books. You've got such a lot – more than we have.'

'I suppose we have.'

'It's just that it's such a lovely room,' Meg blurted out. 'I've never seen anything like it before ... and all the books and the globe and the photographs.' She paused.

On the table by the door was a photograph of a young woman in formal dress, standing stiffly, her train spread out around her, holding a beautiful feather fan.

'Come on.' The woman's voice broke in on Meg's thoughts. 'Let's go and find that jug of lemonade.' She opened the door to the kitchen.

'I'm Colin's mother, Mrs Grierson,' she said. 'And I'm pretty sure he'll have forgotten all about you – he'll be completely absorbed in the horses.'

In the kitchen, a middle-aged woman in a white apron stood by the large table.

'The fish man had only whiting, my lady,' she said. 'But he'll be round on Saturday if you want to order plaice.'

'We'll see.' The mistress of the house smiled.

'Now, Mrs Mackay, can you let Meg here have some lemonade and ginger biscuits, and some to take out to the stable.' She nodded kindly at Meg.

'I hope we meet again.'

Outside in the stable, Colin and Willie hardly looked up as Meg carried the lemonade and biscuits and set them down carefully.

'I'm starving,' Willie said eagerly.

'Tell you what,' Colin suggested, through a mouthful of biscuit, 'I'll show you my new bicycle. Father bought it for me.'

'You were riding it the other day,' Meg put in.

'Yes.' He grinned at her. 'I'm just learning.'

Meg and Willie watched as he wheeled out the bicycle.

'We'll go along the path by the burn,' he decided.

He led them through the stable yard, and down the drive towards the burn that ran through the estate.

Meg had been along the path by the burn once before. That had been in winter, when the branches of the overhanging trees were stark and bare, and you couldn't imagine that the trees would ever be green again.

But now the path was fringed with cow parsley and pink campion and it was cool and shady under the canopy of leaves.

Meg and Willie ran along the path, trying to keep up with Colin. 'Come on!' he called.

At last he braked, and propped the cycle against the trunk of a beech tree. Then he flung himself down on the grass.

'Phew! It's hot! Want to have a shot?' he asked Willie.

Willie's eyes shone. This was a splendid new cycle, and here was Colin, much older, and a hero in Willie's eyes, offering to let him have a turn.

'Oh, yes, please!'

'Come on, I'll show you!' Colin held the bicycle steady while Willie got on.

They turned at the end of the lane and Willie cycled back on his own.

'I did it, all by myself!' he shouted gleefully. 'Didn't I?'

All three sat down on the bank. Colin picked a blade of grass, held it between his thumbs and blew, making an eerie, whistling sort of sound.

Willie was full of admiration. Was there nothing his friend couldn't do?

'You *are* lucky to live in a place like this.' Meg sighed. 'Horses and a bicycle and all those books...' She forgot she wasn't supposed to have been further than the kitchen.

'It gets a bit boring sometimes, in the holidays from school,' Colin said.

'Boring?' Meg sat bolt upright. 'How can you be bored?'

'Well, not exactly boring,' Colin admitted. He brushed back a lock of fair hair, and his pleasant round face looked serious for a moment. 'Lonely, maybe.'

Meg understood, though Willie was too young to grasp what Colin meant. It was no use having all this, if you didn't have anyone to share it with.

And yet – Colin had so much. How wonderful it must be, never to have to wonder how much things cost, never to hear the words, 'We can't afford it.'

'Haven't you any brothers and sisters?' she asked.

'I've a stepsister, but she's years and years older than me. Grown up. She doesn't often come here.'

'Oh.' Meg lost interest. 'Well, you've got us for company,' she said cheerfully.

'Do you want a turn on the bicycle?' Colin asked her suddenly.

'Oh, yes. Please.' Meg had been longing to try the cycle, but hadn't wanted to ask.

'Girls don't ride bicycles,' Willie scoffed.

'Oh, yes, they do,' Meg said. 'I've seen lots of ladies riding cycles. Anyway, it's easy. There's nothing to it.'

As soon as the words were out of her

mouth, she regretted them. What had made her say a stupid thing like that? She'd never ridden a bicycle before. She had no idea where to start – or how to stop.

'On you go,' Colin said.

Meg got to her feet. She clutched the handlebars, and pressed down one pedal, keeping the other foot firmly on the ground.

'That's not riding a bicycle,' Willie said scornfully.

'Just till I get round the corner,' Meg remarked airily. 'Then I'll be able to get up some speed.'

Once out of sight of Colin and Willie, she stopped by a log and climbed on to the bike. It was really difficult, encumbered by her long serge skirt, but she managed to get both feet on the pedals, and by working hard, she could make the wheels spin round.

The bicycle wobbled from side to side, but Meg was triumphant – she was moving. It wasn't so hard after all!

'I'm getting the hang of it!' she told herself proudly. 'I can go faster than this!'

Faster, faster – oh, this was fun! And then Meg realised, to her horror, that she had no idea how to stop the bicycle. Brakes – where were they?

Looking down, she swerved off the path. The bicycle careered down the slope, hit a stone and came to a stop all of a sudden, throwing Meg over the handlebars into the burn.

'Oh!' She cried out with the sudden shock of the cold water. Luckily, the burn was shallow at this point, but the water was muddy – it had rained heavily the previous week.

Meg hauled herself out of the burn, clutching at the branch of a willow tree. She slipped on the grass and sat down heavily.

The bicycle! Colin's precious bicycle! Was it all right? She picked it up. The wheels were still spinning – that was a good thing. It didn't seem to be damaged.

Feeling sore, and scratched by brambles, Meg pushed the cycle back on to the path.

'I'm sorry,' she called out, as she rounded the corner. 'I fell off, into the burn. I think your cycle's all right.'

'Are *you* all right?' Colin was anxious, and Meg thought what a nice person he was, to be more worried about her than his precious cycle.

'If it's damaged,' Meg was going to say, 'I'll pay...' but she hesitated. She had no idea how much bicycle repairs cost.

Colin examined the cycle.

'The mudguard's a bit bent,' he said, 'but don't worry – that can easily be sorted out.'

'I'm sorry,' Meg said again. She would never be invited back to the Big House. Never. Oh, how stupid she'd been! She was nearly in tears.

'It's all right,' Colin said kindly. 'Anyone can fall off. But hadn't you better go home? You're pretty wet...'

Meg's skirt was dripping, and her boots were sodden with mud. There was a scratch on her cheek and her hair ribbon had come loose.

'I suppose I'd better,' she agreed disconsolately.

She set off along the path. Her shoulder was aching from the fall, and her boots made a squelching sound as she walked.

It was lucky that she didn't meet anyone she knew, as she took the road under the railway bridge, past the station, and on towards the main street of the village. She was in no mood to answer questions.

She rather expected to find her father working out of doors. She knew he wouldn't be cross – he was too easy-going to be angry very often. He'd just say, 'You're an awful lass! What have you been up to now?'

But there was no sign of him. Maybe he'd gone down to the village shop, or had stopped for a cup of tea.

As she entered the scullery, Meg heard her parents' voices. She paused, her explanation ready.

'I fell in the burn. I'm not really wet – well, just a wee bit. It'll soon dry.'

And then she remembered. She'd better

take her boots off. She grimaced. They were filthy – they'd take some cleaning.

She leaned against the doorpost, undoing the laces, easing off her boots...

She pushed open the door. Her parents were sitting one on either side of the table, but neither saw her.

She was about to say, 'I fell in the burn,' when to her astonishment, Meg heard her own name.

'Most days,' her mother said, 'I forget Meg's not like the others.'

'You've got to make allowances,' Matt reasoned.

Meg froze, listening.

'We knew that when we adopted her.' Lily's voice trailed off.

Meg couldn't move. But she knew nothing would make her enter the kitchen.

She had to get away – quickly. She forced herself to back away from the door. Still clutching her boots, she turned and ran. At the end of the street, she paused to draw breath. The words she'd heard were still pounding in her brain. It couldn't be true – could it?

Her thoughts raced around in her head. It seemed as if the world was spinning about her.

'If I'm not me,' she said aloud, 'who am I?'

Chapter Two

Adopted? Was that really what her parents had said? Meg couldn't believe her ears. She rushed blindly out of the house and along the street. She didn't know where she was going; she didn't care, either.

Her thoughts whirled round in her head. I'm not me. I'm not Meg. So who am I?

'You're in a rush!' a voice called to her suddenly.

Meg halted in her flight. There was Janet, rosy-faced and smiling, flushed after an afternoon in the warm sunshine. Beside her, Ellen was skipping, happily turning a length of rope from an old clothes line.

'What's the matter?' Janet asked, concerned.

She'd never seen Meg like this before. Her sister was angry at times, sulky at others, and often very excited about something. But she'd never been like this – gasping, sobbing…

'What is it?' Janet's hand flew to her mouth. 'Is it – is something wrong with Mother or Father?'

Meg shook her head, still unable to speak.

'Come on,' Janet said. Always practical, she

knew that Meg needed comfort and help right away. She turned to her little sister.

'Ellen, you go on ahead. Meg and I will follow. See how many turns you can skip before you get home.'

'Right. I'll start counting.' Ellen was proud of being able to skip so well. She started chanting. 'One, two, three…'

Janet watched her and sighed with relief. Thank goodness Ellen hadn't realised something was seriously wrong – she probably thought Meg was just in one of her difficult moods.

'Now, what's the matter? Calm down.' She put an arm round her sister's shoulder.

'Stop crying, Meg, and tell me what it's all about.'

'I went home to get changed,' Meg blurted out. 'I was wet – I fell in the burn. And when I opened the door, Mother and Father were talking.' She stifled a sob.

'What is it, Meg?' Janet asked, really concerned now.

'They didn't hear me come in,' Meg went on. 'They were talking about me – about how I'm different, because … because I'm adopted!' Her face crumpled as fresh tears began to fall.

'Oh, Meg!' Janet patted her sister awkwardly on the shoulder. 'Ssh … don't cry.'

Her voice was reassuring, but her thoughts were racing ahead. Could it be true? Was

Meg really adopted? And if so, why…?

Janet could hardly take in what Meg had just told her. This was quite astonishing, and completely unexpected.

She was overwhelmed by dismay, and pity for Meg. She knew, though, that she must keep calm, and not let Meg see how shaken she was by the news.

'Let's sit down,' she suggested. The two girls sat on a low wall outside one of the cottages.

Meg twisted the material of her skirt between her fingers.

'I don't belong,' she said blankly.

'That's stupid,' Janet retorted. 'Of course you belong. You did yesterday, didn't you? So where's the difference today?'

'What am I going to do?' Meg sobbed.

'I'll tell you,' Janet said, suddenly resolute. 'We'll go right back to the house and ask Mother. She'll tell you the truth, one way or another. Come on.'

'Oh, no, I couldn't possibly…'

'Why not?' Janet demanded. 'It's better to know, one way or another.'

'No, you don't understand. They didn't know I was there.'

'That's not important,' Janet said firmly.

'Look, we're all one family – you, me, Willie, Ellen. They've always treated us just the same.

'Oh, sometimes one gets a treat or a

special present,' she said, trying to be honest as she remembered the money in the pirlie pig, and how Mother had promised her a new dress.

But they didn't have favourites – that was the best thing about Mother and Father, they were always fair.

'No, you don't understand!' Even in her distress, Meg had reasoned it out.

'Once things are out in the open, everyone will know I'm different from the rest of you. Just think how the neighbours will gossip. But if it's kept a secret, no-one will treat me any differently.'

'You've told me,' Janet pointed out.

'Yes, but you won't tell anyone else, will you?' Meg gripped her sister's arm. 'It'll be our secret – promise!'

Janet stared at her.

'I think you're wrong. Who cares, anyway? It's you that matters, not where you come from.'

'It's all very well for you to say that – you know where you come from. I don't.' Meg's tears welled up again.

'All right,' Janet said hastily. 'But I still think you're being silly. Mother would make it all clear, and you know it wouldn't make the least difference to any of us.'

'Promise,' Meg urged. 'Please.'

'All right.'

'You've got to say it. "I promise solemnly

never to tell anyone about Meg being adopted"…'

Janet repeated the words. Meg had stopped crying by now.

'Swear it.'

'I swear. Cross my heart and hope to die.'

'Thank you.' Meg gave a deep sigh.

One of the farm carts rumbled up the street and the driver waved to the girls. Janet waved back, but Meg was too distracted to pay any attention.

Janet rose to her feet, still feeling a little shaken. Was it true, what Meg had told her? Surely it must be – and yet…?

Meg had such a vivid imagination. She was always making up stories.

She'd once told all the other children that old Libby Mackay was a witch, who flew on her broomstick over the rooftops at night. Even Ellen, who loved all animals, had walked a little warily past Libby's black cat after that.

And, when Meg was younger, she'd been convinced there were fairy circles in the cabbage patch. It came from reading too many stories, Janet thought indulgently.

'Let's go home,' she said, handing her sister a handkerchief.

'I can't – not like this.' Meg mopped her eyes.

'We'll say you fell over,' Janet suggested.

Their eyes met, and Meg felt oddly

comforted. It was good to have someone to share her secret.

That evening, Janet watched Meg closely. Her sister was quiet, but then she often was.

After the family meal, Matt took up his concertina and played a number of old favourites – 'The Bluebells of Scotland', 'Flow Gently Sweet Afton' and others.

'Sing to us, Father,' Ellen said, who was nursing her old rag doll by the window.

'Sing "Aiken Drum,"' Will chimed in.

'I wish we had a piano.' Meg had been silent up to now. 'Or one of the new pianolas,' she added.

'One day, maybe.' Lily's glance fell on the pirlie pig and Matt laughed. It was a joke between them – that the pirlie pig would provide for everything.

Janet, humming tunefully, noticed that Meg was very pale. She'd eaten little, but then she was finicky about her food.

'I think I'll go to bed early,' Meg announced suddenly.

Lily glanced at her. Meg was growing fast, she noticed. Look how she'd grown out of her new school blouse already – her thin wrists weren't even covered by the sleeves.

'Off you go. Sleep well,' she said fondly.

When Janet went to bed much later, she climbed into the big flock bed, easing the covers back so that she didn't disturb her sister.

44

'Are you asleep?' she whispered. 'Meg?'

There was no answer. Janet turned on to her side and soon fell asleep.

But Meg lay awake for hours, her thoughts in a turmoil. What would she do? What would happen to her?

Of course, things couldn't ever be the same again.

Her thoughts raced ahead. Oh, if only she could start a new life – put all this behind her.

After all, she was twelve now. Soon she would be able to start work. I could pass for fourteen, she told herself.

She lay very still, trying not to disturb Janet. Oh, lucky Janet, how simple life was for her, how uncomplicated.

At last, exhausted, Meg fell into a troubled sleep.

Next day, she hung around the house. No-one paid much attention to her. It was Sunday, so there was church, and Sunday School, and then the walk home.

No-one sewed or knitted on a Sunday. Meg was rather glad about that, for she hated any kind of sewing, and as for knitting…

No-one read a newspaper either, or any book except one that was thought to be suitable for the Sabbath. But there was plenty to do – relatives to visit and plans to be made for the next week.

It was going to be an exciting week, for

Janet was starting work at the flax mill.

A plan was growing in Meg's mind. Yes, Monday was a very good day. No-one would notice.

On Monday morning Janet was awake early.

'My first day at work!' she said gleefully. Then she turned to Meg, who was sitting on the edge of the bed, yawning.

'Are you all right?' she asked.

'Me? Yes, of course I'm all right.'

'Don't worry about it – yesterday, I mean,' Janet said quickly.

'Of course I won't.' Meg was rather offhand. 'Can't think why I got so upset. You'd better hurry – you don't want to be late on your first morning.'

'No, that wouldn't be a good beginning,' Janet agreed, brushing her hair.

The house seemed very quiet after she'd left, and Ellen and Willie had both disappeared to see their friends.

Willie was going up to the stables at the Big House, even though Colin wouldn't be there today. He was going to the dentist in Kirkcaldy.

All day, the plan grew in Meg's mind. At last, in mid-afternoon, when Lily had gone up the street to the village shop, she hurried upstairs, stuffed a few things into her schoolbag, and glanced around.

Downstairs, she remembered she'd need

food. She took one of Lily's soda scones from the tin, and a bottle of ginger ale from the pantry. Then she hurried down the path to the gate.

She glanced up the street, but at this time of day, even the houses seemed asleep in the drowsy sunshine.

Slowly, she made her way to the railway station just beyond the village. She had no idea when a train was due, but she was prepared to wait. Sooner or later, one would arrive. Meg, impulsive as ever, had thought no further than that.

'I'll take the train to Dundee,' she'd planned. 'Then they'll be sorry. I can write to them from my new address.'

A little voice inside her head asked, 'What new address?' but Meg ignored it.

She sat down on a bench at the far end of the platform, trying to look as if she travelled by train every day. In fact, she'd only been on a train journey once before, across the Tay over the rail bridge, for a treat.

Beside her, a pink rambling rose swayed slightly in the soft breeze. Meg felt drowsy in the sunshine, but she knew she must stay alert until she was safely on the train.

She didn't dare ask the porter what time the next train arrived; he would wonder why she was there. She would just have to wait.

But it wasn't long before a train was

signalled. Meg rose, clutching her school-bag.

'I'm running away, running away,' the wheels of the train seemed to say, echoing her thoughts.

Someone leaned out of a carriage window, opened the door and jumped out on to the platform. The figure, dressed in a grey flannel suit and wearing a school cap, was somehow familiar.

'Hello, Meg,' Colin said. 'Fancy seeing you.' He took off his cap.

'Gosh, it's hot. Thank goodness I'm home again. It's such a fag having to go to the dentist – it's the same every holiday.

'Still, that's it over for a while, thank goodness.' He grinned at her.

'I'm glad I saw you. I was going to send a message with Willie, but he'd probably have forgotten to tell you.'

'He can't think of anything but horses,' Meg said, finding her voice.

'And why not? Horses are much more important than school books and boring old lessons. What was I going to say?'

'You had a message...'

'So I did. My mother said I was to tell you to come up to Pitlady any time you like and she'll be pleased to let you look at the books in the library. If you want to, that is. I don't think they're very interesting myself.'

'Oh, thank you!' Meg said, eyes shining.

48

'Don't thank me. It was my mother's idea.'

Meg gazed at him, entranced. What an opportunity, and to think she might have missed it. She didn't notice the stationmaster waving his green flag, and she hardly heard the engine hoot as the train pulled out.

'I say – were you waiting for someone? There doesn't seem to be anyone else on the train,' Colin pointed out.

'Oh, no,' Meg said. 'Not really. It wasn't important – and it's time I was going home.'

'Me, too,' Colin agreed. 'See you some time.'

He waved cheerfully and disappeared through the gate.

Meg made her way home. The village of Pennyglen looked a much more pleasant place than when she'd left it.

Would the family have missed her? It wasn't likely – she hadn't been away for long. Tea would be ready the remains of yesterday's mutton, with lettuce from the garden and hard boiled eggs. She began to hurry.

When she got home, Meg found that Janet was back from work. It seemed no time since she'd left that morning.

'Sit down,' Lily said to her eldest daughter. 'You'll be ready for a cup of tea.'

Janet sipped the tea gratefully. She was tired with the unaccustomed standing all day.

The noise of the power looms had given her a headache, and it was hard to remember all she'd been told. But she was a working girl, and there would be a wage at the end of the week.

No-one had noticed Meg had been away. She replaced the bottle of ginger ale in the pantry and the soda scone in the tin.

She paid little attention to Janet's description of the day's work, and the overseer, Mr Meikle, and the other girls. Her thoughts were far away.

She wasn't going to run away ever again, she promised herself. She was going to make a life for herself.

She was going up in the world ... and to the Big House, too. One day, she'd be one of them...

Spring, 1911

'In a few months, I'll be working, too,' Meg said, her eyes sparkling.

Janet smiled. She was sixteen now, slim and graceful. Working in the flax mill hadn't coarsened her, as it sometimes did the other girls.

Oh, it had been hard at first, Janet thought a little ruefully. Those early days had been bewildering.

She'd come home exhausted, half deafened by the noise in the shed, her feet swollen with standing. The overseer, Mr Meikle, had been hard to please, too.

At the beginning, Janet had found it difficult to keep up with the work, and she was afraid of Mr Meikle.

'Hurry up,' he'd shouted at her one day. 'How do you think we'd ever get the order finished if everyone was as slow as you?'

Janet was mortified. What a disgrace! All the other girls seemed to manage, their fingers flying nimbly backwards and forwards.

But when the overseer had moved on, the girl next to Janet leaned over.

'Don't you fret over what old Meikle says,' she told Janet kindly.

Janet, nearly in tears, turned gratefully towards her.

'He's like that all the time – but he's a comic really.'

At break time, Janet's new friend sat down beside her.

'My name's Bess,' she said. 'You'll soon get the hang of it, don't you worry.'

It wasn't long before Janet and Bess became firm friends. Bess was so placid and cheerful, nothing ever seemed to upset her.

Janet had settled in well at the mill, but she wasn't sure how her sister would fit in there. Meg could be so impetuous and hot-headed. She was also very bright…

'You could perhaps stay on at school, Meg,'

Miss Macintosh, her teacher, had suggested.

The girl had a feeling for words. She was quick with figures, and observant, too. She would be wasted going into the mill, the teacher thought.

'See what your parents say,' she suggested. It was rare for her to have a pupil as bright as Meg.

But Meg had already decided she wanted to leave school. She didn't know what she was going to do, but she knew she was going up in the world.

She wanted to travel, and she wanted to be grown up as soon as possible.

Meg had finished with school – she'd learned all they could teach her. So she said nothing to her parents about the teacher's suggestion.

Already she was living in a different world. On her visits to Pitlady House, Mrs Grierson had let her take books down from their shelves.

Meg especially liked to read about distant countries – India, the Pacific Islands – and find them on the big globe that stood in the corner of the room.

Lily was a little surprised that Meg made no objection to starting work in the mill. She didn't know that, for Meg, it was only a beginning, a first step into the grown-up world.

'You should see the fine cloths they have on the dining-table at Pitlady,' Meg said one day. 'You'd like one of those, wouldn't you, Mother?'

Matt, hearing this, smiled at her. As manager of the mill, he was proud of the interest Meg showed in the flax spinning and the weaving of linen.

'You'd need to work in Dunfermline if you wanted to make fine linen,' he told her.

'The factories round here make the coarser stuff. It's either ticks – that's a strong, hard linen – or checks – that's linen with a cross pattern.'

'Oh.' Meg was a little disappointed. But it still seemed romantic to think that the flax came all the way from the Baltic to Kirkcaldy or Methil. She looked up the Baltic countries on the globe, next time she went up to Pitlady.

Matt enjoyed his work and, in return, the mill owners recognised that in their manager, they had a skilled man who was clever with his hands and good with machines.

'Machines are the future,' he said now, smiling at Meg.

He was pleased she was going to work in the mill, and proud that Janet had settled so well there. Even Meikle, the overseer, who wasn't usually given to praise, admitted Matt's eldest daughter was a good worker.

Janet, lost in a daydream, wasn't listening to the conversation between her father and Meg. She was too excited about the forthcoming weekend…

'I'm going to visit my aunt and uncle on Saturday – they've a farm just beyond Cupar,' Bess had told her earlier. 'Do you want to come? We'll get a lift on Bob's cart..'

Janet loved an outing.

'Oh, yes,' she'd accepted eagerly. 'But I've to mind my wee sister. Mother's going to Pitlessie to see a friend.'

'That's all right,' Bess said. 'Bring her along – she'll be no bother.'

Ellen was thrilled with the idea of a day's outing. As they clip-clopped through Cupar, along the Bonnygate, Janet felt her spirits rise.

She sat in the back of the cart, her fair hair ruffled by the breeze. What a pleasure it was to have a day out in the fresh air.

'It's not far now,' Bess said, as they left the town behind.

Years later, Janet was to look back on that spring day. She could remember the wild daffodils nodding by the wayside; the trees just beginning to show the first green buds; the odd pheasant strutting across the path of the cart.

Bess's Aunt Alice and Uncle Joe at Glendores were pleased to see them. When Bess had delivered the jar of honey and knitting pattern she'd brought, and passed on some family news, Aunt Alice suggested they look round the farm.

'But mind you don't go running through the fields – and leave old Grumphie alone. He's a fine pig, but he's a bit of a temper.' She reeled off instructions to Ellen, who sat quietly, listening.

'She'll behave,' Janet said quickly. 'She's always good.'

'Bairns are bairns,' the aunt replied sternly.

Janet bit her lip. She was glad to get outdoors, away from this rather stern woman in her spotless white apron, with her hair drawn back in a bun and her lips tight and disapproving.

They wandered round the farm. Uncle Joe showed them the pigs and the stables, then left them to look around on their own.

'I wonder where Cousin Rab is?' Bess said loudly.

'Were you talking about me?' A young man with fair, curly hair and a fresh open face appeared behind them.

'So there you are! I thought you were off having a wee rest somewhere,' Bess teased him.

'Rest? Me? Early morn to late at night, that's the hours I work.' He grinned at her. 'I heard you before I saw you.'

'What a cheek!' Bess grinned back at him. It was clear the two of them were good friends.

'So who's this?' He turned to Janet and Ellen.

'My friend Janet, from Pennyglen, and Ellen, her wee sister. Janet and I are in the mill together.'

Rab pulled a face.

'That wouldn't suit me, cooped up all day... Have you seen the stables?'

Bess nodded.

'Uncle Joe took us round.'

'Willie would have enjoyed it here – my wee brother. He's mad about horses,' Janet put in.

'They're fine horses, but we'll not always be using them on the farm,' Rab told them.

'Why's that? Uncle Joe's not selling up, is he?' Bess asked.

'No, no. The farm's been in the family for generations. But we'll be using machines before another ten years are out. That's the future...'

'He's all for machines, is Rab,' Bess explained. 'Motorcycles especially.'

Rab laughed.

'I saw an aeroplane flying over the fields the other day. You could see the pilot's feet sticking out below it.' He grinned. 'The poor horses didn't know what it was!'

'Father took us to the cinematograph to see the film of Blériot crossing the Channel,' Janet said. 'You could see the plane quite clearly over the water. I'd have been terrified...'

Rab's eyes shone.

'I'd love to fly – but I don't suppose I'll ever get the chance.'

He was so easy to talk to, so quick to laugh. He was kind to Ellen, too, and answered all her questions patiently.

'Come and see the new pups,' he said. 'They're in the shed. They're a bit young to leave their mother yet, but maybe...' His eyes met Janet's.

'Do you think your mother would let her have one?' he asked as they watched Ellen down on her knees, gazing in delight at the small wriggling bodies.

'I'll ask her.' Janet smiled back at him. 'I know Ellen would love to have a pup of her own.'

'Aunt Alice is calling us,' Bess said from the doorway. 'The tea's ready.'

The girls were hungry after the drive and tucked into the spread. Aunt Alice seemed to unbend a little as she watched them enjoy her pancakes and fruit cake.

But Janet felt rather ill at ease with this highly critical lady as she tried hard to think of things to say that would meet with her approval. She was thankful when at last it was time to go.

'You'll come again,' Aunt Alice said as they left.

Janet nodded. She was relieved that no great disaster had happened. Neither she nor Ellen had spilled jam on the spotless white tablecloth, and they hadn't dropped too many crumbs on the floor.

'She must like you,' Bess said on the way home. 'She doesn't often ask people back.'

They waved to Rab as they set off.

'I'll come over to Pennyglen one day,' he said. 'On the motorcycle.'

'You and your machines.' Bess laughed.

'He's nice, your cousin,' Janet said dreamily as they turned towards Cupar.

Bess gave her a sharp look.

'He's got nothing on his mind but machines. He's no time for anything else. Not for girls anyway.'

'I didn't mean that,' Janet protested, but she was rather quiet for the rest of the evening. She was thinking of a fresh, open face, and a cheerful laugh, and the way Rab had looked at her across the shed.

She chided herself for being silly. He was only being polite, after all. But she hoped she'd see him again...

Lily leaned over the gate, enjoying the sight and sound of a blackbird singing on the branch of a nearby cherry tree.

Spring was her favourite time of year. Already, the young shoots of wheat were appearing in the fields, and there was a springing into life everywhere.

She glanced at the white lilac by the gate. It wouldn't be long now till it was in bloom.

And, she thought, all seemed well with her family. Janet was settled at the mill, and becoming more of a young woman every day.

And as for Meg – she'd be starting work at the mill in the summer. She was brighter than most fourteen-year-olds, and quick to learn, though she'd become a little quieter recently.

Lily hoped there was nothing wrong. She pushed the thought away, telling herself she was just imagining things.

She let her thoughts drift lazily as she leaned over the gate. It was nearly time to go back indoors, to hang out the washing and begin to think about the midday meal.

As soon as she could spare a moment, she promised herself, she'd be out in the garden.

Soon it would be time to plant out the pansies and petunias she'd raised from seed. It was tempting to set them out early at the first hint of sunshine, but Lily knew quite well that there could still be frost at night. It was only late April, after all.

'Morning, missus.' It was old Walter, the postman. Very little post came to Matt and Lily, so she was surprised when he fumbled in his bag and brought out a letter.

'Letter for you,' he said, putting his bag down on the wall. 'From the States – that's an American stamp, isn't it? You got family or friends in America?'

'Never you mind,' Lily said tartly. Walter could be too nosy for his own good sometimes.

She took the letter and turned to go indoors. Suddenly, the sunshine didn't feel so warm; the blackbird's song seemed almost an irritation.

Indoors, Lily wiped her hands and sat down at the kitchen table, the letter in her hand. She knew very well who it was from.

'Better open it then,' she muttered, 'and see what she's got to say.'

My dear Lily... Lucille's handwriting was as clear and attractive as ever.

Lily skimmed the contents.

Lucille was married now, *but you know that, Lily, and I can tell you that my Elmer is the best and kindest of men. I wish you could meet him...*

They had two small boys. *They're growing up real little Yankees, but I want them to get to know the old country, too – maybe one day they'll pay a visit.*

Miss Lucille sounded contented, that was plain, thought Lily. Her husband was a wealthy steel magnate, so Lucille had no problems with money.

Lily read on. Lucille's happy, busy life, with its social gatherings and charity work, was so different from her own. But then, the rich were different, Lily reminded herself.

She wondered if she'd ever see Lucille again.

Then she read the next paragraph, and it was as if an icy finger had touched her heart.

And now to little Meg. I have a great longing to see her, Lily, for soon she will be little Meg no more, but a young woman. I've missed so many years of her life.

Suddenly, in spite of the warmth of the day, Lily shivered. She and Matt loved Meg as if she were their own. If Lucille came back, would she want to claim Meg as her daughter? That would be too much to bear...

She scanned the rest of the paragraph for further clues to Lucille's intention, but there were none. Instead, the letter continued in chatty tone.

Lucille was coming to England in June for the Coronation festivities – *we are determined to see King George V crowned* – and after the celebrations in London she'd return to Scotland to visit her old home, and see her sister.

May I come to visit? You know this is our secret – not even my husband knows, and you may be sure I will not breathe a word to Meg. But I should like to see her again...

Lily re-read the letter, then folded it carefully and put it away in the dresser drawer.

All that day, as she washed and cooked

and cleaned, she thought about the proposed visit. Out of doors, she could find no peace or comfort in her garden.

Late that night, as she was unbraiding her hair, she turned to Matt.

'I had a letter today. From Miss Lucille.'

'Ah,' Matt said. 'I thought you had something on your mind. What does she want?'

'She's coming to Pitlady this summer. They're going to be here for the Coronation in June, in England, I mean...' It all poured out.

'She wants to see Meg. Just as a visitor. She wouldn't want her told. Oh, Matt, I don't know what to do.

'Should I let her come? I can't tell her to stay away. Meg's her daughter, after all. But I'm scared! I can't help wondering whether Miss Lucille will want her back. And if she does, will Meg want to go?'

She turned to Matt, her eyes distraught.

'Calm down, love,' he said gently, putting an arm around her shoulders. 'You're letting your imagination run away with you! All Lucille wants to do is visit – I can't see any harm in that. And once it's over, she'll be going back home to America.'

Lily felt calmer. Matt was always so sensible, so reassuring.

'It'll all work out,' he said. 'Try to get some sleep – you'll feel better in the morning.'

Lily decided to take his advice. Where was

the harm in one visit, after all?

The excitement of the King's Coronation spread through the country. Each shop had tried to outdo its neighbour with elaborate window displays, and the small towns in the Howe of Fife were ablaze with red, white and blue.

On a visit to Cupar, Lily admired the crown above the door of one shop, the scroll with the words 'Long Live the King' above another, and the windows decorated in patriotic colours.

'Flags 1d to 7 ½d,' proclaimed one shop, and Lily went in and bought a tuppenny flag for Ellen, who was going to be part of a procession from the school.

Even the smallest village was caught up in the excitement. There were to be bonfires, fireworks, games and souvenirs for the children, and dinners for the old folk.

Willie was full of plans. His friendship with Colin still flourished, even though the older boy was away at boarding school in term time.

Colin would be home for the celebrations and had entered for the slow cycle race in the Coronation sports at St Andrews. Willie, proud to be part of the great event, spent hours running alongside Colin as he slowly cycled round obstacles, practising for the race.

Lily's pleasure in the celebrations was clouded by the shadow of anxiety.

'I think,' she said to Meg, 'that it's better if you don't go up to the Big House for a while. Mrs Grierson's sister, Miss Lucille, is coming home for a visit.'

'But–' Meg began.

'You heard what I said.' Lily was quite firm.

Meg didn't argue, but she fumed inwardly.

'Why shouldn't I go up to the Big House?' she muttered crossly.

The day of Lucille's visit drew nearer. Lily planned to serve tea in the parlour, using the silver teapot an aunt had left her. There would be feather-light scones and a sponge cake, all set out on the best lace cloth.

But it didn't happen like that. The day before, when Lily was busy ironing in the kitchen, there was a tap at the brass knocker.

She pushed back a strand of hair, and went to the door. She didn't trouble to take her apron off, assuming it would only be a neighbour.

'You don't mind? I happened to be passing through, and I couldn't wait to see you, Lily dear.'

Lucille stood there, slim and elegant in a costume of sea-green crêpe with lace insets and a cream straw hat trimmed in green. She looked as graceful as ever. Lily felt drab and unkempt beside her.

'Come in.' Lily's plans dissolved as she led her guest into the kitchen.

'May I sit here? It looks so comfortable.' Lucille settled herself in the rocking chair and looked about her approvingly.

'It's so pleasant here – what a lovely, homely kitchen.'

'How are you, Miss Lucille?' Lily said, a little nervously.

'I thought we said you must drop the "Miss".' Lucille smiled at her.

'Oh, Lily, it's good to see you. I wanted to come before, but I didn't know whether it would be wise...'

There was a silence.

'How is she?' Lucille asked at last.

'Growing up,' Lily said. 'Matt and I – we've done our best for her...'

'I know you have,' Lucille said. 'She's lucky – she has the best parents in the world.'

'But I think,' Lily went on carefully, 'that she feels different from the rest.

'She's much brighter – she's quick to learn. She's just started work in the mill this month, alongside Janet, but I doubt if she'll stay there.

'In fact,' she said briskly, 'they'll both be in soon from work. I'll make a cup of tea.' She took down the everyday cups and the big brown teapot from the shelf.

Lucille looked about her as she took off her elegant grey gloves and laid her hat aside.

'You know I'll always provide any money that's needed,' she said.

'We don't require it, thank you,' Lily replied with a flash of spirit.

'We've got enough, though we're not rich. And anyway, money only makes a difference between the children.' She glanced at the pirlie pig on the mantelpiece.

'In any case, there's always some over and to spare.'

There was a sound of laughter, and the door burst open.

'Mother, guess what? Miss Fraser let me try her typewriter and she said I'd be good at it and I should go to Skerry's and get lessons...' Meg stopped short, suddenly noticing the visitor.

Janet, behind her, put down her piece box and came forward to shake hands.

'This is Janet,' Lily said.

'Hello.' Lucille held out her hand. 'And you–' she said, and no-one would have noticed the slight tremor in her voice '–you must be Meg.'

'This is Miss Lucille,' Lily put in quickly.

'I once lived at Pitlady,' Lucille explained. 'I'm back visiting from the States.'

'I know the Big House,' Meg said. 'And Colin, and Mrs Grierson. She lets me look at the books...'

'Mrs Grierson's my sister,' Lucille told her, unable to take her eyes off the girl.

'You don't look a bit alike,' Meg said boldly.

'Meg,' Lily warned, 'don't be so forward.'

'That's all right.' Lucille smiled at the girl. 'Sisters don't always look alike,' she said slowly.

'So you want to learn to type?' she went on.

'Oh, yes,' Meg said. 'If I have lessons, I can get a better job. There are lots of jobs for ladies that can type.'

'There are indeed,' Lucille agreed.

'I'm not going to stay in the mill for ever,' Meg added.

Lily poured out the tea, her hand shaking a little. Lucille, sitting in the shabby old chair, looked like some rare bird of paradise.

'And Janet–' Lucille turned to the older girl '–do you like being in the mill?'

'Oh, yes, it's fine,' Janet said in her soft voice. 'There's plenty of good company.'

She could hardly take her eyes off this elegant woman. Look at how the bodice of her dress was cut, and the lace – it was so fine.

And her hat! Janet had seen pictures of hats like that in the papers. And such soft gloves! Lucille was the most fashionable person she'd ever seen.

'So you were at the Coronation?' Lily asked.

'We watched the procession from a box,' Lucille told her. 'Oh, Lily, it was splendid! The horses and the guards and the bands and the coach with the King and Queen – London is the most exciting place on earth, don't you agree?'

Lily said nothing. She listened to Lucille talking too much and too fast, and she watched Meg hanging on the words of this exotic stranger.

'I'd love to go to London, and to America,' Meg said eagerly. 'You can sail from Glasgow to Boston. I saw the advertisements in the paper. I could maybe come and visit you...'

'Maybe you could, Meg,' Lucille agreed, suddenly much quieter.

Lily could see the warning signs. Meg's eyes were sparkling, her colour was high, and she was showing off as only Meg could.

'I must go,' Lucille announced. 'Your father – Matt – will be coming in for his tea and he'll want it right away, I'm sure.'

The girls shook hands politely.

'Goodbye,' Lucille said. 'I – I hope we meet again.'

Lily wiped her hands and showed her guest to the door.

'Oh, Lily.' Lucille took both Lily's hands in hers. 'What a daughter to have – she is so

68

lively, so attractive. I wish...'

Lily was deeply troubled. Whatever Matt had said, the visit had turned out to be a mistake. And yet – Lucille had the right...

'I think,' she said slowly, 'that it might be better if you didn't come here again.'

Lucille's eyes filled with tears.

'Oh, Lily – please!'

'I mean it.' Lily could be determined when something was worth fighting for. And she'd do anything to keep her family together.

But the tears in Lucille's eyes weakened her resolve.

'One day, maybe,' she conceded.

That evening, Lily's thoughts were miles away.

The girls exchanged glances, puzzled. When anyone spoke to her, Mother replied shortly. What was wrong with her? She was usually so reasonable, so good-natured.

Once the girls had gone to bed, Lily told Matt all about Lucille's visit.

'She's so anxious to see Meg again,' she said. 'I had to give in. But, oh, Matt, I can see trouble ahead. I wish she'd never come back.'

The scent of Lucille's perfume still hung about the kitchen. Lily flung the window wide open, as if she could blow away all traces of Lucille's visit – and blow away, too, all her anxieties about Meg's future.

Chapter Three

'Don't worry about it,' Matt repeated the next morning. He knew that Lily was troubled about Lucille's visit and he wanted to comfort her, though he, too, felt anxious.

Would Lucille come back next year? Would she want to take Meg away with her? Had her visit unsettled Meg even further? So many questions ... and all unanswered...

'Miss Lucille's seen Meg,' he reassured Lily, pushing his own doubts aside, 'but she's got her own life now. She won't try to take her back.'

'I hope not.' Lily sighed.

'You can be pretty sure of that,' Matt said. He sounded very definite – much more so than he felt.

'I expect you're right.' There was no point in worrying about the situation, Lily knew. All she could do was try to put the disturbing thoughts out of her mind and enjoy the rest of that golden summer.

And there was plenty to enjoy. Lily's precious garden was thriving and, greatly daring, she entered for the amateur classes in the local flower show.

She was thrilled to win a second for an

arrangement of mixed perennials, beating competitors from Freuchie and Pitlessie and even further afield.

And Janet was growing prettier every day. Rab certainly thought so, anyway! Lily smiled at the thought.

She'd been a little surprised when she answered the door one afternoon, to find herself looking at a stocky young man with fair curly hair and a rather bashful expression.

'Is Miss Janet in?' he asked, all in a rush.

'She's not back yet,' Lily replied. Then, taking pity on the lad, she asked, 'Do you want to come in and wait for her?'

He wiped his boots carefully on the scraper by the door and seated himself on the edge of a chair, his cap clutched between his hands.

'You'll be Rab?' Lily asked, putting two and two together. 'Bess's cousin?'

He nodded.

She filled the kettle, hiding a smile. It was clear he was anxious to see Janet, and disappointed to find she wasn't at home.

'Janet said you'd kindly offered Ellen one of your pups,' she said.

'If you're agreeable...' he began nervously.

'Of course,' Lily told him. 'Ellen's a real one for animals – she knows all the cats and dogs in the street! She'd love to have a dog of her own.'

'I'll bring it next time I come,' the young man said eagerly.

He drank his tea slowly. Lily offered him one of her scones spread with treacle. His eyes lit up.

'These are really good,' he told her.

Lily picked up her knitting and chatted of this and that, trying to put the young man at his ease, whilst all the time listening out for Janet.

'She's only gone a message to a neighbour – she won't be long,' she reassured him. 'Have another scone.'

When Janet arrived at last, the young man leapt to his feet, upsetting his cup of tea and dropping his scone, treacle side down, on the rug.

'Oh!' He went red, and tried to scrape it up, spreading treacle over the rug as he did so.

'I'm sorry, Mrs Barclay,' he apologised.

'That's all right.' Lily couldn't help feeling for him – the poor lad was so anxious to make a good impression.

'Don't worry,' she told him. 'That rug's had a good few things split on it – and soon we'll have a pup chewing it, no doubt.'

Janet was standing uncertainly by the door. Lily realised that she was as shy as the young man. Was she to do all the talking herself?

'Rab's here to see you, and he's kindly

offered to give us a pup for Ellen,' Lily told her daughter.

Janet found her tongue.

'She'll be pleased. Ellen's fond of animals.'

'So your mother said.' Now that the ice was broken, Rab was more confident.

'There were four pups – my father's picked out one to train as a working dog. The mother's a real winner. We've had her at the sheepdog trials.'

'It must be a lot of work, training a dog,' Janet said.

'It is that,' Rab agreed.

'I've never been to sheepdog trials,' Janet said, 'but they say the dogs are so clever, the things they can do.'

'You could come with us some time,' Rab offered eagerly. 'If that's all right, I mean...'

Lily smiled.

'Of course it is. Would you like more tea, Rab?'

'I've had enough, Mrs Barclay, thank you.'

'Why don't you two go for a walk?' Lily suggested. 'It's far too good a day to be sitting inside. Have you been to see Bess and her mother?'

The young man blushed.

'No, I thought – that is – I was just passing through. I thought I'd drop in – see about the pup.'

'Away you go, both of you,' Lily said. 'And bring Rab back for his tea, Janet. You'll have time to stop?'

'Thanks.' He smiled; he had a nice, frank, open sort of face, Lily noticed approvingly.

When they'd gone, she sat down and laughed to herself. Oh, she wished Matt was here to share the joke.

Just passing through, indeed! Pennyglen was miles from Rab's home at Glendores. He wasn't on his way anywhere – he'd come specially to see Janet.

But she liked the lad, and his bashful way of speaking, and she was amused, too, by Janet's sudden shyness.

Oh, it took her back! The first time she met Matt, she couldn't think of anything to say, either!

Janet had lots of admirers – she was never short of a young man to walk her home from the mill. But Rab was different – and less confident than the rest. Lily liked him for that.

And so the summer slipped happily past.

There were regular letters and cheques from Lucille. Lily opened the envelopes tremulously, fearful of reading that Lucille was planning another visit.

It was with a sigh of relief that she opened the letter in the spring of 1912.

We will be in London this summer but, alas, we won't have time to come north, as Elmer has to return to the States almost immediately on a matter of business.

Lily felt as if a great burden of worry had been lifted from her shoulders. She was thankful that Lucille was on the other side of the Atlantic – for the moment, anyway. It was better that way.

She wished, though, that she felt happier about Meg. The girl said little about her work in the mill, but Lily sensed that she was restless.

'It's as if she was a pot boiling, and the lid was about to be blown off,' she said to Matt, who told her not to fuss so much.

He'd heard from Mr Meikle that Meg was a good enough worker – a bit dreamy, maybe, but she did her share.

Still, Lily felt that Meg was biding her time. The girl often went up to the Big House, Pitlady, and she'd come back with stories of how they did things there.

Matt laughed at her.

'We'll have none of those fancy ways here,' he'd tease.

The months wore on. Meg was fifteen now, nearly sixteen, and growing tall. She was attractive, too, with her dark hair and eyes.

One day Mr Meikle asked her to run an errand.

'Take this invoice to the office, Meg. Miss Fraser's away, so just leave it on her desk.'

'She's away all this week,' one of the girls chipped in. 'She's on holiday – she's visiting her sister in Largs.'

Meg hadn't been in the office for a long time. She laid the invoice on the desk and looked around at the panelled walls, the dark green paint, the calendar on the wall, the photographs.

But her glance was drawn to the desk and the typewriter under its cover. She looked around. There was no-one in sight. The manager was on his dinner break.

The heat of the midday sun warmed the room, and she could hear only the throb of the looms very faintly in the distance.

Greatly daring, Meg lifted off the cover and looked at the typewriter. Oh, what wouldn't she give for a chance to learn to type!

She noticed a heavy wicker wastepaper basket on the floor – and in it were a few scraps of paper. With a quick glance to see that no-one was coming, she unfolded a piece of paper and put it carefully into the machine.

Now she picked out the letters: *M ... e ... g.* It was like magic!

She tried her surname: *B ...a ... r ... c ... l ... a ... y.* That was more difficult; she made one or two mistakes.

Now the date. She glanced at the calendar on the wall.

Capital S. She experimented until she found the shift key, then typed *September 20.*

Then the year – *1913*.

Perhaps she could type her name again, all in capitals? Better not. Reluctantly, she took the paper out of the typewriter, folded it carefully and tucked it into the pocket of her overall.

She replaced the cover of the machine, looked round the office and then carefully closed the door behind her. Her head was whirling with plans...

Back in the shed, she made casual enquiries.

How long was Miss Fraser away?

'All this week,' Bess said. Bess always seemed to know everything.

A plan was taking shape in Meg's mind. Why shouldn't she learn to use the typewriter while Miss Fraser was away?

No-one would know. No-one would mind.

That evening, at home, she went round the house, gathering up scraps of paper – pages from an old jotter, a grocery list, even old paper bags. Next day she put the paper into her piece tin. She said nothing to Janet – she had the feeling that her sister wouldn't approve.

All morning she could hardly concentrate on her work. She was waiting eagerly for the midday break.

'Coming down by the burn, Meg?' one of the girls asked her.

'Not today.' Meg shook her head.

Her friend shrugged. Meg could be moody sometimes. It was best to leave her alone.

Once they'd gone, Meg opened the door of the office – good, the room was empty.

She stood for a moment, listening. There was no-one around. As she lifted the cover off the typewriter, she felt a little tremor of excitement.

'Today I'll practise doing spaces,' she said to herself.

The time went past so quickly that it seemed only minutes before the dinner break was over. She replaced the cover and gathered up the pieces of paper. She glanced over them. Yes, she was definitely improving.

Every day that week, Meg stole away at the dinner break to practise on the typewriter. Oh, this was wonderful! If only she could type all the time – how exciting her job would be!

She typed very slowly, biting her lip in irritation whenever she made a mistake. But what a sense of triumph when she got it right!

At last, on the Friday, she managed to type a whole letter.

It was one she'd made up, but she thought it looked very professional and business-like. *Yours faithfully*, she finished – with no mistakes.

'And what do you think you're doing here?' Mr Meikle stood in the doorway.

'Oh!' Meg jumped up and clapped a hand to her mouth. 'I was just...'

'I can see what you're doing,' the overseer said. 'And you've no right to be here, let alone using that typewriter.'

Meg knew he was right, of course. But inside her there was a feeling of injustice. She wasn't doing any harm. No-one else needed the typewriter this week. Why shouldn't she use it?

A small voice of conscience spoke inside her head. 'You should have asked...' But Meg ignored it.

'I wasn't doing any harm,' she said defensively.

The overseer's face went red.

'How dare you answer back to me!'

Meg's temper rose.

'I said I wasn't doing any harm. I want to learn to type – Miss Fraser said I'd be good at it. And why shouldn't I? I might be some use to the mill as a typist.'

They stood glaring at each other.

'You've no right. This office is private,' he insisted.

'I've every right!' As soon as she said it, Meg knew she'd gone too far.

'I'll tell you what your rights are, miss,' the overseer said, incensed. 'You can take your lines and go, and you needn't bother coming back.

'You're an impudent hussy, and you needn't think that because your father's a manager, you've got a job here. You're dismissed!'

Meg picked up her things and walked out, head held high. She wasn't going to cry, she was nearly grown up. She walked out of the mill gate.

'Hey, Meg, where are you going?' Jessie called out to her. Meg paid no attention.

At home, Lily was about to go out. She stopped when she saw Meg come in, looking white and shaken.

'Meg, what's the matter?' Lily was surprised. 'It's only just after two. What's brought you home so early? Are you ill?'

Meg shook her head.

'I've been dismissed.' Her voice trembled.

'Oh, Meg – never!' The colour drained from Lily's face. 'You can't mean it! Dismissed?'

Meg nodded.

'Yes, it's true,' she said, and she burst into tears.

Lily stared at her daughter.

'What happened?' she said at last.

Meg drew a deep breath and tried to explain. But she could see that Lily – who was usually so sympathetic, so ready to champion her children – just didn't understand.

80

'Oh, Meg, what have you done? What's your father going to say?' she repeated over and over again.

When Matt came home that evening, it was plain that he already knew what had happened. Normally cheerful and smiling, tonight his face was grave.

Meg waited, nervously twisting her fingers together, as he took his boots off.

'Oh, Matt, something terrible's happened!' Lily burst out.

'I know. I've heard it already. It's all round the mill.' Matt sat down heavily at the kitchen table.

Meg was a little frightened. She'd never seen her father so angry.

'And what have you got to say for yourself?' he demanded.

That was like Matt, Lily thought. Even though he'd heard all about Meg's dismissal already, he was willing to let her speak for herself.

'I just wanted to learn to type,' Meg said, flustered. 'What's wrong with that?

'Lots of girls are learning to type and do shorthand and have proper jobs. That's what the suffragettes are fighting for – freedom and votes for women.'

Matt thumped his fist on the table.

'Stop that nonsense! It's *you* we're talking about – not the suffragettes! You've lost your job and disgraced the family, through sheer impertinence. You should be ashamed of yourself!'

'Well, I'm not! Why shouldn't I say what *I* want to do?'

There were spots of colour in Meg's cheeks. She faced her father across the table, just as angry as he was.

'I'll have none of that talk in this house,' Matt said. 'You'll write and apologise to Mr Meikle, and you'll stay and help your mother at home till we decide what's to be done with you.'

'Oh, Meg.' Lily was nearly in tears. 'How could you?'

'The damage is done,' Matt finished. 'There's no more to be said. We'd best have our tea.'

'I don't want anything to eat,' Meg sobbed, and with that she fled upstairs.

'I'm not very hungry myself.' Matt sighed.

When Janet came in that evening, she found Meg lying on the bed, gazing at the ceiling. Janet had spent the afternoon with Rab. They'd walked and picnicked, and talked of their plans for the future.

Rab was full of enthusiasm. At last, he'd saved enough money to buy a new motorcycle. Next week, he'd go over to Christie's in St Andrews.

'They've got the new Triumph and the new Abingdon,' he told Janet, his face glowing with excitement.

She thought again how cheerful and open he was. There was no need to put on airs with Rab – she could just be herself. It was a lovely feeling.

But now, the happy, peaceful mood of the day was shattered.

'What's wrong?' Janet asked her sister.

'Haven't you heard?'

'I've been away all afternoon, with Rab. You know I had a half-day's holiday to take.'

'You'll hear soon enough.' Meg sniffed. She sat up and explained between sobs what had happened.

'And Father's so angry – I've never seen him so wild. But I was only speaking up for myself – and why not? I've got the right–' she said defensively.

Janet drew a deep breath.

'Will I tell you what I think?'

Meg nodded. Janet was always so sympathetic. She was sure to see her sister's point of view.

'I think you're being selfish,' Janet said. 'I think you've behaved very badly.' Her voice rose.

'Don't you realise how good Father and Mother are to us all? And they don't make any difference between us,' she hurried on.

'Yes, I know I promised not to speak about you being adopted, but you've been so lucky. And yet you're never away from the Big House, copying their ways.

'You're a snob, Meg, that's what you are, and if you don't say you're sorry to Mother and Father, then I'll never speak to you again!' She stopped, flushed.

Meg was taken aback.

'I'm not selfish. Or snobbish or ungrateful,' she protested.

Janet shrugged.

'Maybe you don't see it, but you are. Think about it.' She hung her jacket on the back of a chair and took the pins out of her hair. 'I'm going downstairs.'

When Janet came to bed, Meg was asleep. Next morning, she got up slowly, while Janet was preparing for work. She felt limp and exhausted, and her head ached.

'Janet–' she began.

'Yes?' Janet's tone was polite but distant.

'You were right. I'll say I'm sorry to Mother and Father – but it won't make any difference. I won't get my job back.'

Janet didn't know what to say. She gave her sister a quick hug.

'Friends again?' she asked.

Meg nodded.

Later, when Janet had gone to work and the younger ones to school, Meg made her way downstairs.

Lily was busy at the stove.

'Mother...'

Lily turned round.

'I'm – I'm so sorry.'

84

Lily had never heard Meg speak like this before. Her warm heart went out to the girl – how pale she looked, how woebegone.

'I've caused you and Father a lot of unhappiness,' Meg said. 'I'll try harder, I promise.'

Lily put her arms round the girl.

'I know you will,' she said.

'Now listen to me. Your father and I have been thinking. If you're so anxious to learn to type, wouldn't you like to learn properly?'

Meg stared at her, her hopes rising.

'You could go to secretarial college in Dundee,' Lily said. 'Oh, I know there are evening classes in Cupar, at the Castlehill – but maybe you'd like to go full-time.'

'But,' Meg faltered, 'wouldn't it cost a lot?'

'There's money for it,' Lily said firmly, thinking of Lucille's regular payment.

She reached up to the mantelpiece and lifted down the pirlie pig.

'Take a seat, dear.' She sat down at the kitchen table and Meg followed suit.

'Now–' Lily shook the pig, and bright coins tumbled out on to the scrubbed wood.

'The pirlie pig's never let us down yet,' Lily said kindly, counting the money. 'And I dare say there's enough here to start you on your way.' She looked up and smiled at Meg, a deep, warm smile that touched her daughter's heart.

'Oh, Mother!' Meg blinked back the tears

that threatened suddenly to fall. She could hardly believe that everything was going to turn out well, after all.

'I'll try. I really will,' she promised.

'Yes,' Lily said. 'I know you will.'

Rab and Janet were meeting more and more frequently. Rab would often come over to Pennyglen on some pretext or other.

Willie was fascinated by the new motor-cycle and Rab patiently explained the finer points of the wonderful machine.

Rab was always cheerful and friendly, but Janet wondered if anything would come of their friendship.

He'd taken her to the Lammas Fair, and bought her a little enamel heart – surely that meant something, Janet thought, looking at her reflection in the mirror as she fixed the clasp.

She couldn't help recalling her friend Bess's warning: 'Rab's only interested in machines...'

She smiled, thinking of his enthusiasm. Every time they met, he had some new mechanical marvel, some wonderful invention to tell her about.

'Just imagine,' he said one day, as they sat on the bank of the burn. He lay back in the sunshine, chewing a piece of grass and gazing at the sky.

'Captain Longcroft – you know, the

Montrose airman – he set a new record from Farnborough to Montrose. Ten hours! Just think of that! Isn't it great?

'I wish I could learn to fly. Some hope!' He tossed the piece of grass away.

'I'd like to join the Royal Flying Corps, but I don't suppose I'll ever get near a 'plane.'

For a moment he looked rather downcast, but then his cheerful good temper surfaced.

'Oh, well – there'll be other things to do.'

Janet shivered.

'You're not cold, are you?' he asked.

She shook her head, and he leaned over and put an arm around her.

'It was a great achievement. Of course, it wasn't ten hours' actual flying. More like eight in the air. But it's a terrific record.'

Janet smiled, but her heart was heavy. Didn't she mean anything to Rab? Didn't he ever think about their future? He seemed far more interested in motorcycles and aeroplanes than in her...

Rab spent the next day hard at work on the farm. When he finally stopped for a break during the afternoon, he was surprised to find his mother had a visitor – and a bit put out when he recognised who she was.

'Oh, I'm sorry,' he excused himself, ready to turn round and head back outdoors.

'No, no.' His mother stopped him. 'Stay

and have a cup of tea and a chat with Elsie.'

'Hello, Rab, you're a great stranger! We haven't seen you at the dances for ages.'

The girl sitting in the chair by the fireside had tight, dark curls and a highly-coloured complexion. Her voice was shrill as she chattered away.

'I was just saying to your mother that you haven't been across to visit us lately, either. What's got into you, eh?' She gave him a roguish glance.

'Nothing,' Rab mumbled. 'I've been busy.'

'Here's your tea,' his mother said. 'Just you sit down and have a bit of a blether with Elsie – you haven't seen her for such a long time. You two will have a lot of things to talk about.' She beamed at the girl.

'I haven't time,' Rab said bluntly.

'Nonsense,' his mother retorted.

'What's wrong, Rab – are you scared of me?' The girl gave a chirping little laugh.

Rab gazed morosely into his cup, while she chattered about the soldiers in the town, the soirées and socials she had been to, of the treat it was to get away for a day from the bustle of the farm, how her father had just bought a fine new car, how they were going to Rothsay or maybe Dunoon this summer...

'You'll need to excuse me.' Rab rose suddenly, pushing his chair back. 'I'm needed in the stables.'

'Here, Rab!' his mother called after him, but he ignored her.

'I'm sorry,' she apologised to the girl.

'He's shy,' Elsie said. 'They're all the same, these lads.'

'But I'm sure he likes to talk to you,' Rab's mother went on, a little desperately. 'Maybe another time...'

When Rab came in later on, the visitor had gone.

'I was black affronted at you,' his mother said. 'Fancy you being so rude to that fine lass, and her so smart and trig. I didn't know where to look.'

Rab shrugged.

'She's got too long a tongue on her, that one,' he said.

'You're far too particular,' his mother told him roundly. 'She's a fine lass and she'd be a good match for you.

'That's a grand farm her family has – and no sons to inherit it, either. You'd be right well off there. I tell you, you'd be a fool to let her go.'

Rab rose from his seat and thumped the table. He disliked the girl and her endless chattering. He thought in that moment of Janet, who seemed so cool and quiet, with such a gentle voice.

'You'd better understand this,' he said, in a voice that neither of his parents had heard him use before. 'I'll do my own courting and I'll choose my own girl. Is that clear?'

He stomped out, slamming the door behind him.

'Well, now,' his father said wryly. 'That's not like him. I think, Alice, you'd be best not to meddle. He's a deep one, is Rab – I wouldn't be surprised if he had a girl in mind, of his own choosing.'

A few months later, Meg began her studies at the secretarial college. It was a long day, with an early rise to catch the train from the station to Dundee, but she didn't mind – she was much too excited.

When she came home at night, she hardly stopped talking – about the big room where all the students sat; about the teacher who praised her grasp of the first shorthand out-lines they'd learned; about the other girls.

Every evening she pored over her books, and practised her shorthand – and tried, whenever she could, to get Matt or Janet to read to her from the day's paper.

'It's for practice,' she said. 'So that I can get my speeds up.'

'All right.' Matt smiled at Lily over Meg's head. They were both pleased that she seemed so busy and happy.

Matt scanned the paper.

'There's this trouble in the Balkans,' he said. 'It doesn't sound too good.'

Lily looked up.

'But the Balkans are a very long way away,' she said comfortingly. 'How could it possibly make any difference to us?'

But, as the long summer of 1914 wore on, people talked more and more about the likelihood of war.

'Don't trust that Kaiser,' the older folk said.

'If the Germans attack Belgium, we can't stand by,' others put in.

In early August, war was declared. People looked at one another, bewildered.

At first, life seemed to go on as normal, but already the Territorials had been called up.

While children built sandcastles and enjoyed donkey rides at St Andrews, three planes made practice landings on the sands – a reminder that war wasn't far away from the peace of a Scottish seaside resort.

Young men from all over the country were flocking to enlist.

'Listen to this,' Matt read from the local newspaper.

'"With the close of harvest rapidly approaching, a fine body of recruits, well used to horses, should be readily forthcoming in so large an agricultural district."' He looked grave.

'Brings it near home, that.'

'Thank goodness Willie is too young to go,' Lily said.

As soon as the words were out she felt ashamed of herself. Maybe Willie was too young, but there would be other mothers' sons already joining up.

Janet was silent. Lily glanced at her. Was she wondering about Rab? How long would it be before he joined up?

During the long summer days, the harvest continued. It was a good harvest this year for wheat and barley, though the farmers shook their heads and said that the oats weren't as good as in past years.

Farmers worked on Sundays to get the crops in.

'They'll be commandeering the horses soon, for the cavalry,' Rab's father said.

But, at last, the harvest was in.

The harvest supper at Glendores was one everyone would remember for a very long time.

Trestle tables were laid out in the barn, with cold meats and a ham and stovies, and trifle and apple tart and fruit cake to follow – enough to satisfy the heartiest of appetites.

And then, when everyone had eaten enough, the tables were cleared away and the band tuned up.

Rab danced with all the girls, but though he swung them in the Lancers, and birled in the reels, his thoughts were miles away. He couldn't help thinking of Janet.

August turned into September, and the pace of the war seemed to quicken.

Rab's mother, Alice, had joined a working party whose members were already knitting khaki socks and helmets.

There was disturbing news from the front of the retreat from Mons.

When Rab took Janet to the cinema, there were newsreels showing scenes from Belgium. As they watched the flickering screen, the war seemed very near.

Early in September, the posters appeared and notices were published in the papers. *Join the Second Army now. Your King and Country Need You.*

A few days later, Rab spoke to his father.

'I've decided to enlist,' he told him.

'I thought you'd be going.' His father drew thoughtfully on his pipe.

'Will you manage the farm on your own?' Rab asked.

'We'll manage all right.'

'I couldn't let the others go without me,' Rab said seriously.

Later that week, he went down to the recruiting office in Cupar. Home again, he took down from the dresser a bottle of ink, pen, paper and an envelope. He seldom wrote a letter, but this one was important.

It was delivered at Pennyglen the next day.

'There's a letter for you, Janet,' Lily said, when the girl came in from the mill.

'For me?' Janet was surprised.

Her hand trembled slightly as she opened the envelope.

'It's from Rab,' she said bleakly, without looking up. 'He's joined up. He's leaving on Saturday.'

All that Saturday morning, Janet found it hard to attend to her work. When stopping time came, she hurried out of the mill gate, her thoughts in turmoil.

She was lucky in getting a lift to Cupar. Meg had offered to go with her, but Janet had refused. This was something she had to do by herself.

At the railway station at Cupar, people were already waiting for the volunteers to arrive.

Janet found a place on the platform. Around her, people chattered in excitement, and some lads were setting off fog signals to welcome the soldiers.

'They're here!' A small boy came rushing into the station forecourt. 'They're coming down the Crossgate! And there's a piper!'

The men who marched into the station were a small group, heads held high – some looking proud, others a little embarrassed at the attention.

'Our brave boys! God bless them!' a woman cried out.

And there was Rab, in the midst of them.

Friends and relatives crowded round, wishing them luck.

Rab's eyes scanned the platform. His face lit up when he saw Janet.

'I was sure you'd come,' he said.

Janet was tongue-tied. Oh, this was stupid, she thought – just like the first time they met. She wouldn't be seeing Rab for a long time, and she couldn't think of anything to say.

He took her in his arms, and she looked up at him.

'It's a stupid time to ask you,' he said, 'but I wondered – that is...' He stopped, confused.

'Yes?' Janet prompted.

'When I come back,' he said, all in a rush, 'would you – wait for me? I mean, what I'm trying to say is...'

Janet smiled up at him. He took her face in both his hands.

'When I come back, would you marry me?'

'Oh, yes!' Janet reached up and covered one of his hands with her hand. 'Oh, yes, Rab, I will.'

'Then I'll go off to fight, knowing you'll be here,' he said, his face serious. He held her close and they stood, quite oblivious to the crowds around them.

'Oh, come back to me,' Janet said. 'Come back safe...'

'Here's the train!' A cheer went up as the men climbed on board. The guard blew his whistle and, in a puff of steam, the train drew out of the station.

Janet waved until the train was out of sight, her heart pounding.

She knew she'd remember this day for as long as she lived. She'd never forget the feel of Rab's arms around her ... the sound of his voice as he whispered that he loved her...

She hugged the memory to her fiercely.

As she turned and made her way slowly out of the station, she realised, with a shiver of apprehension, that nothing would ever be the same again.

Not for her, newly-engaged woman; nor for Rab, off to risk his life in the fight for freedom – and certainly not for the people of the Howe of Fife, touched as never before by what was happening in the outside world.

Without a backward glance, she turned down the Crossgate and headed for home.

Chapter Four

December 4, 1914. Lily dipped her pen into the inkwell and paused.

Dear Miss Lucille, she wrote carefully, still unable, after all these years, to call her former employer anything else.

We are all well, though the news from the war is bad, and every day we hear of young men from the district who have been killed or wounded.

Janet's young man, Rab, is at training camp, and will soon be home on leave. After that, he may be sent to France – we don't know. Poor Janet looks so anxious, though she never says anything.

On a happier note – Meg is doing well at the business college in Dundee. She's learning short-hand, typing, book-keeping and commercial English.

Thank you again for your generous gift, which has made it possible to pay her fees.

She paused, listening for Matt's footsteps. He would be home for his tea soon.

She was concerned about Matt. He often looked worried these days. Already the mill's orders from America had dwindled – and there were no supplies of flax coming from the Continent.

She resolved to finish the letter later, and picked up her knitting.

Lily's fingers were never idle, and now she was busier than ever.

Soon after war had been declared, almost every village and town had formed a working party. The women met weekly, and produced socks and scarves, mittens and helmets for the men at the Front.

'I've none of my own to knit for,' old Miss Macpherson had said, holding up a sock. 'But I can still hold a pair of pins – and there are plenty lads who'll need warm socks in the trenches.'

'It's keeping their feet dry, that's the problem,' another woman had added.

'That's just what my Jamie said,' a third chimed in. 'I've got his letter here. *Socks would be warmly welcomed,* he says, *as we cannot get enough to keep our feet dry.*'

'It must be awful for those poor lads,' Lily said with a shiver.

Sometimes one of the women would slip a little note into a parcel destined for a hospital, or pinned a message to a bed-jacket or woollen shirt. *To the soldier who wears this, I wish you a speedy recovery.*

'Poor lads,' one woman said with a sigh. 'It's all we can do for them.'

The day came for Rab's leave. Waiting for his train to arrive at the station, Janet felt suddenly shy.

Rab had been gone for three months – would he have changed? Would he already be different from the cheerful, sunny-tempered lad she'd known?

But she needn't have worried.

'Janet!' he called from the end of the platform, waving his bonnet as he broke into a run. People around them smiled and nodded, and Janet blushed. Fancy, in front of all these folk!

He swept her into his arms.

'Oh, it's grand to see you!'

'Here, careful!' She laughed. 'You're knocking my hat off, and I put it on specially for you.'

'Oh, never mind your hat. My, you're as bonnie as ever!'

Janet, held close against the rough serge of his jacket, wasn't sure whether to laugh or cry. She was engulfed with happiness at just seeing him again.

'Oh, Rab,' she whispered. 'It's seemed such a long time. I've missed you.'

'And I've missed you...'

She clutched his arm as they made their way along the platform, past the ticket barrier.

'So you're home then, Rab,' old Geordie the ticket-collector said. 'Glad to see you, lad.'

'Good to see you, too.' Rab put down his

kitbag and shook the old man's hand.

'When you get out there,' Geordie said, 'see you knock them to Jericho, or wherever!'

'Aye, well, we'll see...'

Janet trembled a little, and Rab patted her hand consolingly.

'Let me have my leave first,' he said. 'I'm going to have a grand time – enjoy some home cooking and all that, while I can.'

'Rab–' Janet grasped his hand tightly, as they left the station '–are you going to the Front?'

'I'm not allowed to say,' he told her. 'But forget about all that.' He gave her a hug. 'We're going to have a grand time, you and I.'

The days passed in a happy haze. Janet knew, even then, that she would treasure the memory of them for ever.

She and Rab spent almost every hour together, walking through the woods, and marvelling at the frost patterns on the bracken and hedgerows as if they'd never seen such things before. They went to the cinema in St Andrews, and to concerts in Cupar.

Sometimes, they just sat in Lily's kitchen and drank tea and laughed and joked as if the war was not uppermost in everyone's mind.

One afternoon, Rab held a skein of wool

for Lily as she wound yarn for yet more socks.

'There's a pair for you, Rab, and a muffler. Make sure you don't go without them,' she said.

Young Willie listened with excitement to Rab's tales of Army life.

'It sounds great,' he said enviously. 'I wish I could be a soldier.'

Lily drew in her breath. How thankful she was that Willie was too young to enlist.

'It's anything but exciting,' Rab said. 'It's hard work, and pretty dull – marching, cookhouse duties, polishing buttons. Oh, there's nothing exciting about it, I can tell you.'

One day, shortly before the end of his leave, he asked Janet if she'd go to Dundee with him for the day.

'That would be a real treat,' she said. Of course, Meg was at secretarial college there now, but Janet hardly ever went to the town.

How busy it seemed after Pennyglen! And what crowds of people thronged the pavements! Janet could hardly take her eyes off the shop windows.

'Oh, isn't that beautiful!' She stopped to admire a black velvet hat in Draffen's window. It was so elegant, trimmed with a rose of black velvet. Twenty-one shillings! A whole guinea!

'Here!' Rab teased her. 'I didn't bring you

to Dundee to look at hats.'

'I'm sorry,' she said. 'I got carried away.'

He tucked her hand into the crook of his arm.

'I've seen a ring I think you'd like... An engagement ring, of course.'

'Oh, Rab!' She gazed up at him, her eyes sparkling with happiness. 'Do you really mean it?'

'Of course! I want everyone to know that you've promised to be my wife,' he declared proudly.

'It's only a small diamond,' Rab said later, a little apologetically, as Janet admired the ring on her finger, 'but...'

'Sh...' she silenced him. 'It's just beautiful.'

'Come on.' Rab smiled at her. 'We've just time for a cup of tea before we catch the train.'

'It's a special occasion – let's celebrate,' he said, so they went to D. M. Brown's tea-room.

As they sat, listening to the music, Janet looked around her. A few tables away, a young man, no older than Rab, sat with a girl about Janet's age.

Ordinarily, Janet wouldn't have noticed him, but for the empty sleeve pinned to the shoulder of his jacket – and the way the young woman cut up his food for him, and put his cup and saucer within easy reach.

The waitress nodded sympathetically.

'Aye,' she said, as she took Rab's order, 'there's a good few lads who've been wounded and sent back to the Eastern Hospital. That'll be one of them.'

Janet looked at the young soldier.

She felt heart-sorry for him, and for the girl, too, who was no older than herself, but who was smiling and laughing as though everything was quite normal, and there was just as much to smile about as ever.

A small cloud passed over the sunshine of her day. What if something happened to Rab?

Rab's hand enclosed hers, as if he knew what she was thinking.

'Don't you worry,' he said. 'I'll take good care.' But she knew that nothing he could say would reassure her...

The first thing they did when they got back to Pennyglen was share their news with Matt and Lily and the rest of the family.

'Engaged? Oh, what wonderful news! I'm so happy for you both!' Lily's eyes filled with tears of joy.

'Congratulations!' Meg hugged her sister warmly. 'Be happy.'

'Welcome to the family, lad.' Matt shook Rab's hand, his eyes twinkling.

He liked the open-faced, honest young man – he'd make Janet a good husband. If...

There was always that 'if' now. No-one

knew what the war would bring; how many lives it would shatter.

But this wasn't the time for thinking like that.

'This calls for a celebration,' Matt announced. He opened the cupboard and brought out the glasses and the bottle that was kept for the New Year.

Rab, looking round the circle of happy faces, and enjoying the warmth of the welcome, wondered what sort of reception he would get back home when he broke the news to his parents.

'I hope you'll make Janet welcome, Mother,' Rab said.

Alice hadn't uttered a word since he'd announced that he and Janet were engaged.

'Oh, aye,' his father assured him. 'We're glad you've found such a fine lass.'

There was a silence.

'Mother?' Rab said.

His mother busied herself at the stove.

'I said, I hope you'll make her welcome,' he repeated.

'She's your choice,' Alice snapped, stony-faced.

'Yes, she's my choice. What have you got against her?'

'I've told you – nothing. Except...'

'Except what?' Rab asked.

'Well, she's a mill girl, and she's not from

104

farming folk.'

'A mill girl?' Rab laughed incredulously. 'For goodness' sake, Mother – that's an awful snobbish thing to say.'

'I don't mean it to be snobbish,' his mother retorted sharply. 'She's from a perfectly decent family. All I'm saying is she's not like us.

'You'd have done better to have chosen a girl from a farm, someone who knew how to milk, how to churn butter, who could help me with the work.'

Rab sighed.

'That's unkind – and uncalled for,' he said firmly. 'I'll expect you to make her welcome and not treat her like she was an outsider. After all, she's part of the family now.'

Even as he said it, he had doubts. He knew his mother, and her rigid, unbending nature, too well. She'd made up her mind about Janet, and she wasn't going to change.

'Anyway,' he went on, 'I'm bringing her over here on Saturday, so I'll expect you to make her welcome.'

Next Saturday, Janet and Rab arrived early in the afternoon.

'You've not to make any special preparations,' he'd told his mother, knowing that she would set tea in the parlour, no matter what he said.

'Janet's one of the family now. Just a cup of tea in the kitchen – that'll be fine.'

'A cup of tea in the kitchen, indeed!' His mother bridled. 'I'm not having folk from Pennyglen saying we don't know how to do things properly here.'

So it was tea in the parlour, a formal meal with a strained atmosphere. Alice spoke little.

'I'm very pleased to hear your news, I'm sure,' she'd said when Janet arrived, but there was no warmth in her voice, no welcoming embrace for the girl.

'We might go for a walk up the road. There's a fine moon tonight,' Rab announced after tea.

His mother was silent.

'We'll help you clear away and do the dishes first,' Janet offered.

'I'll manage.' Alice lifted the heavy wooden tray. 'You go off and have your walk.'

It was a clear, frosty night as Rab and Janet strolled up the track from the farm towards the main road.

They hadn't gone far before they saw a figure turning off and heading towards them.

'Oh, dash and bother it,' Rab muttered. He'd wanted to be alone with Janet.

'Hello, Elsie,' he said wearily, as the figure drew near.

'Well, it's never you, Rab?' The girl stopped and greeted him effusively, ignoring Janet.

'I was just on my way up to the farm with a message. You're on leave, then? We've missed you at the dances lately.'

'This is Janet.' Rab introduced the two girls. 'We're engaged to be married.'

'Oh, my!' The girl's gaze swept over Janet, who suddenly felt rather dowdy in comparison with this breezy, confident young woman.

'Congratulations,' Elsie said briskly.

Janet had the uncomfortable feeling that she was being looked up and down and found wanting.

They made polite conversation for a moment or two. Then Janet and Rab continued on their walk, while Elsie headed for the farm.

Suddenly Janet saw the whole situation very clearly.

'That's why your mother doesn't like me, isn't it?' she asked.

'She does like you–' Rab began.

'Not really.' Janet turned to him. 'That girl – Elsie – she said she was going up to the farm. Did your mother think she'd be – suitable for you?'

'My mother's got nothing to do with my choice,' Rab said defiantly. Then he shrugged.

'But you're right – she does have a soft spot for Elsie. Oh, you know what mothers are like.'

Janet was silent. Her own mother was so different.

She thought, thankfully, of the simplicity of her own home. This planning and scheming was something she'd never encountered before.

'It makes no difference,' Rab said. 'Mother will come round, you'll see.'

'I hope so,' Janet said, rather soberly. 'It's going to be awful if she and I can't be friends.'

Rab's arms went round her and she felt secure in his love, but inside, she knew she faced a struggle. Rab's mother wasn't the kind of person to make her future daughter-in-law's life easy...

It was very quiet after Rab's leave was over and he'd gone. Janet looked at her precious ring, and wondered if it had all been a dream.

'I'll write as often as I can,' he'd promised. 'But you're not to worry if you don't hear from me for a bit. Sometimes it might be difficult to write...'

At home, things were very quiet. Matt often came back from work looking worried.

The mill had gone over to producing heavy-duty cloth for Government contracts. All the mills were finding things difficult, and the price of flax had risen to four times its pre-war level.

'There's no call for damask now,' Matt told Lily. 'We're lucky we do the coarser stuff.'

'Look at the Dunfermline mills – there are no orders coming in from America. Someone was telling me just the other day that four of the mills there have closed down.'

Only Meg seemed to be leading a normal sort of life, and she was engrossed in her studies at the college. And Ellen, soon to leave school, was as cheerful and sunnynatured as ever.

Lily often wondered what she'd do without her girls. They brightened up the home and made it a little easier to cope with the constant worry of news from the Front.

It saddened Lily to see how much quieter Janet had become. She waited daily for news of Rab, and sometimes she would go over to Glendores to visit his parents.

Janet always returned from these visits with very little to say.

Lily had met Alice, Rab's mother, and found her a dour, uncompromising sort of woman. Her heart ached for poor Janet, and she wished that somehow she could help her.

Meg still went up to the Big House whenever she could.

Now, more than ever, she was grateful to Mrs Grierson for allowing her to browse freely among the bookshelves. The Pitlady library was a welcome refuge from all the talk of war.

Today, Ellen had asked if she could go to the Big House with her sister.

Meg tapped at the kitchen door as usual.

'It's Meg, Mrs McKay. Is it all right if I come in?'

The cook turned from her work of trimming the edges of a pie.

'Oh, it's you. Come away in.' She smiled at the girls. 'My, the house is busy today.'

'Oh.' Meg hesitated. 'Maybe it's not convenient.'

'Don't be daft!' the cook said. 'Mrs Grierson's always pleased for you to come up. But you'll maybe not see her today – she's got company. Mr Colin's about, though.'

'Is he?' Meg's face glowed. 'Perhaps we'll see him.'

'You certainly will.'

Meg turned quickly at the sound of Colin's voice. She hadn't seen him for a while, and at first she hardly recognised the tall young man who smiled down at the two girls.

'You're quite grown up, Meg. And as for this young lady here – I hardly know who she is.'

'It's Ellen,' the younger girl said seriously. 'You remember me...'

'Of course I do! I'm only teasing.'

He smiled at them again.

'Come on through, you two. You'll want to

110

look at the books, Meg? We'll find something for Ellen to do.'

'What are you doing here?' Meg asked.

'Me?' He grinned at her. 'Well, I live here
for a start.'

'I didn't mean–' She blushed.

'I know you didn't. I've joined the RFC –
Royal Flying Corps – so I'm waiting for my
papers before I start training.'

'Flying,' Meg echoed. 'That's what you
wanted to do, isn't it?'

'It certainly is,' Colin said. 'I can't wait to
get up in the air.'

'Rab – Janet's young man – is in the Black
Watch,' Meg told him.

'Is he at the Front?' Colin's face was
serious.

'We don't know. Janet hasn't heard for a
bit.'

Meg's voice trembled. She felt for Janet, so
anxious and strained, waiting every day for
news.

'Come on.' Colin tried to lighten the
mood. 'Come and say hello to my mother.
She's got a friend here, but she won't mind.'

Mrs Grierson's friend was in her thirties,
and dressed in the height of fashion.

Meg instantly noticed the fine wool suit,
the elegant lace fichu, while Ellen's attention was drawn to the two lively children
who was squabbling over a Noah's ark of toy
animals.

'He's mine – the sheep's mine.' The small boy was red with anger.

'I had him first,' his sister insisted.

'Oh, dear.' The children's mother twisted her hands helplessly together. 'I'm so sorry about this, Helen, my dear.

'I wasn't going to bring them, but it's Nurse's day off, and we're having such trouble finding servants. There was simply no-one to leave them with.'

In a flash, Ellen was down on her knees beside the children.

'Why don't we put that sheep into the ark?' she suggested. 'The other poor sheep will be so lonely without him. Listen, I can hear the other one inside, baa-ing.'

The small boy stopped screaming.

'I can't hear anything,' he complained.

'You just might, if you listened,' Ellen told him with a smile. 'Isn't this a fine ark? You *are* lucky.'

She picked up one or two of the animals.

'I know a very good Noah's ark game,' she confided.

'Tell us,' the little girl urged.

'Well, it's like this…'

Ellen was soon engrossed in the game. All of a sudden, she looked up, and realised the children's mother was smiling at her.

'Oh, I'm so sorry. I got carried away,' she apologised.

'Don't stop,' the children clamoured.

'Yes, please do go on,' the children's mother said.

Mrs Grierson laid a hand on her friend's arm.

'Listen, my dear, why don't you and I go into the drawing-room and leave the children here with Ellen? I can assure you she's very responsible...'

'I can see that,' her friend said. 'Now, children, don't be a nuisance. I'm very grateful to you, Ellen.'

Colin and Meg had withdrawn, smiling.

'I've got things to see to in the stables,' Colin said. 'You know the way to the library. I'll see you before you go.' He went off, whistling.

Meg looked after him, marvelling at how grown up Colin suddenly seemed. He was different, somehow – more serious, that was it.

As always, once she was in the library, time didn't seem to matter. Meg loved it all – the deep pile of the carpet, the smell of linseed oil, the rich leather bindings of the books. And the books themselves! There was so much to read.

It seemed like only minutes, though it must have been a good hour and a half, before Ellen appeared at the door.

'Meg! Are you ready to go home?'

Meg came to with a start.

'I was miles away,' she admitted.

She put the book carefully back on the shelf.

'Weren't you looking after the children?' she asked.

'They've gone home now.' Ellen laughed. 'It was fun.'

'We'd better go then.' Meg glanced round the library.

'It's beautiful, isn't it?' Ellen didn't have Meg's love of books, but she could admire the dark velvet curtains and the huge leather armchairs.

She wandered over to a sofa table at the far end of the room. On the table stood a group of family photographs.

Ellen gazed at them idly.

'Meg! Look at this!' she called.

'Oh, Ellen, don't be so inquisitive. We must go.'

'No, wait a moment. This lady in the photograph. Doesn't she look like you?'

A little reluctantly, Meg crossed to the table, and looked at the photograph in its silver frame.

A slim young woman stood in a formal pose. She held a fan, and wore a heavily embroidered gown with a short train.

'She looks as if she's being presented at Court,' Meg said.

'But she looks very like you!' Ellen persisted.

'Nonsense!' Meg scoffed. 'Like me? As if

I'd ever be presented at Court! Don't be silly, Ellen. Come on, let's go!'

But she glanced again at the photograph. The girl in the picture wasn't at all like her or was she? Perhaps there was a resemblance – about the eyes? And what about the shape of the chin?

Could Ellen be right? She knew nothing about the secret Meg shared with Janet. Had she stumbled on something? Was there perhaps some sort of link between Meg and the family at the Big House?

At home, Lily knitted busily for the working party, and kept an anxious eye on Matt. He came home exhausted every evening, and sat reading the paper after tea. Now and then he sighed over the news.

Matt didn't play his fiddle quite so often now, and he didn't whistle cheerfully as he came up the path.

But both parents tried to make things as normal and cheerful as they could for Janet's sake. Janet waited daily for news of Rab. She twisted his ring on her finger and thought of his words.

'When I come back, we'll go and see the minister and fix a date for the wedding,' he'd promised.

Winter gave way to early spring. The snowdrops were out in the glen, and the days seemed to lengthen, just a little.

Sometimes Janet went over to Glendores as she'd promised Rab, but Alice, though pleasant enough, was still distant. Janet did all she could to be helpful and friendly, but every time she came away with a heavy heart.

She loved Rab – she had no doubt about that. But why was his mother so hostile, so unbending – surely she could accept her son's choice?

And then Janet heard from Rab. He was being posted with his regiment, but he couldn't tell her where.

Janet's heart plummeted. She knew only too well that he would be going to France.

I may not be able to write often, but I will drop you a line as soon as I can, he wrote. *Keep smiling.* That was so like Rab.

Janet resolved that she would be brave, just as thousands of other wives and mothers and sweethearts had to be. But it was hard.

That night, when she looked out of the window, all was still and quiet. Only a dog barked in the distance. The moon shone on the sleeping village and the frost sparkled on the rooftops.

Where was Rab, she wondered? Was he warm and sheltered? Was he safe? Oh, how she hoped he was.

The postman called one bright morning with a letter from the States. There was

116

nothing unusual about that – Lucille wrote perhaps once every six months, and sent cheques regularly.

Lily finished her ironing and then sat down to read Lucille's news.

She skimmed the first few paragraphs. Lucille was delighted to hear how well Meg was doing at secretarial college, how quick she was to master shorthand and typing.

And then: *Lily, I have a great favour to ask you. Won't you let Meg – and Ellen, too – come to stay with me here in the States for a while? I'd love to see them again, and it makes sense while there's a war on.*

America is full of opportunities for young people. Elmer can find a good post for Meg, and I know many friends who would like to employ Ellen as a nursemaid for their children.

I do so want to see Meg again. You know I'll do my best for her…

Lily's hand trembled. She put down the letter and gazed out of the window at the spring flowers in her garden.

What was she to do?

Lucille wanted to take Meg away from her. She'd been so afraid that this might happen one day…

She picked up the letter again.

Talk it over with Matt, and the girls, too, Lucille continued. *I'm coming to England this year; we can discuss it when I arrive.*

I sail on the first of May – my dear Elmer has

booked me on the most wonderful ship. She has every luxury imaginable – electric lights and lifts, even roof gardens with palms, and she's the fastest steamer of all. The voyage only takes a week!

So, dear Lily, I shall see you very soon, and we can talk things over then. The name of the ship, by the way, is…

But Lily read no further. How could Lucille chatter about electric lights and palm trees, when just a few lines before she'd tried to lay claim to Meg? Meg was *her* daughter, Lily thought fiercely – hers, and Matt's.

All day long her mind was in a whirl.

Was she wrong to want to keep Meg here? A trip to America was the chance of a lifetime for any young woman.

But why was Lucille making the offer now? There was something more to the generous gesture, Lily was sure.

She read Lucille's words once more: *I do so want to see Meg again.*

It seemed like a cry from the heart. Was Lucille ill, perhaps? Or was she simply anxious to see that Meg had the best possible life? But if that was the case, why offer to have Ellen, too?

As the questions whirled round and round in Lily's mind, she was certain of only one thing. A decision had to be made – and soon.

Lucille would arrive in London in early

May; then she'd probably come directly to Scotland. It was now early April. That left only a month.

That evening, she waited until Matt was settled by the fire with his pipe and the newspaper.

'Would you mind putting the paper down for a moment or two?' she began.

Matt looked up.

'Out with it, Lily, my girl.' He smiled. 'What's on your mind? And don't say nothing – I know you better than that.'

'It's Lucille. I've had a letter.'

'What does she want this time?' Matt sighed. 'She causes you so much worry. Why can't she leave us alone?'

'Would you read what she has to say?' Lily asked.

'All right.'

It was very quiet in the kitchen. There was no sound but the ticking of the clock, while Matt read the letter. When he'd finished, he laid it down and looked at Lily.

'I don't think it's our decision. We ought to tell the girls.'

'I expect you're right.' Lily nodded. 'But I'd like a little time to think about it. If Meg goes...' She could hardly put her thoughts into words.

'If she goes ... it would be for good. I don't think she'd come back.'

'You don't know that,' Matt said in his

reassuring way.

'I'll think it over,' Lily insisted.

'Well, don't leave it too long,' Matt advised her. 'Lucille will be here early next month. You'll have to let her know, one way or the other.'

'I will, I promise.'

During the days that followed, Lily's thoughts were far away.

'Mother!' Willie tried to attract her attention. 'Can I go out to play?'

'Yes, all right,' Lily said absently.

That wasn't like her, Willie thought, puzzled. Usually, she'd want to know where he was going, warn him not to tear his trousers climbing over fences, and tell him there'd be no tea if he wasn't back sharpish.

But this time, she said nothing.

'Is there something wrong?' Meg asked one evening. Her mother was standing by the sink looking absently out of the window.

'Nothing.' Lily shook her head.

April drew on. The yellow narcissi by the gate were a picture, and soon the velvety red wallflowers by the gate would be scenting the air.

All winter, Lily had looked forward to their heady perfume – but now, she hardly noticed them.

'Lily,' Matt asked one evening, 'have you spoken to the girls yet?'

'No, I haven't.' Lily flushed.

'You'll need to soon,' he said. 'Next week's the first of May – that's the date Miss Lucille sails, isn't it?'

Lily nodded.

'I'll talk to Meg tomorrow, I promise,' she told him.

A few days later, Meg had a holiday from college. She spent the day helping Lily spring clean the bedrooms. She hung the rugs over the line and beat them until the dust flew out, making her cough and her eyes smart.

It was a good time to talk to her about Lucille's letter, Lily decided.

'Stop that for a moment, and come inside. I've put the kettle on,' she called to Meg.

The girl stopped work, pushing her hair out of her eyes.

'Whew! It's heavy work. I'd rather do typing than housework any day, that's for sure.'

Lily poured the tea, her hand shaking a little.

'Meg, there's something I wanted to ask you,' she began hesitantly.

'Yes?' Meg said cheerfully. She sipped her tea.

'It's … it's about...' Lily broke off as a motor horn blasted on the road outside.

'Who on earth can that be?' Meg jumped up and ran outside.

Sitting at the wheel of his new car was

Colin Grierson.

'Hello!' He jumped out of the driving seat. 'Hope you don't mind my calling. I'm home for a few days' leave, and I've just collected the car. Would you like to come for a run?'

Meg glowed. Oh, this was a treat! She rarely had the chance of a ride in a car, and to travel in this beautiful motor, with its deep brown leather upholstery and shining lamps, would be a real luxury.

And to go with a young man, too – even though it was only Colin, whom she'd known for years and years. It was so exciting!

And then she remembered. She'd been sweeping the rooms and dusting and beating carpets all afternoon. Her hands flew to her hair.

'I must look a real sight! I've been helping Mother with the spring cleaning.'

'You look fine,' Colin assured her. 'I'll come in and speak to your mother. She won't mind you going out, will she?'

Indoors, he shook hands with Lily, and politely declined her offer of a cup of tea.

'You don't mind if I take Meg for a spin, do you?' he asked. 'It's such a grand day. I promise I'll drive very carefully.'

Lily smiled back at him. She liked Colin – he was a fine young man.

'I know you will,' she said. 'Off you go and enjoy yourselves.'

'We'll only be an hour,' Colin promised.

Meg felt like a real lady. She wished the neighbours could see the beautiful car, and Colin holding open the door for her to get in.

'Goodbye, Mother,' she called – and then she remembered. 'You were going to ask me about something...'

Lily shook her head.

'It doesn't matter. It can wait.'

She wondered, afterwards, if Colin's arrival just then hadn't been some sort of sign.

There was no chance to speak to Meg privately that evening. The next day, she was away at college, and didn't return home till late.

Perhaps she would wait until Lucille arrived, Lily thought.

Early the following week, Matt came home a little early from the mill. His face was drawn, and Lily thought, not for the first time, how much the war had aged him already. Tonight, he looked especially tired.

'Tea won't be long,' Lily greeted him cheerfully. 'Sit down and have a read of the paper while I set the table.'

Matt unfolded the paper he'd brought with him.

'There's bad news, I'm afraid. The Germans have torpedoed a passenger liner.' He pointed to the headlines.

'"Two torpedoes sink the *Lusitania*.

Twelve hundred lost."

'Lily,' he went on, his voice strained, 'Miss Lucille was sailing from New York on the first of May. You don't – can't remember the name of the ship? Did she say? Was it the *Cameronia* or the *Transylvania*?'

Lily's hand flew to her mouth.

'Her letter,' she said. 'It's here.'

She unfolded the sheets of paper, her hand shaking. She scanned the letter quickly, then looked up, her face drained of all colour.

'Oh, Matt! She was sailing on the first of May on board the *Lusitania*.'

She stood silent, staring at him, as the full impact of the news began to dawn on her.

Suddenly, she sank down into a chair, quite numb with shock.

'The *Lusitania*. Twelve hundred lost. And Miss Lucille was a passenger.'

Chapter Five

Lily stared at Matt, shocked.

'I can't believe it! Lucille – drowned?' He put down the newspaper with its stark headline, '*Lusitania* Sunk', and tried to comfort her.

'We don't know yet,' he said. 'There may have been survivors.' He scanned the paper.

'"It is believed many lives were saved",' he read.

'Oh, if only Lucille's among them.' Lily clasped her hands.

Matt put an arm around her shoulders.

'Don't give up hope,' he said gently.

But Lily would not be comforted. Lucille had always been so full of life and enthusiasm. That she might be dead was unthinkable.

Lily thought back to her friend's last letter. She'd been so excited about her forthcoming voyage on the luxurious new *Lusitania*.

Lucille's description of the ship echoed in Lily's mind. *She has every luxury imaginable – electric lights and lifts, even roof gardens with palms!* There was a hospital, too, and a nursery – even kennels for dogs travelling with their owners.

Lily shivered. When she'd first read that letter, she'd been angry with Lucille for chattering on about damask curtains and mahogany furniture in the same breath as declaring her intention to take Meg to America. But now...

None of that seemed to matter now. For the grand *Lusitania,* the pride of the Cunard fleet, was sunk off the Irish coast. And Lucille might be lost with her...

The next day, Lily went about her work, numbed by grief. Nothing Matt could say helped.

Janet and Meg were confused by the depth of their mother's grief. It was understandable that she should be shocked – they all were – but they hadn't realised how much their mother cared for her former employer.

'Don't you think it's a bit strange?' Meg asked.

'Strange?' Janet echoed. 'In what way?'

'Well,' Meg said, 'Mother's distraught about the ship, and her friend.

'I mean, I know it's dreadful – but this Lucille wasn't close, was she? Mother was her maid once, long ago. They knew each other in London. But she hardly ever mentions her.'

'She's very, very upset,' Janet pointed out.

'Yes, I know,' Meg said thoughtfully. 'I wonder why.'

Two days later, Matt brought the newspaper home with him.

'There's a list of survivors from the *Lusitania*,' he said.

'Please, let me see!' Lily exclaimed, but Matt shook his head.

'Calm down, love.' He ran his eye down the list.

'Miss Lucille's not among them.'

'Oh!' Lily gasped.

'Wait,' Matt went on. 'That doesn't necessarily mean... Here's the list of passengers.' He read hastily through the names, then looked up, a slight frown on his face.

'She's not among the names on the passenger list, either.'

Lily sank down into a chair.

'I don't know what to think.'

'Don't give up hope,' Matt told her. 'I'll go into Cupar tomorrow, to try to find out more. Maybe I can get in touch with Cunard.'

The cable arrived the very next day. Lily sat down at the kitchen table, afraid to look at it.

'I daren't open it,' she told Matt. 'It's bad news – I know it.'

Matt reached out.

'Give it to me. I'll open it.'

He read in silence, then held the paper out to Lily, his hand shaking slightly.

'Oh, Lily! It's good news. Look! Read it for yourself.'

Lily's eyes could hardly focus on the words on the paper.

SAFE AND WELL IN NEW YORK. WRITING. LUCILLE.

'I can't believe it,' Lily said, over and over again. 'I can't believe it.'

Matt put his arms around her.

'You see, I told you it would be all right.'

Lily smiled up at him through her tears.

'I should have believed you. But what can have happened? Why wasn't she on the ship? I don't understand.'

'I expect we'll hear in a day or two,' Matt said comfortingly. 'The important thing is that she's safe.'

The promised letter arrived a fortnight or so later.

It was all very strange, Lucille wrote.

The very day the ship was due to sail, she explained, a notice had appeared in the New York papers, right next to the Cunard schedules of sailings.

The notice, signed by the German Embassy, warned travellers about to cross the Atlantic that they were in a war zone. If they sailed on British or Allied ships, they did so at their own risk.

As you can imagine, Lucille wrote, *this was hot news in the papers. Lots of people scoffed – they said the* Lusitania *was so fast, she could outdistance any submarine.*

But Elmer wasn't at all sure about that. He

128

went down to the steamship office and cancelled my passage, right away.

Oh, Lily, I was hopping mad, as they say here. I'd looked forward for so long to this trip. I don't mind telling you, I said a few harsh things to Elmer. But he was quite firm. And once Elmer's mind is made up, nothing will budge him.

So I unpacked my suitcases. I was going to write to you, once I'd persuaded Elmer to book my passage on another ship.

But a few days later, we heard the news.

I feel bad that I was spared when so many people – little children among them – perished.

What can I say? Had it not been for Elmer, I would have been on that ship…

Here Lucille's pen had faltered. Lily could imagine her friend writing, her large, sprawling handwriting becoming almost illegible as the tears welled up.

Lily picked up the letter again.

So, Lily, you will understand that my visit will have to wait. Who knows when this dreadful war will end?

I am sure you will agree that it would be foolish to make plans to bring Meg and Ellen to the States.

I am truly sorry about this, for you know how I would have welcomed them. Elmer and I would have done our best to make them happy. But that now cannot be – at least for the present.

Your loving Lucille.

Lily folded up the pages. She'd show the

letter to Matt later on, when he came home from work. She smoothed down her apron, and picked up the bucket of scraps she'd saved for the hens.

Out of doors, with the hens clucking around her feet, she felt the warm spring sunshine on her face.

Her mind was in a whirl. She thought of the poor people who had died in the disaster; and of Lucille, who seemed different now, quieter and more reflective.

And she thought of Meg. Meg was eighteen now, and had nearly finished her secretarial course. By the time the war was over, she could be grown up, perhaps even married. Would Lucille and Meg ever meet again?

She pushed the thought away, and began to tackle her household chores.

'I've had some wonderful news!' she told the girls that evening, her face glowing with happiness. 'I've had a letter from Miss Lucille.' She quickly explained all that had happened.

'Isn't it strange that her husband should have stopped her sailing?' she went on.

'And Miss Lucille says...' She broke off, remembering just in time that Meg and Ellen knew nothing of Lucille's plan to invite them to the States.

'It's wonderful news,' Meg said, giving her mother a quick hug. 'We know how worried you were...'

She'd been more than worried, Meg thought. Her mother had been shattered by the news of the sinking of the ship, and the belief that her friend was lost. It was as if Lucille had been her dearest, closest friend.

Mother, who was normally so calm, so much in control of things, had been heartbroken – because her former employer was thought to be missing.

They must, Meg told herself, be a good deal closer than anyone had imagined. And again, she wondered why...

After that, life seemed to return more or less to normal – with one exception.

The days without Rab passed slowly for Janet – and there was nothing Lily could do to help her, except hope and pray that he would come home safely. So many homes in Pennyglen and the surrounding villages were already darkened by sorrow.

Every fortnight, Janet took herself off to Glendores, the home of Rab's parents. How she dreaded going! But she'd promised Rab she'd visit his family regularly, and she meant to keep her word.

Her latest visit was no different to all the rest. Rab's mother was polite enough – but it was perfectly clear that Janet wasn't welcome.

Every time the girl walked up the road to

the farm, she reminded herself that it was hard for Rab's mother, too. She must be missing him as well.

But the older woman showed no signs of anxiety.

'You must be missing him badly,' Janet said gently, as she stirred her tea.

'Me? Oh, we manage.' Rab's mother wiped the table, dusting away imaginary crumbs. She didn't look at Janet as she spoke.

Janet went home that day more disheartened than ever. She wished she could do something to help the war effort. She felt so useless. She couldn't even bring comfort to Rab's mother.

When she reached home, she took off her hat and sank wearily into a chair.

'I'll make a cup of tea,' Lily said sympathetically.

She longed to speak out. She knew only too well that Rab's mother was a difficult sort of woman. Oh, no doubt she was secretly anxious about her son, but why did she have to be so aloof and unfriendly towards poor Janet?

Ellen glanced at her older sister. They were close, the two sisters, and the younger girl often wished she could do more to help the older.

Just then there was a shriek from outside.

'Mercy, what's that?' Lily hurried out of the door and down the path, followed by

132

Janet and Ellen.

Willie and a smaller boy had been playing in the road, but now, the smaller boy lay on the ground. Willie stood over, looking rather pale and shaken.

'It wasn't my fault. I never touched him,' Willie told them.

'What happened? Is he hurt?' Lily asked.

'He fell off the wall,' Willie said. 'I never touched him.'

'Never mind that.' Surprisingly, it was Ellen who took charge. She knelt down beside the younger boy.

'It's Tommy, isn't it? Let me have a look.'

Tommy opened his eyes.

'It's my knee. It's bleeding. It's his blame. He dared me.'

'Thank goodness he can speak,' Lily said.

'I don't think he's badly hurt,' Ellen decided confidently.

Lily had never been so grateful for the first-aid classes Ellen had taken last winter.

'Come on, Tommy, see if you can walk.'

Supported by Ellen, the small boy hirpled into the house.

'There,' she said kindly, once they were indoors, 'it's only a graze. I'll put a bandage on your knee, and it'll soon heal up. There, that wasn't sore, was it?'

Lily looked on in surprise. Could this capable young person be her little Ellen?

'And you're not to go jumping off walls

again,' Ellen warned him, as she tidied up. 'Next time, you could be in trouble.'

When Tommy had been comforted with a treacle scone and sent on his way, Lily smiled at her youngest daughter.

'You did very well, Ellen,' she praised.

Ellen paused, the basin in her hands.

'I like doing it,' she said simply.

Ellen had always been the same, Lily thought. An injured bird, a dog with a sore paw – Ellen had always been there, soothing and quietly helping the injured bird or animal. She never seemed the least afraid.

She was good with younger children, too, always playing with them, and drying their tears when they tumbled.

'You ought to be a nurse,' Lily said proudly.

Ellen put down the basin.

'That's what I want to do,' she told her mother. 'I don't want to go into the mill, like all the other girls.'

'But,' Lily said gently, 'you're too young. You're only just leaving school.'

'I'll soon be old enough,' Ellen replied eagerly. 'Oh, I wish I was old enough now. I could go to France or Serbia with the Scottish women's hospitals...'

'There's time enough for thinking about things like that,' Lily told her, frowning. It was selfish, she knew, but she couldn't bear the thought of Ellen, too, being drawn further into the war.

'Anyway,' she went on, changing the subject, 'I've got some news for you. Mrs Grierson's sister spoke to me after church last Sunday. She'd heard how much you enjoy looking after children, and wondered if you'd be interested in working as nursemaid to her own family.'

'I'd like that,' Ellen said eagerly. 'And I could still train as a nurse, once I'm old enough.'

Lily looked at her daughter's bright face and felt a pang of sorrow. How quickly her family was growing up!

'Looking after children is hard work, mind,' Lily cautioned. 'And some of it – well, it isn't very pleasant.'

'I know that,' Ellen said in her composed way. 'I've thought about that, and I don't mind. It's part of the job. And I'll face worse when I'm a nurse!'

Looking at her daughter's calm, smiling face, Lily realised that Ellen knew just what she wanted to do. She'd made up her mind, and wouldn't be persuaded from her chosen path.

At least that was one less thing to fret about. Lily worried all the time about Janet's Rab. Every day, the papers carried news from the Western Front, and of the battle now raging on the Somme.

Looking out at the peaceful fields and

woodlands surrounding Pennyglen, it often seemed they lived in another world to the mud and horror of the trenches. And yet – the war was all too near.

In the local papers, the casualty lists told of the young men who'd been killed or wounded, of those who had died of their wounds in prisoner of war camps. For so many families, life would never be the same – their loved ones would never come home.

It was late one evening when Janet arrived back from her regular visit to Glendores, Rab's home. She looked even more strained and whiter than usual, and Lily's heart went out to her.

Up till now, she'd kept quiet, but she felt she had to speak out. It wasn't fair, it wasn't right that Janet should be treated like this.

'Sit down,' she said gently. 'My, you look worn out.'

Janet didn't reply.

'It's all wrong,' Lily burst out, unable to bear it any longer. 'That woman doesn't have any call to treat you this way. Rab's a lucky lad to have you, and she doesn't realise it.'

'Oh, Mother.' Janet's voice broke. 'Don't – it's not that.'

A cold hand seemed to clutch at Lily's heart.

'What's wrong? What's the matter?'

'It's Rab. He's been hurt.' It seemed for a

moment as if Janet would break down, but then she gulped.

'There was a telegram. He's been wounded.'

'Oh, my dear.' Lily knelt down beside her. 'Where is he?'

'In a hospital behind the lines, in France. He's being brought home just as soon as he can travel. He'll be coming to London next week.'

She rose, more composed now.

'I've decided I'm going down to meet him. I want to be there when he arrives.'

'But...' Lily faltered. She could see that Janet's mind was made up.

'I've got to go,' Janet said.

'Rab needs me. And if I don't go, he'll be all alone down there. There's no way that his parents can leave the farm at this time of year – they're working all hours as it is.'

Lily smiled wanly.

'I understand, love. If there's anything I can do...'

'Thanks.' For a moment, tears glittered in Janet's eyes.

'Anyway, I'd better start getting some things together,' she said briskly. 'I'll see about taking my holidays now – and I'll have to find out about trains...'

'Do you want anyone to go with you?' It was such a long journey, Lily thought, concerned. Janet had never been further than

Edinburgh before.

'Meg would go, I'm sure,' she suggested.

Janet shook her head.

'No, thank you all the same. I want to go on my own...'

The next few days sped by in a flurry of preparation. The minister's wife knew of a respectable boarding house in London, which was run by someone she knew.

'Your Janet will be fine there,' she re-assured Lily. 'Mrs Macnab's the soul of kindness.'

Lily could hardly hide her anxiety.

'Janet's never been so far away before,' she said. 'I know she's twenty-one, and sensible, but to be going all on her own...'

'Don't you worry,' the minister's wife said. 'I'll write to Mrs Macnab and tell her to expect Janet. She'll look after her for you.'

Matt had looked up the train times for Janet.

'There's one that will get you into London about tea time,' he told her.

Meg busied herself helping Janet to get her clothes ready – sponging and pressing, and folding things neatly.

Even Willie, who couldn't help feeling it was all rather exciting, was caught up in the bustle.

'I could go with you,' he offered. 'Fancy, going on a train all the way to London.

'If I was you,' he told Janet, 'I'd be sure to

get a proper look at the engine. Maybe you could speak to the driver?'

Janet laughed outright and pretended to cuff him.

'You and trains!' She was smiling for the first time in days. 'All right, I promise. If I can possibly have a word with the engine driver, I will.'

The night before Janet was due to leave, Lily was busier than ever. As she packed sandwiches in waxed paper, she thought back to her own time in London as Miss Lucille's maid.

How carefree life had seemed when she was Janet's age, walking in the park, listening to the band, feeding the ducks.

She sighed. How different it was for poor Janet!

Before Janet left for the station, Lily took the pirlie pig down from the mantelpiece. There was quite a sum inside.

'Take this, love.' She pressed some money into Janet's hand.

'Mother! That's far too much!'

Lily shook her head.

'Just take it. Things cost a lot in London. You're sure to need quite a bit.'

'Oh, thank you!' Janet gave her mother a warm hug. 'I'll be fine; don't worry!'

There were only a few people waiting at the station.

'Write to us as soon as you get there – if

you can,' Lily begged her daughter. Then she launched into a list of last-minute instructions.

'Do be careful of the traffic – and hold on to your purse.'

'All right. I'll remember.' Janet smiled.

Matt gave her a handful of coins.

'For porters – when you get there,' he told her.

Tears sprang to Janet's eyes. How like her father to think of little things like that. She squeezed his arm.

'I'll be all right, Father,' she assured him.

Over the hiss of steam from the engine, Lily and Matt called out their goodbyes. But their words were lost as the station master blew his whistle and the train moved out.

'That's it! She's off!'

Matt took Lily's arm, and together, they watched and waved until the train was out of sight.

Janet sank down into a corner seat in the compartment, trying to compose her thoughts. She fought down any feelings of panic. It was Rab who mattered now, not her.

The journey seemed to last for ever. But, as the green Border country gave way to rows and rows of back-to-back houses in the North of England, Janet relaxed a little and leaned back in her seat.

'Are you going far?' the elderly lady in the other corner asked.

'To London.'

'Then you've no fear of missing your stop.' The lady's bright blue eyes twinkled, and Janet smiled back at her.

'I should rest while you can. It's a long way. Here – I've a little cushion you can borrow. It's so much more comfortable on your neck.'

Janet was touched by this kind gesture from a total stranger. She began telling her companion about Rab, and the telegram, and the family she had left behind at Pennyglen.

The lady was a sympathetic listener, and Janet found it easy to talk to her.

When they parted, the lady shook Janet's hand warmly.

'God bless you, my dear. I'll be thinking of you and your Rab.'

Once outside the station, Janet was bewildered – there were so many people, so much traffic! And the noise and the dirt!

She felt a moment's pang of homesickness for the tranquillity of Pennyglen. Then she told herself robustly that she was being fainthearted.

She waved her umbrella at a cab and, much to her surprise, it stopped and the driver jumped down. He picked up her suitcase and opened the door for her.

'Where to, Miss?' he asked.

Janet gave him the name and address of the boarding house, then leaned back against the upholstery, her mind a jumble of impressions.

Although she was tired and anxious, she was still interested in all that was going on about her. So this was London!

The streets were crowded, and it was so noisy – the traffic, the newspaper-sellers shouting out the headlines, the clatter of hooves and the squeal of brakes.

She was thankful when they reached the boarding house and there was a kindly rosy-faced woman on the doorstep.

'You'll be Janet. I'm Mrs Macnab. Come away in.'

She showed Janet upstairs into a little bedroom.

Mother would approve of the snowy white bedspread and the fresh cotton curtains, Janet thought. Her spirits lifted further at the sight of a cheerful coal fire burning in the grate.

'I thought it would be a comfort for you, after your long journey,' Mrs Macnab said, in her soft Borders accent.

Later that night, Janet lay in bed watching the firelight glowing. Tomorrow, she would see Rab again. She had no idea how bad his wounds were, but at least he'd be home – and safe.

She was at the station in good time the next morning, waiting for the troop train to arrive. She glanced round at the others – mothers, wives, sweethearts. People stood in little groups, chatting quietly or anxiously straining for a glimpse of the train.

At last, the train drew in, and people surged forward to the barriers.

'Make way,' a porter called, and the crowd parted as the first of the wounded – those who were able to walk – stumbled along the platform.

Some were on crutches, helped by VADs, others were on stretchers. Janet scanned the faces anxiously. Where was Rab?

And then she saw him. Two orderlies carried him on a stretcher, and a nurse walked by his side. His face was grey, but there was no mistaking the shock of fair, curly hair.

'Rab, oh, Rab. It's me. Janet.'

The nurse looked at Janet sympathetically. 'Your young man?' she asked.

Janet nodded, unable to take her eyes from Rab's face.

All the way to the convalescent home, she sat beside him, every nerve taut when the ambulance jolted over a rut in the road, making Rab wince with pain. All the time, he hardly seemed to realise she was there.

After an age – it seemed like hours, but it must have been only minutes – they reached their destination.

It wasn't until much later, as Janet sat by Rab's bedside, that there was any progress. All of a sudden, he opened his eyes and looked directly at her.

'Janet?' he asked, puzzled. 'Is that you?'

'I'm here, Rab. You're safe now.'

He sighed and closed his eyes again without saying another word.

A slim, red-haired nurse tapped Janet on the shoulder.

'He'll sleep now. Why don't you go and get some rest? You can see him tomorrow.'

Janet rose stiffly.

'I'll be back soon,' she promised Rab, but he was already sleep.

The next morning, the red-haired nurse was already on the ward.

'You've come to see your young man,' she said. 'Can I have a word with you first?'

The girl was scarcely older than Janet, but she seemed so capable and confident.

'I know he must seem different to you just now,' the nurse began. 'You'll need to be patient – I'm sure you realise that. He needs plenty of rest and to be allowed to get over this in his own time.'

'He is going to be all right, isn't he?' Janet asked anxiously.

'His wounds are healing, though he's still in a lot of pain,' the nurse reassured her.

'But–' she hesitated '–you've got to

remember that he's probably seen and experienced things he won't want to speak of, even to you…'

There was a pause.

'I nursed in France,' the girl explained, 'at a hospital near Etaples.

'You never got used to it, really. Those fine young men – and there was only so much you could do for them. They were so brave.' She sighed.

'Don't be surprised if your Rab is edgy and short tempered, or if he suddenly bursts into tears,' she finished, putting a comforting hand on Janet's arm.

'He doesn't seem to want to know me.' Janet's voice trembled a little.

'He'll come back to you,' the nurse assured her. 'Just give him time.'

'At least,' Janet said bravely, 'I've got him back. He's home and he's safe.'

'Yes,' the girl agreed. Then she turned away. 'You're lucky in that.'

That day, and over all the days that followed, Janet tried to remember what the nurse had told her. She sat quietly beside Rab, talking of things far from the war. She tried hard to think of reminders of happier days.

She told him about the Big House, and how they were growing potatoes where there used to be roses.

'The fields round Pennyglen are all a mass

of blue,' she went on. 'They're growing flax there now, because they can't get it from abroad. They've already been picking up at Luthrie – they bring in the pickers, just like for the berry picking.'

She tried to think of other things that had happened during the summer.

'Willie went to the Lammas Market at St Andrews,' she said.

'Remember the day we went to the Market – and you bought me a red sugar heart?'

Slowly, a flicker of interest came back to Rab's eyes. He sighed and reached out for Janet's hand.

Every day after that, he grew stronger. Soon, they were able to walk in the gardens, enjoying the warmth of the late summer days.

'I'll soon be able to throw away these crutches!' Rab joked. 'Just you wait – I'll be competing in the Games next year. Just the hundred-yard dash, you understand!'

Janet smiled, bending her head so that he wouldn't see the tears in her eyes.

One day, when she arrived at the con-valescent home, the red-haired nurse was waiting for her.

'It's good news! Your Rab can go home next week.'

'That's wonderful!' Janet glowed.

'Yes.' The girl smiled. 'It's always a great day when our patients are well enough to leave us.'

'I can't thank you enough,' Janet said. 'You've done so much for Rab – and you've helped me, too.'

Suddenly, she noticed how tired the girl looked.

'And you – will you get leave?' she asked. 'You seem to work so hard.'

The girl shook her head.

'I'd rather be at work. My fiancé was killed – at Verdun.' She was silent for a moment, then smiled bravely at Janet.

'I wish you both every happiness.'

Lily smoothed out the pages of Janet's letter.

'She sounds so much brighter,' she said, looking up.

'That's good,' Matt put in, lighting his pipe. 'Go on, read us what she says.'

'*My dear Mother and Father... You will be pleased to hear that Rab is doing well. He was discharged from the convalescent home on Friday, and is able to walk with a stick, though very slowly.*

'*We are planning to stay for a few days in London before coming back to Pennyglen. It will be good to be home – I've missed you all! We'll be arriving at the station at...*'

Lily's voice tailed off.

'They're coming on Saturday. That's only two days away – the letter's taken five days to get here. Oh, I'll need to get ready, to have everything nice for them…'

'Lily,' Matt interrupted. 'Wait a moment. Maybe they'll want to go to Rab's home first.'

'No.' Lily shook her head. 'She says they're coming to Pennyglen first. Oh, it'll be grand to have them back.'

Lily was up early that Saturday, making last-minute preparations.

Matt had arranged for a cab to meet Janet and Rab at the station. Though it was only a short distance, he knew Rab would probably be unable to walk far.

At last the train appeared round the bend in the track.

'There it is!' Lily called out eagerly. She scanned the faces looking out of the windows. 'I can't see them…'

'Yes, there they are!' Matt waved and hurried forward to help with the luggage.

'Oh, Mother! It's good to be back!' Janet gave Lily a quick hug, then turned to Rab, anxious to make sure that he could manage the step without too much difficulty.

'Rab, it's grand to see you!' Secretly, Lily was shocked by Rab's appearance. Was this gaunt figure the sturdy young man who'd gone off to the war?

He smiled at her and she could just recognise the open grin that was so like the old Rab.

'Your tea's waiting,' she said. 'I've got some of that ham you liked, and there's potato scones.' She chattered on, trying not to show her dismay.

'Now just put your things by, and I'll get the tea right away,' Lily said once they were home.

'I'll help you.' Janet, still in her coat and hat, followed Lily into the kitchen.

'Oh, Janet, take a seat at the fire. You'll be tired,' Lily said.

'No, Mother. Just a minute. There's something I want to tell you.'

Slowly, Janet took off her left glove and stretched out her hand. She spoke quickly, her cheeks flushed.

'I wanted to tell you, but we decided in such a hurry – we got a special licence. You see, I want to be with Rab all the time. And now that we're married, I can be.'

Lily could think of nothing to say. Her heart filled up with love and compassion as she held Janet's hand, gazing at the shining gold band on the third finger.

'What a happy day this is,' she whispered at last, hugging her daughter close. 'Let's tell the others – it's about time we all had something to celebrate!'

Chapter Six

While Janet was in the kitchen, telling her mother all about the wedding, Rab blurted out the news of their marriage to Matt.

'Married? Well, well.' Matt tapped down the tobacco in his pipe, the way he always did when faced with unexpected news that he needed time to think about.

'I'm sorry it's too late to ask your permission,' Rab went on. 'But I hope you wouldn't have refused it. There just wasn't time, what with us being in London. But I'll do my best to make her happy.'

'I know that.' Matt had always liked the young man with his frank, open smile, and he, too, had been shocked by the change in the cheerful lad who'd gone off to war only a short time ago.

'Lily and I would have liked to be there – but that can't be helped now. You've my blessing, lad – I hope you'll both be happy.

'Ah, well, that's the way of it in wartime,' he went on.

'And your own folks – they're pleased, too, I take it?'

'We haven't told them yet,' Rab said. 'We'll go over to Glendores tomorrow.'

That evening was a cheerful affair. Lily spread a snowy white cloth over the table, and set out the meal she'd been planning all week. There was a meat pie, and scones, and a featherlight sponge cake – they could still get plenty of eggs, despite wartime shortages.

Meg wanted to know all about London.

'But we were hardly there!' Janet protested. 'And there was no time to look at the shops. Anyway, no-one troubles much about the latest fashions just now,' she explained.

Willie was eager to learn all about the fighting and what it was like at the Front. He chattered away until Matt shook his head.

'That's enough, Willie,' he said in an aside. 'No more questions.'

Next day, the young couple travelled on to Rab's home with the local carter.

'I hope your mother will be pleased,' Janet said, a little hesitantly.

'Of course she will, she'll be as pleased as punch,' Rab assured her, but he said it a bit too heartily, and Janet felt a pang of anxiety.

'My, this is grand.' Rab took a deep breath of fresh air. 'This is what I missed all that time in the trenches.' He shivered a little.

Janet hastily pointed out a couple of finches on a nearby branch, and a partridge ambling across the road a few yards ahead, to distract him.

'My parents are expecting us,' Rab told her. 'But my father will be out in the fields – we'll see him tonight.' He winced, and Janet was immediately anxious.

'Are you in pain?'

He shook his head.

'Not much. It's just the cart going over the ruts in the road – I never noticed them before...'

When they reached Glendores, old Sandy helped Janet from the cart and lifted down their bags.

'I'll take these inside for you, then I'll be off,' he said.

'Rab, why don't you go on in, and speak to your mother? I'll follow later,' Janet suggested.

He looked at her gratefully and she knew all too clearly how much he was dreading this reunion.

After the cart had disappeared down the lane, Janet sat down on her suitcase, feeling suddenly forlorn. A black and white collie came bounding up to her and she fondled the dog's head.

Dare she go in yet? She decided to wait a little longer. She wanted Rab and his mother to have the first few minutes to themselves.

The day was warm and sunny, and she leant against the wall, enjoying the autumn sunshine on her upturned face. From the farmyard she could see the rolling fields of the Howe, and she felt so thankful that Rab had been spared to come back home.

She was roused from her thoughts by Rab's voice.

'Are you there, Janet? Come on in.'

A little shyly, and with a final pat for the collie, she turned to go into the farmhouse. Rab was at the door, holding out his hand to her with that smile that always made her heart turn over.

Rab's mother was busy in the kitchen. She wiped her floury hands on her white apron.

'Rab's told me the news,' she said. 'Ah, well...' There was a pause. 'You'd best take your things off.'

She hardly looked at Janet, but her eyes followed Rab all the time, as though she couldn't bear to let him out of her sight.

Janet looked at Rab for support, and he put his arms around her.

'It's great to be back,' he said as cheerfully as he could, 'and I've brought you a daughter-in-law, Mother. How about that?'

'So you told me.' Alice glanced at Janet. 'Well, I hope you'll be happy.'

'I'm sure we will be.' Janet was determined to be friendly and cheerful.

In the pause that followed, she wondered if she could ever make this woman like her. Was there room for the two of them at Glendores? And despite her happiness, and her joy at Rab's return, she felt chilled.

For Meg, life was changing, too.

'You've done very well,' the supervisor told her at the end of the secretarial course. 'Top of the class.'

Meg knew how high Miss Martin's standards were, and she glowed under the unexpected praise.

'I think we can find you a very suitable post,' Miss Martin continued, glancing at a letter on her desk.

'Baillie's are looking for a lady to take over the post of secretary to the chairman – the present lady is retiring.'

Meg gasped. She'd heard of the well-known jute firm – that would really be a top post. And what was more, one with a good salary!

Her thoughts raced ahead. She saw herself handing her first pay packet over to Mother.

She imagined, too, shopping in Draffen's – perhaps she'd buy a new hat for the spring. She'd seen such a pretty one in a magazine, trimmed with silk roses. A hat like that would be so elegant...

'Did you hear me, Miss Barclay?' Miss Martin asked.

'Oh, yes.' Meg hastily abandoned her dreams and came back down to earth with a thud.

'So they'd like to arrange an interview. Of course, a candidate from this college with a good recommendation stands an excellent chance...'

'Yes, Miss Martin. Thank you.'

The night before the interview, Meg could hardly sleep. She'd been through her simple wardrobe time and again. What should she wear? She wanted to look smart, but not flashy, she told herself.

Oh, if only Janet were here. But Janet was over at Glendores.

Meg badly missed her sister, and their friendly chats after they'd turned down the paraffin lamp and huddled under the big patchwork quilt.

She missed Janet coming home from work with funny stories of what had happened that day, and her sweet voice singing around the house. Janet would have known just what to wear.

At least Meg had a smart new pair of patent leather boots.

When she'd heard about the interview, Lily had smiled.

'You'll need a new pair of boots now you're going up in the world,' she'd said.

'I think there's enough in the pirlie pig for me to be able to treat you.'

Meg was thrilled. She'd seen the boots in a shop and had longed to have them.

Next day, Meg dressed smartly in a light wool jacket and skirt in soft grey and a white voile blouse, with a bunch of artificial violets

155

pinned to the lapel of the jacket.

It was a pity she hadn't worn in the new boots, though. They pinched just a little, and the soles were still new and shiny.

'Good luck. You'll do fine.' Matt patted her shoulder as he went off to work. 'You'll be quite the grand lady if you get this job!'

'Not too grand.' Meg gave him an affectionate smile.

'Miss Barclay. We're expecting you.' The commissionaire at the entrance to the offices greeted her. 'I'll tell Miss Keith you're here.'

Miss Keith was brisk and efficient. There was no nonsense about her, Meg thought. She couldn't imagine the present secretary ever being anything but completely in charge.

Trying hard to calm her quaking nerves, Meg followed the older woman up the wide staircase to the dark, wood-panelled corridor. Pictures of past chairmen of the firm lined the walls.

Meg thought they looked down on her rather sternly. No-one would ever dare to skip along this corridor.

'Here we are,' Miss Keith said.

Meg had never seen an office quite as imposing as this one, with its big desk, rows of filing cabinets, neatly ranged trays of pens and pencils, the latest typewriter – and the luxurious Indian rug on the floor. It was a far cry from the shabby little office at the mill.

Miss Keith tapped at the inner door.

'Come in!' a gruff voice called.

Meg took a deep breath and crossed the polished floor. As she shook hands with Mr Baillie, her thoughts raced ahead again.

What would he be like to work for? He looked very distinguished and had a somewhat abrupt way of speaking.

'Sit down,' he told her. He glanced at the papers in front of him. 'You come with excellent references from the college.'

Meg blushed and looked down at the toes of her new boots.

'Well, let's see.' He picked up a letter. 'I'll just dictate this and then Miss Keith will show you to a machine.'

'We work at speed here,' he said, glaring at her from under bushy white eyebrows.

'There's no time for daydreaming. Invoices have to go out promptly, letters and inquiries have to be answered without delay. We have important customers world-wide.

'Quality and efficiency – that's our motto.'

'Yes, sir,' Meg said.

She produced a notebook and pencil from her bag and waited for him to begin. Luckily, she had been well trained and had no difficulty in taking dictation. Her pencil flew over the paper. Then she paused.

'I'm sorry, sir. I didn't quite get that word,' she said, frowning a little.

He glared at her.

'Were you not listening?' He sighed and repeated the word.

'Thank you, sir.' Meg rose with more composure than she felt. Well, she could only do her best.

Miss Keith showed her to a desk and typewriter and left her to begin transcribing her shorthand.

Meg began, quite confidently. Then, to her horror, glancing back over the few lines she had typed, she saw that she had made a stupid mistake.

She rubbed hard with the eraser, and in a panic saw that she had rubbed a hole in the paper. There was nothing for it. She would have to start again.

She tore the paper out of the machine, screwed it up, and aimed it at the wastepaper basket. She missed.

Just then, Miss Keith came back into the room. She picked up the discarded letter with a sniff, and put it into the wastepaper basket.

'Dear me, Miss Barclay, we are much more economical in this office.'

Her heart thudding, Meg began typing again. This time, she took extra care. Yes, it looked all right, she thought, as she rolled the paper out of the machine.

'Have you finished?' Miss Keith asked.

Meg nodded.

'Very well.' Miss Keith tapped at the inner door and Meg, hands shaking, went in.

'Is this it?' Mr Baillie asked. He ran his eye over the page.

Meg hoped that there were no mistakes, but her confidence was waning, and she couldn't be sure it was perfect.

'Thank you, Miss Barclay. We'll let you know.'

Meg turned, reached for the door handle and slipped on the polished wooden floor. My boots, she thought desperately. The leather soles were still new and the floor was highly polished.

'There! Careful now!' A strong arm caught her, and she found herself looking up at a fair-haired young man in officer's uniform.

'Are you all right?' he asked, concerned. 'It's so easy to slip on these floors.'

'Yes, thank you,' Meg gasped.

The young man opened the door for her.

'Goodbye,' he said politely.

'Goodbye,' Meg gulped.

As the door closed behind her, she heard the young man say, 'Sorry I'm late, Father. You wanted to see me?'

In the outer office, Miss Keith hardly looked up from her typewriter.

'I'm sure you can find your own way out,'

she said. 'We'll be in touch with you.'

Meg was nearly in tears as she went down the stairs and past the uniformed commissionaire.

How stupid and undignified she must have seemed! Oh, why hadn't she worn her new boots in first?

'How did you get on?' Lily asked, when Meg arrived home. But a glance at the girl's woebegone face told her it would be unwise to ask any more.

A few days later, Geordie the postman called at the cottage.

'It's not for you, missis. It's for the lassie,' he told Lily, handing over an envelope.

Lily realised at once that this was the letter Meg had been waiting for.

'Oh,' Meg said a little flatly. 'It's come.'

She opened the envelope.

'I expect Baillie's write the same letter to everyone. *Thank you for your attendance...*' Her voice tailed away, and then she let out a shriek of joy.

'I've got the job. They want me! I can't believe it!'

'That's wonderful.' Lily gave her a warm hug. 'Oh, Meg, I'm so pleased for you.'

'This is just the beginning,' Meg said. 'I can go up, and up, and up...'

That night she took out the new boots, which she'd thrown into the back of the cupboard.

'You brought me luck,' she said with a smile.

Mrs Grierson's sister and her children were staying at the Big House, and Ellen went there every day now. In a starched white apron and cap, she became the children's nursemaid, Miss Ellie, who could play all sorts of wonderful games and knew lots of marvellous stories.

Lily wasn't the least bit worried about Ellen – she knew the girl had found her niche. Life, she believed, would be tranquil and straightforward for her youngest daughter.

But for Janet, the eldest of her children – and Lily acknowledged in her heart that Janet, being the first, was a little bit special – for Janet, life would never be straightforward again.

She tried, without success, to persuade her eldest daughter to talk on the occasions when she visited Pennyglen.

'You're settling down all right?' she asked anxiously.

Janet nodded, not looking at her mother.

'Oh, yes. The cottage is fine.

'Of course, it needs a bit doing to it, but I've distempered the walls, and I bought a piece of material at the sales, to make kitchen curtains. A nice bright cotton...'

That was not what Lily wanted to know.

'Have you made any friends there?'

Janet's face lightened.

'Oh, yes. Mrs Mackie – she's the grieve's wife – took me to a meeting in the village hall.

'It's a new kind of meeting, for women who live in the country. They call it the Scottish Women's...'

'...Rural Institute,' Lily finished. 'I know. There's a branch at Pennyglen.'

'They were all so friendly,' Janet said. 'There was a demonstration, and a cup of tea, and a chat...'

Just for one evening, she thought, the companionship had taken her mind off her troubles. Although she would hardly admit it, even to herself, she often felt lonely.

Walking home afterwards, by the light of the full moon, she'd felt more cheerful, and already she was looking forward to the meeting next month.

Rab's cousin, Bess, was more outspoken than Lily. When the two girls met up again, Janet felt she was able to speak more freely.

'So how are you?' Bess asked. 'It's not the same without you at the mill. We don't have so many laughs. And how's Aunt Alice?'

Janet paused.

'You don't need to be tactful with me,' Bess said. 'I know what she's like.'

Janet turned aside, but not before her friend had seen the tears in her eyes.

'Here, she's not upsetting you, is she?' Bess was instantly compassionate. 'She can be right sharp, but don't let her bully you.

'The thing is, Rab was always the apple of her eye.'

'I know,' Janet said. 'But it's so unfair. I've tried my best to be pleasant to her, and it isn't as if I'm taking Rab away from her.

'But she's always picking on me and criticising me, just because I didn't grow up on a farm.'

'Listen–' Bess took her friend by the arm '–you've got to stand up to her. Don't let her get away with it.

'If she sees you've got a bit of spirit, she'll respect you. If you behave like a little mouse, she won't.'

'But I hate rows and upsets,' Janet told her.

Bess shrugged her shoulders.

'It's up to you,' she said. 'But don't let her make your life a misery.'

The days went by, with Rab growing stronger all the time. Janet learned to milk and to churn butter and her quick fingers soon made curtains and cushions for the little cottage. She was proud of her home.

Rab fretted that he couldn't return to the Front. Every day there was news of casualties.

Many local lads had fallen or been injured,

and there was news, too, of others who'd been taken prisoner. But Rab knew, and so did Janet, that he wouldn't be fit enough to return to the Front.

Janet watched him every day. Although he was growing stronger, he would never be quite able to manage the heavy work on the farm.

She realised, too, that he was restless. She guessed he wanted a change from the farming life.

His eyes would light up when he scanned the newspaper for advertisements for motorcycles and cars, and he talked sometimes of opening his own garage.

'That's the coming thing, after the war,' he said. 'But that's all a pipe dream. I couldn't let Father carry on with the farm alone,' he added.

Janet kept busy. In the evenings she knitted socks and scarves for the Red Cross Appeal. She was a good cook, and a careful manager, and Rab came home every day to a nourishing meal.

'That smells good,' he'd say with a grin, giving her a hug.

There was only one cloud on Janet's horizon. Rab's mother, Alice, was still cold and distant in all her dealings with her daughter-in-law.

Eventually, things came to a head over a trivial matter.

Janet had brought the crock of butter she'd churned into the farm kitchen, proud it had turned out just right.

Rab's mother, who was working at the stove, turned round.

'Oh, there you are. Just put it down, will you?' She glanced at the butter, and sighed.

'Is it all right?' Janet longed for some word of approval.

'It'll do.'

Suddenly, Janet's temper flared up.

'It'll have to do, won't it?' she said. 'I work so hard to please you, and to do everything right, but nothing's ever good enough for you.'

The older woman stared at her, astonished. She'd never seen Janet like this before.

But now Janet's temper had flared up, and she'd quite forgotten her resolve to ignore the older woman's attitude.

'I've never been good enough for Rab, have I? I'm just a mill girl.

'Well, let me tell you, my family's just as good as yours. They're kind and friendly, and wouldn't dream of treating anyone the way you've treated me.

'I want to look after Rab and do the right things, but...' She burst into tears and sat down at the table, burying her head in her hands.

'I didn't know. It's just my way,' Alice said awkwardly.

'Well, I hope–' Janet raised her tear-stained face, '–that you'll be a lot kinder to your grandchildren.'

'Grandchild?' Alice stared at her, quite at a loss. 'You mean…?'

Janet nodded.

'I saw the doctor this week.'

'And Rab? Is he pleased?'

Janet smiled.

'He's thrilled. We both are.'

'I…' Alice reached out a hand and laid it awkwardly on the girl's shoulder. 'I'm pleased for you both.

'I see now I've been a bit hard on you. I don't mean anything – it's just my way.' She bit her lip.

'Would you like a cup of tea?'

Janet smiled at her.

'That would be fine.'

'I'll put the kettle on.'

It wasn't much, but Janet knew this was the older woman's way of saying she was sorry.

'So you'll be a grandmother,' she said. 'How will you like that?'

Alice paused, the kettle in her hand.

'My, but I'll like it fine,' she murmured.

'I'm a private secretary!' Meg repeated to herself, over and over again. She could hardly believe it.

Miss Keith had suggested she go into

Baillie's for a few days to see how the office was run, and Meg was eager to learn.

'This is the letter book,' the older woman explained. 'Copies of all letters go in here, and they're sent round the directors. And this is the "bring forward" file. You'll know what that is...'

'Oh, yes,' Meg said brightly. She'd learned in secretarial college about checking on outstanding queries and invoices.

'And we could put a note in the diary,' Meg added.

Miss Keith's tone was a little sharp.

'We've always done it this way and it's always worked satisfactorily,' she insisted.

Meg knew by now when to hold her tongue. If things had always been done in a certain way, she could let them go on like that – until Miss Keith retired, at least.

She had all sorts of ideas for ways of running the office more efficiently after that. After all, she told herself, she'd had the most up to date secretarial training available.

At the little party for Miss Keith's retirement, Meg stayed in the background, making herself useful by handing round cups of tea, and carrying trays of sandwiches.

'Milk and sugar, sir?' She halted in front of two men who were deep in conversation. One of them spun round, almost knocking the tray from her hands.

'Oh, I'm sorry!' He smiled at her. 'I beg

167

your pardon. We seem to make a habit of this, you and I.' It was the young man she had met on the day of her interview.

'We met before, remember? And you are?'

'Meg Barclay,' Meg told him. 'I've been appointed to replace Miss Keith.'

'I'm very glad to hear it – that you're joining us, I mean, not that Miss Keith's leaving.

'I'm Philip Baillie,' he went on. 'I'm home on leave just now – just for the weekend. As soon as I'm out of the Army, I'll be joining the firm again.

'And this–' he introduced the older man '–is Jim Mackenzie, the works manager.'

'So where are you from?' he asked her, as if he really was interested.

'Oh, just a small place near Cupar,' Meg said.

'You'll be in digs in Dundee then?'

Meg nodded, her cheeks burning at the memory.

Lily had insisted on inspecting the lodgings, even though they'd been recommended by Miss Martin.

'She's a widow lady, three children all still at school. She's a good plain cook, and her house is spotlessly clean – she'll keep an eye on your daughter...'

Meg had felt resentful about that. She was nearly twenty; she didn't need anyone keeping an eye on her. But Mother and Mrs

Maclean were soon chatting away over a cup of tea.

Meg brushed the memory aside as she realised that everyone had turned towards the end of the big room.

'It's the presentation,' Philip Baillie said. 'We'd better stop chatting for a bit. Here, let me take that tray – I don't want you dropping it.'

He smiled, and Meg blushed again – oh, when would she ever grow out of that silly girlish habit?

He took her by the arm and steered her to a place at the front of the room.

After Miss Keith had been presented with a silver tea service, and had stammered her thanks, young Mr Baillie led three cheers for her, and insisted on giving her a kiss on the cheek.

Meg, watching, wondered if she would be in the same job in 30 years' time?

It was a bright spring day when Meg looked up from her typewriter to find Philip Baillie standing at the door, gazing at her.

'Surprised to see me?'

'Yes! Are you on leave?' she asked.

He nodded.

'I'm going back to France next week.' There was a pause.

'My brother-in-law was in the trenches,' Meg told him. 'He's been invalided out, though.'

'Poor chap.' He seemed as if he was about to say something more, then changed his mind.

'Is my father in?' he asked abruptly.

'Mr Baillie's at a meeting. I'm not sure when he'll be back.'

'Never mind.' He sat down on the chair beside the desk.

'So how do you like the job? I expect you're the most efficient secretary they've ever had!'

Meg had been practising being cool and sophisticated, but in no time, she found herself telling him about Pennyglen and her family and the Big House, and all the books, and how she'd been allowed to go up there and read whenever she wanted.

'I know Pitlady,' he said. 'At least, I've been there once. And my mother's spoken of it.'

'Oh!' Meg's eyes lit up. Although she loved her new post, and being grown up, she couldn't help the occasional pang of homesickness.

Often, in the evenings, sitting with the kindly Mrs Maclean, and listening to her stories of the islands, she would wonder what they were doing at home.

It was good to meet someone who had heard of the Big House – it made it all seem so much closer, somehow.

She glanced at the clock on the wall.

'I mustn't stop. I've a lot of letters to finish.'

'And I mustn't keep you from your work, but ' He paused.

'I wondered if you'd like a walk on Saturday or Sunday afternoon? We could have a cup of tea somewhere.'

'I'd like that.' She smiled at him.

That weekend, they strolled in Baxter Park in the early spring sunshine.

'Well, I'm off next week,' Philip said suddenly. 'But before I go, my mother's having one of her coffee evenings, in aid of the Belgian refugees. Would you like to come?'

Oh, wouldn't I just! Meg said to herself. She was thrilled at the thought of seeing the large house where the Baillies lived, with its wonderful views across the Tay.

'Thank you. I'd like to come,' she told him.

'Good.' He smiled at her. 'I'm sure my mother will be pleased to meet you.'

Meg shivered a little.

'Are you cold?' he asked at once.

She shook her head. How could she explain that this was what she had looked forward to all these years? This was her big chance to make her way into society.

Her head in a whirl, she wondered what she could wear.

Mrs Maclean was as excited as Meg about the invitation.

'I wish I had something new to wear,' Meg said. But she'd just bought a thick winter jacket, and couldn't afford to splash out on a new dress just yet.

And Mother had been generous enough. She wasn't going to write home and ask for money from the pirlie pig. No, her plain white muslin would have to do.

Mrs Maclean washed and starched the dress for Meg, and produced a length of emerald green taffeta from a trunk.

'I bought this years ago,' she said, 'and never used it. It might make a sash.'

Her skilful fingers pleated the material.

'There, how does that look?'

Meg gazed at herself in the mirror. The vivid green of the sash set off her dark colouring.

'It's wonderful,' she said. 'Thank you so much.'

When the cab drew up at the door of the house, Meg felt a sudden rush of panic.

Her hand trembled as Philip helped her out of the cab, and she was suddenly swept into the warmth of the house.

It reminded her a bit of Pitlady, she thought, but it smelt different – rich, opulent. There was the scent of roses and lilies, the aroma of the gentlemen's cigars, the smell of leather upholstery and beeswax polish.

Meg, looking about her, forgot to be nervous.

'Come and meet my mother,' Philip said.

Mrs Baillie was a little woman, with a soft west coast accent. Her grey hair was already escaping from a bun, and she wore a dress of plain grey silk.

'My dear.' She took both Meg's hands in hers. 'I'm so glad you could come. Now you must meet some of my friends. My son tells me you're from Pennyglen – and you know the family at Pitlady?'

Meg opened her mouth to say, no, she didn't really know them very well, but she was allowed to go and look at the books in the library there. But her hostess hurried on.

'So you will know Lucille – one of my dearest friends. Such a fortunate escape she had! It doesn't bear thinking of.

'Oh, I would like to see her again. Perhaps, after the war...'

'We met – once,' Meg said, trying to recall the graceful figure who had come to Pennyglen all those years ago.

The evening passed in a whirl. There was dancing, and coffee and sandwiches and little cakes and ices – and all the time Philip Baillie was at Meg's side.

'Would you like some lemonade?' he suggested. 'It's rather hot in here.'

'Yes, please.' Meg wished she had a fan like some of the other ladies.

'I won't be a moment.' He vanished, and

173

Meg leaned back against the wall.

'Who is that girl?' she heard a voice say.

'In the white with the green sash?' It was Mrs Baillie's voice. 'She's my husband's secretary.'

'A most attractive girl,' the first voice remarked.

'It's strange,' Mrs Baillie said. 'She reminds me a little of my friend Lucille, when she was young. You remember Lucille?'

'Indeed,' her friend said. 'Now that you mention it, she does resemble Lucille.'

They moved on, and Meg trembled a little as she stood behind the pillar.

'She does resemble Lucille.' What could they mean?

Chapter Seven

Dear Lucille,

It is a long time since I last wrote to you. Lily dipped her pen in the inkwell, then paused to gaze out of the window, smiling happily.

So much has happened...

The best news of all was that Janet was expecting a child in the summer.

It was late spring now, Lily's favourite time of the year. By summer, when the old-fashioned roses were scenting the air, there would be a new member of the family.

Thank goodness, Lily thought, that things seemed to be working out well for Janet. She deserved every happiness.

She smiled to herself as she recalled the day Janet had broken the news of the baby. Lily had given her daughter a warm hug, unable to find the words to express the joy she felt.

'You're keeping all right?' She'd held Janet at arms' length, studying her closely.

'I'm fine.'

'And Rab – is he pleased?'

'Oh, yes.' Janet had grinned.

'And what about his mother?' Lily had paused, not wanting to pry. She knew things had been difficult for Janet at the farm.

Rab's mother was not an easy woman to get along with; she'd always disapproved of Janet, wishing that Rab had chosen a girl from a farming background instead. From the start, Alice's manner had been distant and unfriendly.

To Lily's surprise, Janet had smiled.

'Oh, that's all right. We're better friends now. She'll always be–'

'A bit sharp,' Lily put in.

Janet smiled.

'Yes, but I can manage that. She's going to be the most besotted grandmother. Since we told her about the baby, she'd been much easier to talk to. Even if she does still tell me what to do!'

Lily returned to her letter. She had so much to tell Lucille.

There was Meg's new job as private secretary at Baillie's. How elegant she looked now – quite the young lady! Lily knew Lucille would love to hear how she was getting on.

Then Lily hesitated. There was something about Meg these days that concerned her a little. It was nothing she could put her finger on, but…

Matt had noticed it, too. He listened, with that half-smile Lily knew so well, to Meg talking eagerly about her new friends; about the lunch parties she'd attended; the fine dresses the ladies had worn; the business acquaintances she'd met.

'She's getting above herself,' Matt said suddenly one evening, when he and Lily were alone. 'She's not born to that kind of life.'

Lily had silenced him, a finger to her lips.

'Well, maybe she *is* born to that way of life,' Matt added after a moment. 'But it's not the way we brought her up.'

'They're decent people, the Baillies,' Lily pointed out, trying to reassure him. 'Straightforward. Kindly, too.'

'Perhaps,' Matt conceded. 'But she's rising too far, too fast. I'm worried no good will come of it.'

Of course Lily didn't mention these doubts in her letter to Lucille.

As for Ellen, she wrote, *she is happy in her work.*

Lily always smiled when she thought about Ellen. 'Miss Ellie' was a favourite with the children at the Big House. They'd welcomed her as their nursemaid. No-one else knew as many exciting stories as Miss Ellie. No-one else could make up such splendid games.

It was a wonderful job. Ellen came home each evening, her face glowing, her eyes sparkling.

But one day, everything was turned upside down.

'I've got some news for you.' Mrs Moir, her employer, called Ellen into the little sitting-room. 'And I want to make you an offer.

'We're going to return south, to Surrey, to stay near my parents. It seems best for the children.'

Ellen was dismayed, though she tried not to show it. She'd grown so fond of the little family.

She knew, too, though her employer never spoke of it, that Mrs Moir's husband was a prisoner of war. Bewildered and anxious, the young woman had returned to Scotland to stay with her sister. Now, it seemed she'd decided to move on.

'You see,' Mrs Moir went on, 'Alfred will be going to school soon, and I'd like him to attend his father's old school in Surrey. We'll be leaving here in a month's time.'

'Oh.' Ellen couldn't think of anything to say.

'There's something else,' her employer continued. 'Pitlady is going to be turned into a hospital – a convalescent home for wounded servicemen.'

Ellen shook her head.

'I didn't know,' she murmured.

Mrs Moir paused.

'You've been so wonderful with the children – would you come south with us?' She took Ellen's hands between hers.

'Please say yes, Ellen,' she begged. 'It would mean so much to me. And yet – I haven't any right to ask you to leave your home.

'Why don't you talk it over with your parents? You can have a little time to decide. We'd make you feel at home, and the children are so fond of you. They're going to miss you terribly.'

'I'll think about it,' Ellen promised. Her heart seemed to beat a little faster. What a wonderful chance!

If she accepted, she'd be able to see more of the world, instead of staying in Pennyglen. And there couldn't be a kinder employer than Mrs Moir.

Ellen was very quiet that evening. As the family sat round the fireside, she looked at them as if she'd never seen them before.

Matt, her father, had greying hair, and was rather stooped now – how much older he looked!

And Mother – she was always the same. But too often these days, her smile was an effort, and Ellen noticed wrinkles around Lily's eyes and mouth that hadn't been there before.

She was worried, of course; anxious about Matt, and concerned about Janet, too. For although Rab was gaining strength all the time, and he and Janet were looking forward to the baby's arrival, Ellen knew that things were often difficult at the farm.

Next day, Ellen could keep her news to herself no longer.

'Mrs Moir's taking the children back to Surrey,' she blurted out. 'She wants me to go with them.'

There was a long pause.

'They must think a lot of you, the folk at the Big House,' Matt said at last.

'Of course they do!' Lily sprang to her daughter's defence. 'She's worked hard for them, she's a good nursemaid to those children.'

'Calm down.' Matt had a twinkle in his eye. 'You've no need to stand up for Ellen. I reckon she can do that for herself.'

'Well–' he turned to his daughter, '–it's up to you. Do you want to go?'

'I'd like to,' Ellen said slowly. 'I've never been anywhere, and it's a fine chance…'

'Think it over carefully,' Matt advised. 'We'll not stand in your way, will we?' He glanced over at Lily.

'It's like your father says,' Lily agreed. 'If you want to go–'

'But I can't leave you!' Ellen protested.

'Nonsense.' Matt tapped his fingers on the arm of his chair. 'We're not in our dotage yet, are we, Mother?' he joked.

That night, Ellen tossed and turned, unable to sleep. At breakfast next morning, she sat listlessly over her porridge, saying little.

All day, Ellen's thoughts were in a whirl. If Pitlady was being turned into a convalescent home, they were sure to want staff. This might be her big chance to train as a nurse.

If she went south, what would happen when both children started school? She wouldn't be needed as a nursemaid any more.

Oh, she was sure Mrs Moir would find her another post with a family, but she *did* want to train as a nurse.

And then there was her father and mother... Ellen remembered how white Matt had looked the night before. He wasn't well, she was sure, even though he insisted he was all right.

Who would help if he fell ill? Janet was going to have her hands full once the baby was born, and she lived a little distance away.

And Meg? She was so busy with her job in the city that Ellen couldn't imagine her coming back to live in the village and help out.

Ellen took a deep breath. Yes, she knew what her decision would be.

'I've made up my mind,' she told Mrs Moir later that day. 'Thank you for giving me the chance – but I can't go to England with you.'

'I understand, Ellen.' Mrs Moir smiled gently. 'But I'm sorry you're leaving us. What are you going to do? I – I don't like to think of you working in the mill – I know you'd find it hard...'

'I'd like to train as a nurse,' Ellen told her. 'Yes, I know it will be hard – just as hard as mill work – but it's something I've always wanted to do.'

'Come in!'

Ellen stepped into the large sunny room at Pitlady that was now the office of the matron of the convalescent home.

'Sit down.' The matron nodded towards a chair and Ellen sat down, crossing her ankles neatly and folding her hands in her lap.

Her hands were trembling slightly and she tried not to show that she was nervous. She'd pinned all her hopes on becoming a nurse, and this interview was her big chance.

'You've been looking after the Moir children, I understand?' The matron glanced at her notes.

'Yes.' Ellen explained that they were going back to England and, though she'd been offered a job, she was anxious to train as a nurse.

'What else have you done?' Matron wanted to know.'

'This is my first job.'

'I see.'

'I really do want to train,' Ellen said. 'I'm used to hard work, and I don't mind long hours.'

'Looking after children is not the same as our kind of nursing,' the matron explained. 'I wonder if you have any idea how hard the work is.' She looked across the desk at the slim, fragile girl sitting opposite her.

'I doubt very much you'd be strong enough – a lot of the work is hard and physical, with heavy lifting and so on.'

'But I don't mind. I'm willing to try,' Ellen told her eagerly.

'And,' the matron went on, 'you'd find that a good deal of the work is rather unpleasant. These are men who have suffered severe injuries. Many of them are maimed for life. I need someone who can cope with tending wounds, without being squeamish.'

'But I...' Ellen began.

The matron shook her head.

'No, I'm afraid this sort of nursing isn't for you. You'd be far better to look for another job as a nursemaid. Thank you for coming to see me.'

The interview was at an end. Ellen, outside the door, felt her knees trembling. She couldn't believe it. Rejected! She wasn't going to be a nurse after all.

She stumbled out of the door and down the drive, feeling stunned. She was near to tears but she wouldn't cry, she wouldn't.

How could she tell them at home? She'd gone off with such high hopes that morning. She'd planned to come back and share her excitement about the new job – when she was to start, and what she'd be doing. And now...

'Well?' Back home, Lily was eager to know how Ellen had got on. But one glance at the girl's face made her pause.

'Is something wrong?' she asked.

The tears which Ellen had fought to control welled up.

'They don't want me!' she burst out, and rushed upstairs to fling herself on her bed.

The next morning, Lily tried to comfort her daughter as she prepared to set off for the Big House and her day's work.

'Never mind,' she said kindly. 'You're doing a fine job, looking after the children. And you'll get another post...'

To her astonishment, Ellen whirled round, her eyes flashing.

'I don't want just any job! I want to be a nurse. And it's not right – she just looked at me and said I'd be too weak, not tough enough.

'Well, I'm not going to take that – I'm going back to ask for a job.'

Lily was amazed. This was a quite different Ellen, this determined creature, flushed with anger.

'I know they're short-staffed. She can't

184

refuse me.'

'Well!' Lily sank down in her chair, astonished, as Ellen marched off, slamming the door behind her.

That evening, Ellen came up the path in a rush, eyes sparkling.

'Well,' she exclaimed, 'I did it!'

'Did what?'

'I went to see the matron.' Ellen perched on the edge of the table.

'Oh, I was nervous! But I had my speech all prepared – and I kept thinking, if other girls can be nurses, so can I!'

'What did you say?' Lily gasped.

'I just said I was tougher than I looked, and I wasn't afraid of hard work and unpleasant jobs. And I said she could take me on three months probation, and if I was no good at the end of it then I'd accept that I wasn't cut out to be a nurse.'

Matt, listening, looked up with a quiet smile of admiration.

'So she said yes!' Ellen jumped down from the table and danced round the room.

Matron was right – the work was gruelling. Ellen ran here and there; some days it seemed that she couldn't do anything right, no matter how hard she tried.

One day, she was helping another nurse to fold sheets when she heard a familiar voice.

'Well, if it isn't Nurse Ellen!'

185

'Colin!'

Ellen smiled up at the tall young man in the RFC uniform.

'What are you...? I mean...'

'It's my home, remember? But I'm staying in the lodge now. And I'm up here to see a friend – one of the patients. My, you do look grown up.'

'I *am* grown up,' Ellen said, with as much dignity as she could muster.

'Little Ellen!'

She made a face at him.

'You suit the uniform.' He gazed at her. Ellen blushed.

'I've work to do,' she told him.

'In that case, I'll come back when you're off duty.'

He waved goodbye and Ellen's companion gazed after him.

'He looks nice,' her friend said. 'Very handsome.'

Ellen laughed.

'He's just Colin – just a friend.'

Colin was waiting for her when she came off duty.

'I'll drive you home,' he offered.

Ellen was only too glad to accept a lift in the comfortable car. She enjoyed being handed into her seat as if she were a lady.

She smiled at the thought.

'What's so amusing?' Colin wanted to know.

186

Ellen laughed.

'Oh, it's just that I feel like a lady, but I certainly don't look it. Not with these hands.' She grimaced at her hands, already work-worn with scrubbing.

'They look very nice to me.' Colin took one of her hands in his.

Ellen looked up at him and quickly withdrew her hand.

'We'd better get home.'

'So, how are you getting on?' he asked. 'Are you finding it hard work?'

Ellen nodded.

'I don't like to say anything at home – but well, I don't know if I'm going to make a good nurse. I never seem to do anything right.' She gave a little sigh.

During the days that followed, Colin called regularly for Ellen. Sometimes they walked in the woods, where the paths would soon be fringed with speedwell and campion.

'Oh, Ellen,' Colin said, 'when I'm with you, the war seems a million miles away.' He put his hands on her shoulders.

'Look at me.'

She turned her face to him and he brushed a curl off her brow.

'Will you write to me?' he asked.

'I don't know what you want to hear.'

'Just about this,' he told her. 'About the countryside, and the birds and the fields, and what you're doing. About your family,

187

about the things that matter to you.'

'I'll try,' Ellen promised.

'Little Ellen,' he said. 'You're still so young – very young. But one day–' he took her in his arms '–one day, I hope you'll care for me.'

Confused, Ellen broke from his grasp.

'Come on! I'll race you to the stile!' she called. She ran until she was out of breath and collapsed against the trunk of a tree.

Colin was right behind her.

'I mean it, Ellen. I won't forget you.'

It was a hot June night when Janet awoke. Everything was still, except for the distant hoot of an owl and the sound of small creatures scurrying around outside. It was so quiet she could almost hear her heart thudding.

Should she waken Rab? He was exhausted by his day's work – it seemed a shame. And yet – she caught her breath. There it was again, that pain!

Rab stirred in his sleep.

Janet lay for a little longer, enjoying the stillness, but with the odd pang of apprehension.

At last she leaned over.

'Rab,' she said softly. 'I'm sorry to wake you, but...'

'What is it?' Rab was awake in an instant.

'I think–' Janet gave a gasp. 'I think the baby's on the way!'

'Why didn't you wake me before this?' he demanded. 'I'll go for my mother, and then fetch the midwife.'

'There's no rush.' Janet looked up at him. 'It's likely to be hours yet.'

But Rab was already pulling on his clothes and lacing his boots.

'I'll be as quick as I can,' he promised.

Janet, tossing restlessly in bed, was aware of cool hands stroking her forehead. 'There now, lass, you're doing fine.' She could hardly recognise the gentle voice as that of her mother-in-law. She squeezed the older woman's hand gratefully.

At dinner time, Alice came downstairs to see to the meal.

'She's doing fine,' she told Rab. 'You've nothing to worry about.'

Rab's father tried to distract his son with talk of cattle and the price of wheat, and what was happening in France after Germany's breakthrough on the Western Front a few months before.

But Rab paid no attention; he couldn't take his eyes off the clock.

'I'll see to the milking this afternoon,' his father offered. 'You wait here.'

Rab accepted gratefully. It was warm in the little kitchen, and as his head sank lower on his chest, he soon dozed off...

'Is that you asleep? You should be ashamed of yourself. And you with a fine wee girl, too.'

Immediately, Rab sprang to his feet.

'A girl! And Janet...?'

'She's fine,' his mother said. 'Come away up and see them both.'

Janet gave him a smile as he entered the room.

'We've a daughter, Rab.'

'And you?' He grasped her hand in his. 'Are you all right?'

'She's as right as rain.' The midwife came from the other side of the room. 'And here's the wee lass...'

'Oh, she's bonnie,' Rab exclaimed.

The midwife laid the baby gently beside Janet.

'I think,' Janet said softly, 'it would be nice to call her Alice, after your mother.'

Rab nodded. His mother was standing by the door.

'She's a grand wee girl,' she whispered, then turned aside. For Alice had her pride still, and she didn't want anyone to see the tears – tears of joy – that had welled up in her eyes.

'That's real nice of you,' she murmured.

It was a sombre November day – November 11, 1918.

No-one, Lily reflected, had much heart for the celebrations of the Armistice. In four long years of war, too many homes had been touched by sorrow, too many lives shattered.

Lily was thankful in her heart that she'd had no men of fighting age, thankful that her family had been spared.

But all the same, she felt anxious. Only the visits from Janet, carrying baby Alice, cheered her.

She was deeply concerned about Matt. He no longer played the fiddle in the evening, and would sink into his armchair, looking drawn and tired.

'Is there anything wrong?' she asked him several times.

He always shook his head.

'No, I'm fine. Just busy at work, that's all. It's been a hectic time with the Admiralty contracts.'

Lily wasn't altogether surprised when, one evening a few days later, he collapsed heavily into his chair.

'What's the matter? Is something wrong?' She knelt down beside him, frightened by the look on his face.

'I'm not feeling right,' he said slowly.

She put a hand on his brow, and realised he was hot and feverish.

'Off to bed,' she said firmly. 'And if you're no better in the morning, I'm calling the doctor.'

Matt tried to protest, but he was too weak. He spent a restless night and Lily became more and more anxious. The family rarely called in the doctor – Lily couldn't recall the last time – but she knew Matt was ill.

'It's this influenza – you've maybe heard of it, the epidemic that's laid so many folk low,' the doctor explained to Lily once he'd examined Matt.

She nodded, her face pale.

'He'll be all right in time,' the doctor reassured her. 'He's got a fine strong constitution, your man. But keep him quiet – don't let him go worrying about his work. He'll not be ready to go back for a while.'

During the weeks that followed, Ellen was a tower of strength to her parents. She was always so calm and cheerful.

Matt's eyes followed her as she moved about the room.

'I can see you're a good nurse,' he said one day, as he sat in his chair. 'You'll keep those lads at the convalescent home in order!'

Ellen was deftly changing sheets and smoothing out the pillowcases.

'We'll be losing you to one of them before much longer,' he teased her. Ellen was glad to see the smile back in his eyes.

'No fear of that,' she said briskly, giving him an affectionate pat on the shoulder.

Meg came home every weekend to visit her parents. She sat by her father, reading bits from the newspaper, and telling him about the Baillie family.

Even Willie – now a gangling youth, who cared about nothing but football – was a help to his mother. He'd happily run messages when he returned from his day's work at the farm near Pitlessie, where he'd been taken on as a farmhand.

Yes, Lily was proud of her family.

Meg was now a valued member of the staff at Baillie's. She was efficient and quietly confident, and gradually old Mr Baillie allowed her more responsibility.

'Ask Miss Barclay,' she heard him say one day. 'She knows all about everything – she's a real right-hand woman, you might say.'

Meg's spirits soared at the praise. She couldn't wait to tell them at home.

'A right-hand woman, eh?' Matt beamed with pride. He was growing stronger with every day.

'If you're as good a business woman as all that,' he joked, 'they'll be making you a partner one of these days.'

Meg looked serious. She had her dreams and ambitions. She wanted to be rich one day she knew – and independent, too.

She also knew that she was becoming more and more attracted to Philip Baillie...

When the young man was demobilised and returned to the firm, he and Meg saw a lot of each other.

'Things are going to be different,' he told

her one day. 'I know my father's done a grand job, keeping the business going during the War, but times change.

'We've got to be up to date with the latest methods. New machinery, new ways of doing things...'

She listened with shining eyes to his plans for the firm. They talked a lot, strolling in the park, or driving through the Angus countryside.

It was Meg's friendship with Philip that sparked off the row with Ellen.

Meg had returned to Pennyglen for the weekend. Ellen had just finished night duty followed by overtime, and was sitting on her bed, almost too exhausted to remove her shoes and stockings.

When Meg arrived, she was bubbling over with excitement as usual. She flung her straw hat down on the bed.

'Oh!' She yawned. 'It's been such a busy week.'

'Has it?'

Meg didn't notice that Ellen's tone was rather chilly.

'We had several rush orders, but I can cope with that. The unflappable Miss Barclay, so Mr Baillie calls me. Actually, I have done a lot to make the office more efficient.

'My dear, you should have seen it when I first walked in. Out of the ark!' Meg gave an affected little laugh.

'They're very lucky to have you – what would they do without you?' Ellen said. Meg didn't even notice the sarcasm in her sister's voice.

'Oh, well, I don't know ... and, of course, I've had a busy social life as well this week. Philip and I went to a soirée, a very smart musical evening.

'I wore my new blue muslin – did I tell you? Mrs Maclean made it up for me; she really is handy at things like that. Well, I know I looked elegant because Philip said...'

'Will you be quiet!' Ellen jumped to her feet.

'What do you mean?' Meg was startled. 'Aren't you well? What's the matter?'

'I'm perfectly well, thank you,' Ellen said calmly, 'but I'm tired of hearing about your wonderful job, and your smart friends, and elegant evenings.'

'You're jealous!' Meg said hotly.

'Jealous?' Ellen repeated. 'Why should I be jealous of such a silly, empty snob like you?'

'Me – a snob?' Meg was almost speechless.

'You never talk about anyone but yourself. You aren't interested in my job, and it's a lot more useful than yours, even though it isn't glamorous. You never think of people who are worse off than yourself.

'You never think of Mother and Father, and you can see how ill he still looks. Selfish – that's what you are.'

195

'But...' Meg stared in amazement at her younger sister – Ellen had always looked up to her.

'I'm not selfish – am I?' she asked slowly.

Ellen nodded. Now that she'd spoken out, she was a bit ashamed of her outburst.

'You are a bit...'

'I didn't mean to be.' Meg rose with dignity. 'I'd better leave you alone to have a sleep. I'm sorry if I've offended you.'

She didn't want Ellen to see how hurt she was. Was she really a snob? She hadn't realised...

Most of the employees were glad to see Philip Baillie back in the business. He had a cheerful word for everyone, and if he was a bit of a hard taskmaster, well, he was just his father all over again, wasn't he?

Meg had never met anyone quite like him. How handsome he was, how charming, how fortunate to have been born with a silver spoon in his mouth!

Everyone agreed with her – or so she thought.

One day, she returned to the office after a short dinner break, to finish some letters that Mr Baillie wanted urgently.

As soon as they were ready, she rose to take them into the inner office. Then she realised he had a visitor with him. Never mind, she would just hand them over.

She knocked on the door and opened it.

'Well, they won't stand for it! I can tell you that!'

She paused, astonished. Philip Baillie sat at his father's desk. The young man before him, who'd raised his voice, thumped his fist down on its wooden top.

'I'm so sorry…' Meg began to back out.

'Are these for my father?' Philip asked her.

'Yes, some letters he wanted urgently.'

Philip held out his hand.

'We have a meeting shortly. I'll see that he gets them.'

Meg handed over the letters and thankfully retreated into the outer office. A moment later, the young man pushed the door open and hurried past Meg.

She saw that he was shabbily dressed and very thin. He didn't give her a second glance, and she felt a little put out. She wasn't used to being ignored!

A few moments later, Philip, too, came out of the office.

'I'll make sure my father gets those letters to sign,' he said again.

Meg was puzzled. Who was the young man, and why was Philip being so tolerant of his behaviour?

She turned back to her typewriter, and decided that she would ask Philip, the first chance she got.

Her opportunity came a few days later,

when Philip invited her to his family's house for dinner.

'You know how much my parents like you,' he said. 'My mother keeps asking when I'm going to bring you home.'

Meg blushed. Did that mean he was serious about her?

'I'd love to come,' she said.

She took great pains with her dress that day, and she knew she looked her best in the royal blue skirt and little jacket, with the frilly eggshell-blue blouse.

Philip looked at her admiringly.

'I wondered,' she said idly, 'about that young man in the office the other day. Who was he? I haven't seen him before.'

'Oh, you mean Alec Webster,' Philip said. 'He works for us. He's got a lot of influence with the men – he often speaks for them.'

'But he was shouting at you,' Meg protested.

'That's just his way. To be honest,' Philip continued, 'he's very bright. He's going to be a big asset to the firm. We don't want to lose him.'

Philip's mother gave her a warm welcome when they reached the house. 'My dear, it *is* so good to see you.' She drew the girl into the hall.

Meg looked around her. Such space, such comfort, such taste! This was how she wanted to live!

'Now I want to know about your family,' the kindly Mrs Baillie said. 'Your father – is he feeling better?'

All through lunch, as they talked, the older woman watched Meg closely. Yes, she was an asset to the firm – but...'

'Oh,' Mrs Baillie said suddenly, putting down her spoon. 'I almost forgot to tell you. I've had a letter from my dear friend, Lucille.

'Do you remember, she came from your part of Fife? And you remember she planned to sail on the *Lusitania?* Thank goodness she didn't.

'Well, she's going to visit in the spring. I'm longing to see her. Lucille is one of my dearest friends – we've known each other for many years.'

Meg couldn't help recalling the words she'd once overheard: 'She does resemble Lucille.'

She could hardly wait to meet Lucille again – she had only the dimmest memory of the graceful figure who'd visited Penny-glen all those years ago.

That evening, Mrs Baillie was thoughtful.

'Meg's a charming girl,' she said to her husband. 'I just hope Philip doesn't get too involved after all, she is an employee.'

Her husband looked up from his paper.

'Don't you worry your head about it,' he said. 'Philip's got too much sense.'

'You men!' His wife, rearranging a vase of carnations, snapped the head off a bloom in her annoyance.

'You don't see what's before your eyes,' she went on. 'Oh, Miss Barclay's a pleasant girl, I know, and I'm quite happy for her to come to the house, and help out at functions, too. She's very well turned out.

'But I don't want her getting the wrong idea. And I doubt Philip's got the sense to see what's happening until it's too late.' She turned to her husband.

'Would you have a word with him?'

'No,' her husband said firmly. 'I will not. Let the lad alone. He's got plenty of sense. He won't fall for the first pretty girl who makes eyes at him.'

His wife sighed and changed the subject.

'Did you remember, my dear, that you promised to take me to Mr Barrie's new play – what's it called? Oh, yes, "Dear Brutus." Now you did promise.'

Next weekend, when Meg went home, she told her family about her visit to the Baillies' home – the fine furniture, the flowers, the meal with its delicate soup, chicken mousse and ices.

Meg was more careful now, though – she avoided saying too much in front of Ellen. The sisters were on speaking terms again, but Meg couldn't help feeling a little ashamed of the whole incident. Perhaps she had been bragging – just a little...

'Oh, Mother, guess what! Mrs Baillie's friend, Lucille, who lived in the Big House, is coming over from America for a visit.

'I expect I'll be asked to meet her. I'm sure they'll have a special dinner for her – won't that be fun?'

Lily put down the plate she'd been drying.

'Lucille? Coming back?'

'So Mrs Baillie said.'

Lily turned aside, pretending to be busy, to hide the sudden pang she'd felt at Meg's news. After all these years, and all they'd shared...

And Lucille hadn't even thought to let Lily know of her planned visit. It wasn't fair.

'Mother,' Meg said one weekend, 'I'd like to bring Philip home. Next Sunday, perhaps?'

'That would be fine,' Lily agreed.

'You will–' Meg hesitated '–you will set the tea in the parlour, won't you? I mean – that's what he's used to.'

'Of course. We know how to behave ourselves before the gentry,' Lily said drily.

'Oh, Mother!' Meg flared up. 'It's not like that. Philip's not grand at all. I just want to have everything nice.'

'It will be,' Lily promised.

But somehow, the visit was not a success.

Lily had gone to a great deal of trouble.

The table was set with her best lace cloth, and the china that had been her mother's.

There were freshly baked scones, and a sponge cake and shortbread. Matt always said that no-one could make shortbread like Lily.

The young man ate everything politely, and praised the baking. But he was just a bit too fulsome. He praised the sponge cake, and asked for the recipe for his mother.

'She can have it and welcome. Does your mother do all her own baking?' Lily asked.

'Hardly at all, but we have an excellent cook,' Philip told her.

'I doubt your cook doesn't need me to tell her how to make a sponge cake,' Lily remarked.

It was said lightly, but Meg was aware of the distance between the two families.

With Matt, the young man talked a little more easily about his work, but Matt was ill at ease, uncomfortable in a stiff collar.

It was an uneasy visit, and Meg was glad when it ended.

'Your parents,' Philip said later. 'They didn't like me much.'

'They did,' Meg protested. 'They just take a little getting used to. They're a bit – set in their ways.'

As she spoke, she disliked herself for her attitude. But she didn't know what else to say.

On Meg's next visit home, Lily felt that the time had come to speak to her daughter.

Ever since that Sunday, when Philip had called, Matt had been quiet and a little gruff. Lily, knowing him so well, realised that he was anxious about Meg.

She chose her moment. It was a fine evening and Matt had wandered down to the corner of the street, where one or two of the men gathered for a smoke and a chat, while they sat in the warm sunshine and put the world to rights.

'This young man,' Lily began carefully. 'Is he serious about you?'

Meg flushed.

'I think so,' she said in a neutral tone of voice. 'You liked him, didn't you? He's so brilliant, so charming – everyone likes Philip.'

'Just be careful,' Lily said, laying down the flowers she'd been arranging. 'Because he's charming, that doesn't mean he'll make you a good husband.

'Oh, I've no doubt he's very clever and rich, and has always had it easy...'

'That's it, isn't it?' Meg's voice rose. 'You'd rather he was poor and struggling. You think less of him because he's well off. You'd rather I married someone like Rab.'

'Rab's a fine man, and a good husband to Janet,' Lily said, a note of warning in her voice.

'Oh, I'm not saying anything against him. But–' Meg turned to face her '–can't you understand this is my chance to better myself?'

'I want to have a good life. I don't want always to be scraping and watching the pennies. I want to have a big house and servants and everything pleasant and comfortable. I don't see what's wrong with that.'

Lily drew a deep breath.

'Listen, Meg. Your father and I – well, we didn't feel that this young man was right for you.

'I think you've got carried away by the fact that he's rich. All this grandeur – the big house, the dinners, the fine dresses. You don't really want this sort of life...'

'Yes, I do!' Meg flared up. 'Philip and I get on well. I'd make him a good wife.'

'Think carefully,' Lily begged her. 'You're making a mistake. Your head's been turned – this sort of life isn't what you want, deep down inside.'

Meg's voice trembled with anger.

'How do you know what I want? You don't really know me, how I feel, what I want to do with my life. How *could* you know? You're not my mother!'

The words fell into the silence between them.

Lily sank down into a chair, her shoulders shaking.

As soon as she'd spoken, Meg realised what she had said. Oh, she'd have given anything to take the words back!

'How long have you known?' Lily asked at last. 'That you're adopted, I mean.'

'For years,' Meg admitted. 'I overheard you and Father talking one day.'

'Oh, Meg!' Lily cried. 'Why didn't you say something before? What must you have thought, all this time...?' She buried her face in her hands.

'I'm so sorry, Mother!' Meg wiped tears from her eyes. 'I just say things without thinking – I didn't mean to hurt you...'

Lily stroked the dark head with a gentle hand.

'I know you didn't mean it,' she said, her voice shaking.

'I've always tried to do my best for you. You've been like one of my own – you *are* my own...'

Meg looked up, her face tear-stained.

'I know. I'm truly sorry. Oh, if only I could be more like Janet, or Ellen.'

'We wouldn't want you any different.' Lily forced a smile.

That evening, before Meg left to catch her train, she gave Lily a hug.

'I'm sorry, you know.'

'It's forgotten,' Lily said, giving the girl an affectionate pat on the arm.

But, as Meg hurried down the road

towards the station, she wasn't too sure. She knew that Lily had been deeply wounded by her careless words. Could things ever be the same again?

Chapter Eight

Could things ever be the same again? Meg tossed and turned on her pillow that night. She would have given anything in the world to have taken back the words she'd spoken in anger.

'You're not my mother!' How could she have said that to Lily – even in the heat of the moment? Lily had always been so good to her.

Matt and Lily had never made any difference between herself and the others, Meg reflected. She burned with shame as the memory of what she'd said flooded over her.

And as for the pirlie pig, she thought – her mother could have used the coins she saved in it to buy treats for herself, but she never did.

Instead, there had always been money to spare for Meg's new boots, for fares to Dundee, even a pretty new hat for the summer.

Meg thumped her pillow. I'll make it up to her, I promise, she resolved, just before she fell at last into an uneasy sleep.

In the days that followed, Meg was not herself.

Her colleagues at work noticed that the smiling, confident Miss Barclay was not as serene as usual. She snapped at the messenger boy instead of joking with him, and she sighed audibly when Mr Baillie asked her to retype a letter.

Even Philip noticed that she was quieter than usual.

'What's the matter?' he asked one evening.

They'd been out for a stroll, and Meg had barely spoken at all. Whenever he'd tried to start a conversation, she'd simply answered, 'Yes', or 'No', or 'I suppose so.'

'What on earth's the matter with you?' he repeated. 'You're like a wet Sunday afternoon in January!' The words were spoken lightly, but he looked a little irritated.

'Nothing's wrong.' Meg gazed into the distance. 'It's just that–'

She realised, suddenly, that she couldn't tell Philip. How could she say, 'I spoke in such a cruel way to my mother – well, she's not my real mother. You see…'

Of course she couldn't tell him. She was slowly coming to understand that, if she wanted to be with Philip, it had to be on his terms.

The Baillies would soon put an end to any relationship with a girl whose family background was unknown, even mysterious.

'Well, for goodness sake, do cheer up!' He sounded a little impatient. 'You're usually so lively. It's not like you to be so glum...'

Meg's temper flared.

'In that case, you'd better take me home. No-one wants to force you to spend an evening with someone so dull and dreary...'

'I never said–' he began, realising too late that perhaps something *was* wrong. 'But, well, you have been rather moody lately, always mopping around the office, and snapping my head off...'

'That's enough,' Meg said. She rose to her feet and pulled her wrap around her. 'You obviously don't want to be with me.'

They glared at each other. Normally, Meg would have laughed and teased him. They'd quarrelled before, and had made it up. But this time, it was more serious.

They walked back to her lodgings in silence.

'I expect I'll see you in the office,' Philip said coldly as they parted.

Two days later, he breezed into Meg's office and threw a couple of documents on the desk.

'Ask my father if he'd look at these as soon as he can, would you?' he said.

'Of course.' She smiled at him a little shakily.

'Feeling better?' he asked. 'That's good.'

'Philip,' she began haltingly, 'I'm sorry about the other evening.'

'Don't be. It's quite forgotten.' He gave

her his special smile, the one that always made her heart turn over. 'Must rush. See you soon.'

Meg began to type again, feeling somewhat happier. At least Philip wasn't going to bear a grudge against her.

But she still felt anxious and troubled about Lily. Night after night, she slept badly, going over and over in her mind what she should do.

She hadn't been home since that awful day. Should she go back to Pennyglen at the weekend, and just pretend nothing had changed? If she left early on Saturday, she could catch the one o'clock train...

Maybe she should talk to Janet? No, her sister had enough to think of with the baby...

She decided to leave things alone for the moment. She usually went home once every two weeks, but if she let another fortnight slip by, maybe things would be easier.

But how dreary she felt! It was a cold, damp spring, and all she could see when she looked out of the window was the rain sweeping the pavements, and people hurrying by, the high wind catching their umbrellas.

Tears began to well up in her eyes, and she reached for a handkerchief. Then the door of the office burst open, and she hastily dabbed at her face, pretending that she had a speck in her eye.

But it was only Alec Webster, one of the employees.

'Oh, I'm sorry...' He stopped in the doorway.

'Is there...? I mean – is there something wrong?' he asked, concerned.

Meg shook her head.

'No, nothing. Just a bit of grit in my eye.'

'Oh, I see. I thought you looked a bit down. Look here,' he said kindly, 'don't let old Mr Baillie bully you. He's a bit of a tartar, but decent enough really.'

'It's not that. Oh, no, the Baillies have been very kind to me.' Suddenly, Meg felt the urge to confide in someone.

'It's just – well, a family matter,' she told him, after a pause.

'Ah!' Alec said. 'Families can be the very dickens! If they're not rowing or hardly on speaking terms, they're smothering each other with kindness. With me, it's porridge...'

'Porridge?' Meg couldn't help being intrigued. She managed a little smile.

'What on earth has porridge to do with it?'

'My mother,' Alec said solemnly, 'has a heart of gold, and is the kindest soul on earth. She thinks I need feeding up.

'We lost my father years ago – he was involved in a pit accident. Mother works pretty hard – cleaning, washing, that sort of thing. And she keeps telling me that I need feeding up. I'm far too thin, and so on.'

'She's quite right,' Meg said firmly, forgetting that she hardly knew this young man.

'So she feeds me porridge every morning. I can't bear the stuff – I have to choke it down. Yet she means well. I couldn't hurt her feelings, now could I?'

'I suppose not.' Meg smiled.

'Have you any brothers and sisters?' she asked.

'There's Maisie – she's away from home now. And young Jamie – he's the brightest of us all. He wants to be a doctor. There's plenty time – he's only fourteen. But he's clever, Jamie. All his teachers say so.'

'The trouble is finding the money.' His face clouded. 'But here I am rambling on, and you've work to do.' He sat down on the edge of the desk.

'I wanted to see Mr Baillie. Actually, I want to ask him for a pay rise. Is he in a good mood, do you think?'

'I'm sorry – he's not in,' Meg told him.

'Then I'll just have to come back and hope he's in a giving mood!' Alec gave her a grin and she found herself responding, liking his frank, freckled face and way of chuckling at the end of a sentence.

A few days later, Meg came back from an errand to find a small posy of violets on her desk.

She picked them up. So Philip had remembered that she loved violets! Surely this meant that all was well between them again.

Then she noticed the scrap of paper beneath the flowers. *Perhaps these will cheer you up a little. A. W.*

At first she felt a little disappointed. Philip hadn't sent her flowers after all. But it was thoughtful of Alec – especially when she knew he had very little money to spare.

She carefully put the flowers in a tumbler of water, feeling flattered that two young men were paying her attention. If only Philip weren't so busy these days...

'Have you a moment, Miss Barclay?' Mr Baillie came out of his office, with a box in his hand.

'My wife urgently wants these invitations – they've just come from the printer. Would you mind taking them out to the house? Take a tram – you know the way, don't you?'

Meg's spirits rose at the thought of seeing the beautiful house again, and Mrs Baillie, too.

'Of course. I'd be glad to.'

Meg could have handed the box to the maid who opened the door, trim in her black dress and white cap and apron, but she didn't.

'I've come from the office to see Mrs Baillie,' she said firmly.

'Will you wait, please?'

Meg gave her name and was shown into the drawing-room. She stood at the window, gazing out at the immaculate garden and the sunlight sparkling on the river in the distance.

What wouldn't she give to live in a house like this!

She turned swiftly as footsteps tapped over the polished floor.

'How good of you to bring the invitations!' Mrs Baillie greeted her. 'I wanted them right away.'

'I'm planning a special evening. My good friend, Lucille – of course, you know her – is arriving soon, and I want her to meet all my friends...' Mrs Baillie's voice chattered on, but Meg paid little attention.

So Lucille was to be here! Would there be a chance for Meg to see her again? There was so much she wanted to know...

'Is Lucille to be staying with you?' Meg asked politely.

'I wish she would, but she has so many friends. Now, my dear, I have a great favour to ask you.

'There's such a lot of planning to be done in advance – would you be willing to lend me a hand? Checking the acceptance list, keeping track of the catering arrangements, seeing the hired staff, and so on. I'd be so grateful.

'And you needn't worry that it will

interfere with your work at the office. My husband said, "Just ask Miss Barclay for any help you need."'

'I'd be glad to help.' Meg's voice trembled a little.

This was it! At last, she was accepted as one of the family. She'd be at Mrs Baillie's right hand, interviewing, organising – just the sort of thing she was good at.

'Thank you,' Mrs Baillie said. 'Now, about these invitations…'

The next few weeks were frantically busy. Meg seemed to live in a whirl – keeping things on an even keel, soothing Mrs Baillie when she became anxious over the menu or the delivery of the flowers.

There was no time to go home to Pennyglen. Once this was over, she'd go, Meg promised herself.

One thing puzzled her a little. Mrs Baillie was obviously expecting her to be a guest, chatting to people, making sure everything ran smoothly on the night. Meg would have loved to have an invitation to show to her family, but days passed, and still it didn't arrive.

Once or twice, she wondered if she should ask Philip about it, but he was busy. He didn't often appear in her office nowadays.

'I'd be so glad if you could come along early on the evening of the party,' Mrs Baillie said to Meg.

'There will be a maid to open the door, and someone to help with the cloaks, but could you just keep an eye on the caterers, and make sure all the staff have turned up?'

'And I'd appreciate a last-minute hand with the flowers – just to make sure they're perfectly fresh.'

Meg felt proud. How Mrs Baillie trusted her! It was good to be wanted like this – like one of the family.

Meg planned her outfit carefully. She knew she looked well in her new sea-green georgette, and she'd searched the shops till she found elegant satin slippers to match.

She carefully packed her dress and slippers in her suitcase. She'd leave the suitcase in the cloakroom and change just before the party began.

There was no point in arriving in her evening dress if she was to be out in the kitchen, supervising.

'There you are, my dear!' Mrs Baillie, expensively dressed in black lace encrusted with jet beads, looked pink and flustered.

'I do hope everything's under control. Would you mind just glancing at the lilies? I'm sure they're wilting.'

'Don't worry, I'll see to them right away.' Meg went off willingly.

She couldn't wait to see Philip. She'd bought the new dress with him in mind, and she knew she would look her best.

For the next half-hour, she rushed here, there and everywhere. She pushed back a strand of hair, and looked at the clock. People were already arriving. She'd have to change into her evening dress fairly soon.

Then the front door opened, bringing with it a blast of cool night air. And there was Philip, with a slender fair-haired girl on his arm. She threw back her head, laughing at something he had said, and put her hand possessively on his arm.

'Hello, there!' Philip called out to Meg. 'Are you having a busy evening? Quite a crush, isn't it?'

Somehow, Meg forced a smile.

The truth was gradually dawning on her. She hadn't been invited to the party. She wasn't a guest.

The Baillies had used her as an employee, that was all. There had never been any intention of inviting her!

Tears welled up in her eyes, and she blinked them away. She'd nearly made a fool of herself – she went cold at the very thought of it.

Just suppose she had arrived in her new dress and slippers... How ridiculous she would have appeared!

At least now she could creep away, holding her head up high. She gulped and went in search of Mrs Baillie.

Her employer turned round.

'Yes, my dear? Everything seems to be going smoothly, I think.'

Meg nodded.

'Yes, it's all going very well. If you don't need me any more, I think I'll slip off home. I have a bit of a headache...'

'Oh, dear,' Mrs Baillie said. 'Yes, of course you must go. Do have something to eat and drink first, though.' She turned to the tall, dark-haired woman beside her.

'This is my husband's secretary – she's been such a tower of strength.

'This is my good friend Mrs Lucille Sherman – you'll remember I told you about her visit.'

Lucille, elegant in blue silk, stretched out a hand.

'I'm so glad to meet you,' she said in a voice that had just a hint of an American accent. It was clear to Meg that she had no idea she was talking to Lily's daughter.

'You have organised everything beautifully,' Lucille said kindly.

Meg swallowed. Now was her chance, she thought, as Mrs Baillie turned aside to speak to one of the maids.

'I think,' she said, 'we met once before, at Pennyglen. My mother is Lily Barclay. My name is Meg...'

Lucille stared at her.

'Meg? You're Meg?'

Meg nodded.

'Could I please speak to you? It's very important.'

'Not here,' Lucille said hastily. She fished in her silver evening bag, and held out a small piece of card.

'This is where I'm staying. Can you come and see me? Shall we say Monday evening?'

'Thank you.' Meg took the card.

'About seven o'clock?'

Meg nodded. As she turned to go, she saw Lucille gaze after her.

Hastily, Meg retrieved her suitcase from the cloakroom, and slipped out of the door.

In the long days that followed her confrontation with Meg, Lily longed to confide in someone. She had been more hurt than she would admit, even to herself, by Meg's sharp words.

But she couldn't tell Matt – he'd be as worried and hurt as she was, and he still hadn't fully recovered from his illness. Janet had quite enough to think about. And Ellen was too young to be burdened with this, Lily thought.

And yet – Ellen was growing up. Both Lily and Matt were amazed at the way she'd stood up for herself, and by the cheerful way she was coping with a hard and often distressing job.

And Colin – now there was a fine, steady young man.

'Colin?' Ellen laughed whenever anyone mentioned him. 'Oh, he's just a friend.'

But, just a friend or rather closer, he was often at the house, sitting at Lily's kitchen table and drinking tea and eating potato scones.

'You'd never know he was from the Big House,' Lily remarked one day to Matt. 'He fits in, somehow.'

Matt had laughed.

'And why not? You make him welcome, and any lad would come a distance for your potato scones.

'And of course,' he added, 'our Ellen's not a bad lass either...'

'Oh, you!' Lily shook her head at him.

But it was true – Colin did fit in. He talked about the mill with Matt, and one evening, when Rab and Janet were visiting, the two young men spent a long time talking about the farm, discussing farm machinery and the price of wheat.

'He's a real farmer,' Rab said approvingly, for Colin could tackle any job on the home farm of the Big House. 'Not just a gentleman pretending.

'Though,' he added with no hint of envy, 'he's not short of money. That Morris Oxford two-seater he drives – it costs well over four hundred guineas.'

Though things were easier between Janet and Rab's mother, Janet was anxious about

Rab's father, who was growing frail.

'You're dashing around like a young lad,' she told him one day, only half-teasing. 'I saw you, climbing that ladder. You shouldn't do that, you know.'

'Eh, lass, are you telling me off then?' He smiled at her.

She *was* concerned, though. If Rab's father fell sick, how would Rab manage the farm alone?

She knew his father was often quite exhausted at the end of the day. Surely he must retire soon – but what would happen then?

A week or two later, Rab's mother Alice called at the cottage.

'Can you come round for your tea tonight?' she asked.

Janet was a little surprised. It was unusual for them to be invited formally.

'Yes, of course.'

It was clear, when they arrived at the farmhouse, that Rab's mother was not her usual self. She dandled little Alice on her knee, and spoke absently, with none of her usual sharpness.

'Right,' Rab's father said, 'before we have our tea, I've something to say. It'll maybe come as a bit of a shock to you, but I've given it a lot of thought, and talked it over with Mother, too, and she agrees with me.'

Alice looked up and nodded.

'I'm not getting any younger,' he explained, 'and the work's getting harder. I've decided I'm going to put the farm on the market. It's time to sell up.'

Janet flushed.

'But what about us?' she wanted to ask, but she couldn't speak. She was dismayed.

What would she and Rab do? How could Rab find another job in farming? He wasn't all that strong, and he was still troubled by the injuries he's suffered in the War.

Oh, she was disappointed. Hadn't the older folk thought about their son and his wife, and their grandchild?

'Don't you fret, lass.' The old man turned to her as if he knew just what she was thinking.

'We'll get a good price for the farm – and Mother and I only need a wee place for ourselves.

'There'll be enough money left to set Rab up in a garage somewhere. I know fine that's what you want.'

'Oh, Father.' Rab was deeply touched.

For years, he'd dreamed of owning his own garage. Now, at last, thanks to his parents' generosity, that dream looked like becoming a reality.

'You've a feeling for machines,' the older man went on. 'I remember what you were like as a laddie.

'Well, this'll be your chance. I know you'll

do your best to make it a success.'

Alice rose and put her little granddaughter in her high chair.

'Well, you'll have a lot to talk about, you two, but that can wait.

'The tea's ready. There's ham and eggs, and soda scones, made fresh this afternoon. I'll just put the kettle on.'

'Father,' Rab said later, as they were finishing the meal, 'it's really good of you to give me a chance like this. I can't thank you enough.'

'You'll do all right.' In a rare moment of emotion, the older man raised his teacup. 'Here's to you both.'

'Ah, well.' Alice sniffed. 'If you've all finished, we'll get this table cleared and the dishes done.'

Janet smiled to herself. Alice might be sharp-tongued, and not one to show sentiment, but she knew her mother-in-law was just as responsible for this decision as Rab's father.

Janet was thrilled for Rab. She knew it was what he'd always wanted. A garage of his own – it was a dream come true!

When Rab came in from work, about a week later, she had the local paper open.

'Well, it's advertised,' she said. 'Look!'

He read out the details.

'To be sold by public roup, on June 22, etc. etc. Farm steading and land...' His voice trailed off.

'Well,' he said, 'this is it – our big chance.

'I've been thinking – once we get the garage off the ground, we could hire out limousines, even run charabanc trips, like Johnston's do.

'Our main business will be selling cars, though. There are some great new models – Humbers, Austins, Arrol Johnston...

'I can make a go of this, I know I can.'

She laughed, eyes shining.

'Of course you can.'

There was a silence.

'I know living here hasn't been easy for you. But I'll make it up to you, I promise,' he said haltingly.

'You don't need to.' She stretched out a hand to him.

'I've everything I want – you, and Alice. But the garage will succeed – I'm sure.'

The day of the farm sale arrived.

That evening, Colin was waiting for Ellen when she came off duty.

He jumped out and opened the car door for her.

'Tired?'

'No.' She smiled at him. 'I'm getting more used to the work, I think.'

'Then you won't mind coming for a spin before we go home?'

'I'd like that,' Ellen said. 'It's a lovely

evening.' She was silent for a moment.

'I've been wondering about Janet and Rab. Today was the farm sale – I hope it went well.'

'The sale went well all right,' Colin said casually, stopping the car on a quiet side road.

'How do you know?' Ellen was puzzled. 'Were you there?'

'I can't keep it to myself any longer. Meet the new owner of Glendores.'

'You! You've bought the farm!' Ellen couldn't believe it.

'Yes, I have,' Colin admitted. 'I've learned a bit about farming, since I left the RFC. I thought it was time to start up on my own.

'It's in good shape, Glendores, but I want to try out some new ideas. I'm going to make it the most up-to-date farm in the whole county!

'I'd thought about going to Canada, to try farming there – but I didn't want to leave Scotland. You know why.' He reached out a hand to Ellen.

'It would be perfect if … I had you to share it,' he went on. 'Ellen, you know how I feel about you–'

She pulled her hand away.

'Oh, Colin, it's much too soon to be talking like this. I've only just started nursing. I *am* fond of you, Colin, but I just don't want to be serious about anyone, not yet…'

He sighed.

'I thought you'd say that. But I promise you, Ellen, I won't give up. I'll keep asking in the hope that, one day, you'll care for me as much as I care for you.'

Meg couldn't remember ever feeling this nervous before. She kept telling herself to keep calm, to let Lucille do the talking, but she was still trembling with excitement and fear – and guilt.

She hadn't told Lily about her planned meeting with Lucille, and wondered what she would say if she knew. She'd probably be desperately worried for Meg, and try to talk her out of it...

But Meg was determined to see this through. Lucille had known Lily for longer than anyone. Surely she would know the truth about Meg's real mother?

Anyway, I'm twenty-four – old enough to make my own decisions, Meg told herself. But she couldn't forget the hurt in Lily's eyes...

She'd make it up to her, Meg promised herself. She realised, with a pang, that Ellen had been right. She had been selfish – and snobbish, too.

She thought about Philip and the fair-haired girl he'd brought to the party. Meg realised her friendship with Philip was at an end, and felt hurt.

Why had the Baillies made her one of the family, and then withdrawn like this?

But they hadn't, she told herself firmly. The fault had been her own, for imagining things that were never intended.

The Baillies had been friendly and polite towards her – as they were to any employee. That didn't mean they wanted her as a daughter-in-law.

Philip had called at the office the day after the party.

'Hello!' He greeted her with his usual friendly smile. 'Did you enjoy the party? You were run off your feet, I expect.'

Meg looked up from the letter she was filing.

'It all went very well, I understand,' she said smoothly.

'Thanks to you,' he added, with the grin that had once made her heart miss a beat.

'My mother was just saying what a tremendous help you've been – she couldn't have managed without you.'

'I'm glad I was of some use.' The old Meg would have spoken sharply, sarcastically. But she was learning. There was no point in alienating the Baillie family.

'You certainly were.' Philip turned towards the door. 'I'd better let you get on with your work.'

'Yes, there's quite a lot to do.' Meg gave him a pleasant nod. Her heart was thumping, but she was determined to give nothing away.

She had her pride. No-one would ever know how hurt she'd been, what great hopes she'd had.

Meg dressed carefully for her meeting with Lucille. She wore her Sunday best costume of blue serge, with a white voile blouse, and her new boots.

She boarded the tram for Broughty Ferry, clutching her purse containing the card Lucille had given her.

The house, when she found it, was quite small – nothing like as imposing as the Baillies' home.

She climbed the steps to the front door, and pulled the brass bell handle.

'I've come to see Mrs Sherman,' she told the maid who answered.

'What name, please?' But before Meg could say anything, Lucille, elegant in soft grey crepe, appeared in the hall.

'That's quite all right, Annie. I'm expecting Miss Barclay.'

She took both Meg's hands in hers.

'Do come in, my dear.'

Meg heard a slight tremor in Lucille's voice, and the hands that grasped hers were cold. She realised, with a start, that Lucille was nervous, too. It made her feel slightly more confident.

'This way.' Lucille led her into a large

sitting-room, and Meg gazed around in astonishment.

She had expected to see a room like the Baillies', with heavy, dark furniture, vases of hothouse flowers, pictures in gilt frames and thick Turkey carpets.

This was so different. There was white paint instead of dark walls, and light wood.

The pictures on the walls were not of moors and mists and Highland cattle, but vivid scenes of Mediterranean markets, olive groves, and harbours with boats moored under blue skies.

Lucille noticed Meg glancing around her.

'Yes, it's very different, isn't it? The friends who lent me the house are interested in modern pictures.' She paused.

'Would you like some tea – or coffee?'

Meg shook her head. She wanted to get this interview over as quickly as possible.

'Do sit down and tell me about your mother and your family. Your mother was my best and dearest friend. Do tell her I'll come over to Pennyglen just as soon as I can.

'How is she? And your father? And your brother and sisters? Janet was married during the war, I think?'

What a lot Lucille seemed to know about the family, Meg thought.

'Janet lives quite near now.' She told Lucille about little Alice, and the sale of the farm; about Ellen's work at the convalescent home; and about Willie, who was employed on a farm at Pitlessie.

'And you, my dear?' Lucille asked. 'Tell me about your work. You've done so well.

'Mrs Baillie tells me you've been a tower of strength. They're very lucky to have you.'

Meg found herself liking Lucille. But did they really have much in common?

The older woman was rich, elegant and beautifully groomed. She had everything she could want. But she belonged to the Baillies' world, not to the world of Pennyglen. Meg could sense the gap between them.

And yet – Lucille's dark eyes were troubled. She reached out a hand to Meg.

'You said you wanted to talk to me, my dear. I think I know what it's about...'

Meg twisted her hands in her lap.

'I flew into a temper with Mother,' she burst out. 'I didn't mean to, and I said something quite unforgivable.

'The thing is – if only I knew the truth, then I could start all over again, without this – misunderstanding between us.

'I think you might be able to tell me the truth,' she went on bravely. 'You've known Mother for many years.'

'Yes,' Lucille said slowly, almost to herself.

'If only I hadn't said what I did,' Meg went on. 'But it's too late for that now. I'm so grateful for all she's done, but I have to know.'

'What was it that you said to her?' Lucille asked gently.

'I said–' Meg gulped '–I said, "You're not my mother"'

There was a silence between them.

'I've known for years that I was adopted,' Meg went on. 'But it was my secret – I didn't tell Mother and Father that I knew. I didn't want to hurt them.

'I've always wondered about my real mother, though. And I thought that perhaps she might have been a relative of yours.

'I've heard people say that you and I look a little alike. And I know you were a good friend of Mother's, as well as her employer.' She glanced down at her hands.

'I hope you don't think me terribly forward, asking you this, but you see, don't you, that I have to get to the bottom of things. I can't rest till I know, and Mother – Lily – well, she's unhappy, too.

'So, please, can you tell me – it's desperately important – who *was* my mother?'

Chapter Nine

'Who is my mother?' Meg repeated. 'Please, Lucille – I have to know.'

There was a long silence. Lucille's hands shook as she twisted her handkerchief between her fingers.

Meg stared at her.

Gradually, as the older woman struggled to speak, the truth dawned on Meg.

How could she have been so blind? It was staring her in the face – had been, all along. All these years, Meg thought, and I never even guessed.

'It's you,' she said. It was a statement, not a question. 'You're my mother.' She gazed back at Lucille, this elegant stranger from another world.

Lucille nodded. She sank down on to the sofa, her face ashen. Her voice trembled.

'My dear – oh, you were never meant to know. I'm so sorry. I can explain. Please sit down...'

As though hypnotised, Meg sat down on a small upright chair. She was speechless.

'You see,' Lucille began, 'you had a new life. You were happy with Matt and Lily.

'I would never have tried to claim you as

mine, though I wanted – I still do want – to give you the best I can...'

'I just can't take it in,' Meg whispered at last. 'It's so hard to believe...'

'Let me explain,' Lucille begged her. 'I want to tell you the whole story, right from the beginning...'

'No.' Meg shook her head. 'Please – I've got to talk to Mother–' She broke off, as they both realised she was talking of Lily, not Lucille.

'I need some time to think things over. You understand, don't you?'

'Of course. It's been a shock for you – for both of us. But can't I help? I'd like you to stay.'

Again, Meg shook her head.

'Thank you – you're very kind. But I'll go home to Pennyglen next weekend and talk to Mother.' Her voice was polite but distant, giving no hint at all of the confusion she felt.

'If I were to write to Lily,' Lucille said hesitantly, 'would it help? I could tell her that you know...'

'Yes,' Meg agreed. 'I think that would be a good idea.' She rose and pulled on her gloves.

'Do you mind if I go now?'

'You'll be all right?'

Meg smiled wanly.

'Oh, yes, truly. It's just that I want to go

away quietly and get used to the idea on my own.'

'Of course.' Lucille took Meg's hands in hers. On impulse, she gave the girl an affectionate kiss.

'We'll see each other soon.'

Lucille pulled back the net curtain and watched Meg as she made her way down the steps and along the street.

To the rest of the world, Meg must have looked as she always did – a slim figure dressed in a blue suit, her dark hair topped with a fashionable cloche hat. But inside, her emotions were in turmoil.

How had Lily – Lucille's maid – come to adopt her employer's baby? Why?

Her heart racing, Meg turned the corner, walking faster and faster. When she remembered all the times Lily had spoken of Lucille ... the letters ... the visits ... and she'd never once suspected the truth. Oh, why had nobody told her?

During the next two days at work, Meg found it hard to concentrate. She'd promised to go home to Pennyglen at the weekend, but she was apprehensive of seeing Lily again after all that had happened.

'Miss Barclay?' A voice roused her from her thoughts.

'Oh, it's you!' She looked up from her desk to see Alec smiling at her.

'It's such a fine day – what about a walk in

the park at the dinner break?' he suggested.

Meg had hardly glanced out of the window all morning.

Now she saw that there were buds on the sycamore trees outside her window, and a gentle breeze was stirring the branches.

'I hadn't noticed,' she confessed.

'You were miles away,' Alec said. 'All the more reason to go out and enjoy the sunshine.'

'I have a dinner break from one till two,' Meg told him.

'In that case, I'll call back for you sharp at one.'

At one o'clock, Meg put on her outdoor shoes and hat, and was ready when Alec appeared.

'I brought us a picnic,' he said. 'It's not much – just some bread and cheese, but it means we needn't waste time indoors.'

Meg was touched by his thoughtfulness, and by the way he spread his jacket over the park bench so that she could sit down.

She hadn't realised how hungry she was.

'It's the fresh air,' she said. 'It makes everything taste better!'

They threw crumbs to a robin that hopped around their feet and Alec told her about the tame blackbird that came every morning to the kitchen door at home.

Gradually, she felt less tense, and found herself laughing at his jokes.

'That's better,' he said. 'You've been looking pretty low, if I may say so, Miss Barclay.'

'It's Meg, please.'

'Meg, then. Not at all your usual bright sunny self...'

'So you'd noticed. I suppose everyone has.' Meg realised she sounded a little bitter.

'Oh, no,' he said. 'I don't mean that you weren't as brisk and efficient as ever. It's just that – well, I noticed, because...' He broke off.

There was a long silence between them.

'You're very kind,' Meg murmured, with a tremor in her voice.

'I don't suppose,' Alec went on cautiously, 'that you'd like to tell me what's worrying you?'

Meg brushed away a few crumbs and fixed her eyes on her black patent shoes.

'Suppose someone found out that she didn't belong where she thought she did?' she began hesitantly.

'Yes?' Alec encouraged, though he didn't have the least idea what she was talking about.

'Suppose,' Meg said more firmly, 'that she knew she was adopted, but she'd grown up in a nice ordinary family, and was – well – reasonably happy. She had no idea who her real mother was...'

'And?' Alec prompted.

'Suddenly she discovers that her real

mother is someone so different, she can hardly believe it. Someone rich, elegant, beautiful – all the things she'd always wanted to be herself...'

'Mmm,' Alec said. 'That would be a bit difficult for her.'

'You see,' Meg explained, 'she doesn't know where she stands. Suddenly everything is turned upside down.

'She's always known she's different, but her family have been so good to her and never made it seem as if there was any difference – between me and the others, I mean,' she added, without noticing that she was no longer talking about a vague 'someone'.

'I'm putting this all so badly,' she said, turning to Alec, 'but I'm sure you understand. It's a bit of a shock for someone to find a real mother like – like this person.'

'Yes, I can see that. But at the same time, you know – this friend of yours – well, she's not changed in herself, has she?

'I mean, she's still part of her family, and they're not going to stop being fond of her, just because her real mother has appeared. She's just the same person.

'Oh, maybe she'll have to think a bit about the future, make room for her real mother, but her family – they're still there, aren't they?'

'I hadn't thought of it quite like that.' Meg

turned to him, her face lit with a sudden smile.

'Well, you just think about it,' Alec told her.

'I will. It makes it a bit easier,' Meg said.

'Listen, Meg, I have a suggestion. What about coming home with me for tea – say tomorrow night?

'You could meet my family – there's just my mother and my young brother, Jamie.'

'Well, yes, thank you. I'd like that.'

'Good! Come on, we should be getting back.'

Meg jumped to her feet.

'Is that the time already?' Oh, she felt so much better – Alec was so cheerful, and he made her laugh.

Alec lived in a part of Dundee she hadn't visited before. In the street of small terraced houses, children were playing with a hoop and one or two older boys had started a game of football.

Meg's heart went out to a little lad with rickets who was sitting on a doorstep, watching the game.

'Here, Walter,' Alec called to him. 'Want a piggy-back?' He hoisted the child on his back and galloped the length of the street with him.

An old woman who was sitting at her door, knitting a sock, laughed.

'Eh, he's an awful lad that one,' she said as Alec, red in the face, came back along the street, swerving round the children playing peevers.

'Come on, Alec,' one of the boys called. 'Are you not coming to be goalie?'

'Not now, we're away for our tea.' Alec stopped at one of the doors in the terrace.

'It's us, Mother – we're here!'

Meg just had time to take in the shining brass bell push and the polished lino, before Alec's mother appeared in the hallway.

She was a stout little woman, wrapped in a flowered pinafore, who grasped her warmly by the hand.

'Come away in. The tea's ready. I'm real pleased Alec's brought you along,' she said.

From then on, Meg felt completely at home. There was Alec, teasing his mother till she nearly collapsed with laughter; his younger brother Jamie, a thin, eager lad of sixteen; and of course, Alec's mother herself, brisk and cheerful.

After everyone had had enough to eat and the teapot had been filled and refilled, Alec said, 'Let's have a game of cards,' and brought out an old card table.

It was a shabby little room, Meg noticed as she glanced around – the horse-hair sofa had seen better days, and the curtains were threadbare. But somehow it didn't matter.

They played cards till young Jamie said

he'd Latin to study for the morning. Then Alec's mother sat down at the old piano and played some favourite Scots songs.

'Time for something a bit more modern,' Alec announced once she'd finished. Soon he was thumping out 'Polly-wolly-doodle'.

Finally, they all sang some songs everyone knew – 'The Mountains of Mourne' and 'I'll take you home again, Kathleen'.

Meg was surprised to find how late it was.

'I'll walk you home,' Alec insisted.

'I haven't enjoyed myself so much for ages,' Meg said, and she meant it.

'You'll come again soon,' Alec's mother told her firmly.

'Do you know,' Meg said thoughtfully, as they reached the door of her digs, 'I haven't once thought about this problem – I mean my friend's problem, the one who was adopted.'

'That's good.' Alec smiled at her, and Meg flushed.

Now be sensible. He isn't your type, she told herself, but all the same, she went to bed feeling much happier than she'd done in ages.

She felt more cheerful, too, when she set off that Saturday to catch the one o'clock train from Dundee that would take her to Pennyglen.

Lily was watering her plants when Meg arrived.

'The train's right on time,' she remarked. 'I'll put the kettle on.

'Could you go up the garden and call your father? He's working in the vegetable patch.'

'Yes, in a moment.' Meg put her bag down on the table. She had to speak now.

'But first, Mother – there's something I've got to say.'

'I know. It's about you and Miss Lucille–' Lily caught herself up. 'I can't get out of the way of calling her that. It seems silly, when she's been married all these years.'

'So you know that I went to see her?' Meg said.

Lily nodded.

'She wrote to me.'

'Then you'll know what she told me.' Meg was suddenly flustered.

'Oh, Mother, I should have spoken to you first.'

'Yes,' Lily said calmly, 'you should have. You could have asked me instead of talking to a stranger.'

'She's not a stranger – she's–' Meg flared up. Then she broke off.

'I thought, as she knew you so well, she'd be able to tell me,' she said more soberly.

Put that way, it sounded so lame. Why hadn't she asked Lily? No wonder Mother was upset. She'd every right to be.

'I'm sorry,' Meg apologised. 'The trouble is, I don't always think.'

'No,' Lily agreed. 'But you're learning.'

She smiled at the girl – so smart and very much the lady, yet still the impetuous Meg. She'd never change – and Lily was glad of that.

'This is what happened,' Lily began.

Meg sat in silence as Lily took her back through the years.

She told her all about the young Lucille, whose soldier fiancé had been killed before he could marry her.

'Miss Lucille was already expecting you by then,' Lily revealed, her eyes misting over as she remembered. 'She asked Matt and me to care for you – to take you into our family, and love you as our own. And we did.

'But Meg, she never forgot you. She kept in touch, even when she moved to America, and she sent money, too. There was always something in the pirlie pig for you, now wasn't there?'

Meg smiled, and her mother clasped her hand.

'It hurt her to give you up, Meg,' Lily went on. 'And it was so hard for her to come here and see you, but not say who she was.'

'I know.' Meg brushed away a tear. 'I just wish somebody had told me.'

'We did what we thought was best,' Lily assured her. 'I'm sorry if it hurt you.'

'But now,' she went on, changing the subject, 'you have a chance to get to know

242

Lucille properly. She wants you to go to America with her.'

Lily handed Meg the letter she'd received from Lucille.

'Oh!' Meg's face flushed. This was completely unexpected. But what an opportunity to be given…

'She planned it years ago,' Lily said. 'She was going to ask you that time she was due to sail from America on the *Lusitania*. Then the war came, and now…'

I'm going back to the States in a fortnight, Lucille had written. *I could take Meg with me for a visit to see how she likes the life. I think it would suit her. She might even consider staying for good.*

There was a pause when Meg had finished reading the letter. They both knew that a decision had to be made.

If Meg went to America, there would be no turning back. It would be for ever…

'You've got time to think about it,' Lily said. 'Anyway, the tea's almost ready. Could you go and call your father?'

Meg's thoughts were in turmoil. This was such an exciting opportunity. How many girls got the chance to go and live in America? It was a whole new world.

How she longed for excitement, a chance to see new things, meet new people.

She had just two weeks to decide…

All that week Meg's thoughts were in a whirl, but she was no nearer a decision. She resolved to talk to Janet at the weekend. Though the sisters didn't meet all that often, they were still close.

After dinner the following Saturday, she set out to visit her sister. Rab and Janet had settled happily in a small house, just by the garage, where he was working round the clock to build up the business.

Already, Janet had made the new house into a real home. The brass shone, and the starched net curtains were crisp and fresh. A canary sang in the cage by the window, while little Alice crawled happily on the rag rug in front of the fire.

'I'll come, too,' Willie had offered, when he heard where Meg was going.

Meg was surprised. In his time off from the farm, Willie usually preferred playing football to visiting!

As soon as they reached the house, Willie disappeared into the garage.

'I'm seeing a customer,' Rab greeted him. 'Just take a look round.'

Willie needed no second bidding.

The sisters had plenty of news to catch up on. Janet listened eagerly, as she always did, to Meg's account of life in the office, her descriptions of the shops and the new fashions.

But Janet noticed that Meg hardly spoke

of Philip Baillie now. There was no mention of smart parties and evening functions, either. She wondered if they'd quarrelled, but didn't like to ask.

Meg thought that Janet seemed quieter than usual, a little preoccupied, perhaps.

'Are you all right?' Meg asked, as Janet rose slowly, her hand to her side.

'Me? Oh, yes, never better. I get a bit tired, that's all – well, it's not surprising, with another baby on the way.'

'But that's wonderful! You never said–' Meg grinned.

'I'll tell Mother and Father when I visit next week – it'll be a bit of a surprise for them.'

'They'll be so pleased,' Meg said warmly.

'Yes.' Janet smiled. 'Rab's mother is, too – she dotes on Alice.'

'And when is the baby due?'

'The end of the year.'

'And you're keeping fine?' Meg asked anxiously.

'Oh, yes.' Janet laughed. 'I'm in blooming health.

'Well, that's my news. What else have you been doing?'

Meg drew a deep breath. Should she tell Janet about Lucille's offer? She'd wanted to ask her advice, but was it really fair to burden her sister now, of all times?

As she paused, there were footsteps in the

hall and Rab and Willie burst in.

'My, we're ready for our tea.' Rab grinned. 'It's been a busy afternoon. Wait till I tell you what happened!

'I was busy in the office with a customer, when this man, a visitor from England, came in to look at the cars.'

'The Crossley tourer,' Willie chimed in. 'That was what he wanted to look at specially. My, it's a beauty–'

'Yes, but wait a moment,' Rab interrupted. 'I was tied up with this customer, as I said. There was no chance of getting out to the front. So when I did come out to the show-room I apologised for keeping him waiting.

'"Sorry to have kept you, sir," I said.

'"Not at all," he replied. "I've been talking to your assistant here – he's been most helpful, and filled me in on the details. Now I'd like to take the car out for a spin, get the feel of it."

'He's coming back on Monday.'

'Assistant?' Meg echoed, puzzled.

'Yes, I was a bit flummoxed, too – for a moment.' Rab laughed. 'He meant Willie! And, thanks to him, I think we've got another sale.

'See he gets an extra big helping of pie, Janet.'

They all laughed, but later, Rab was thoughtful.

'He's quick, that brother of yours,' he said

to Janet. 'I wonder if … I think he'd do well in the business. How would you feel if I offered him a job?'

'That would be great,' Janet smiled. 'Willie's always been daft about cars. It would be a real chance for him.'

'Don't say anything to him just yet.' Rab was cautious. 'I'll need to look at the figures, to see what we could pay him. I think he'd do well.

'We've started slowly, but people are coming to us, and recommending the garage to friends. I've my eye on one of those fourteen-seater omnibuses, a Chevrolet.

'We could run tours – lots of firms do it now. Outings to Perthshire for picnic parties, and bowling club trips, works outings…' His eyes shone, and Janet was glad to see him so enthusiastic.

Meg was preoccupied in the days ahead, so preoccupied that she hardly heard when one of the other secretaries said, 'Have you seen the paper? It's in today – Mr Philip's engagement. Look at this!'

'Oh?' Meg looked blank.

'He's engaged, to that Miss Macrae – you must know her. Tall, fair, wears the most beautiful clothes. She lives somewhere up in Angus – her folks are very well off.'

'Oh, that's good news,' Meg said, a little absently, and the other girl went off to chat to someone who would be more responsive.

The next time Philip came into the office, Meg looked up with a smile.

'My congratulations.'

'Thank you.' He smiled back at her. 'It all happened rather suddenly. My mother's delighted, as you can imagine. She thought I'd never settle down.'

Meg laughed politely, and wondered why she felt nothing at all.

How could she have imagined spending her whole life with Philip? Oh, he was handsome, and good company, but that was all. She couldn't grudge him to the fair-haired Miss Macrae.

'I hope you'll both be very happy,' she said, and meant it.

Ellen, like Meg, was struggling with a decision.

Matron had sent for her one day.

'I think you ought to know, Nurse, that the convalescent home is to be closed down in three months' time. We have fewer patients now – our long-term patients will be transferred.'

'Closed down?'

Matron nodded.

'Yes, the house will be taken back by the owners. It was only leased to us, after all. It means you will have to look for another job, I'm afraid.

'I can give you an excellent reference. I'm sure you'll have no difficulty in finding another post. You've done very well.

'Have you any idea where you'd like to go from here?'

Ellen shook her head.

'It's so unexpected. I never thought about moving on.'

When she told Colin later, he leaned forward and took her hands in his.

'I know you enjoyed the work,' he said. 'But now you've proved you can do it. You know how I feel about you. Don't keep me waiting for ever.' His tone was light, but his eyes were serious.

'I want to marry you, Ellen – you know that.'

Ellen was troubled.

'It's not that I don't care for you, Colin, but don't you see – I want to go on nursing. It's the one thing I've always wanted.'

'You wouldn't miss it, I promise,' he said. 'You'd have lots to do with the farm, and your family nearby – it would please them all so much.'

'I know it would,' Ellen said. 'But is that a good enough reason?'

'So what do you want to do?'

'I'm not sure,' Ellen confessed. 'I thought I'd like to work in a city hospital – or maybe as a district nurse. I don't know…'

'Well, you know how I feel–' Colin

stretched out a hand. 'You'll have to decide some time.'

A few days later, they took a stroll by the Eden. Ellen was enjoying the cool, fresh evening air, when suddenly, Colin turned to her.

'I've got a proposal to make to you,' he announced.

'Oh, Colin,' Ellen said, 'we've been through all this before.'

He grinned at her.

'You don't know what I'm going to say. Now listen. Your trouble is that you don't have enough fun – you take life too seriously.

'I've had a wonderful idea. How would you like to come to London next month, with me – and my cousin, Lizbeth to see the Empire Exhibition at Wembley?'

'Oh!' Ellen gasped. 'I've heard so much about it. That would be wonderful! But–' her face fell '–I couldn't take the time off. It would mean too long away from work.'

'No, it wouldn't,' he said. 'We leave St Andrews by train about eight o'clock on the Sunday evening and travel through the night.

'There's time for breakfast and a sight-seeing tour of London before we go to Wembley. We have five hours there, then catch the train about seven. We'll be back on Tuesday morning.

'We've got a spare ticket. I was going to hand it back – but would you like to come?'

'Oh, yes, please!' Ellen's eyes shone. 'I've never been to London, and it all sounds so marvellous.

'I'm due some time off – I'll ask Matron. And I'll pay for myself,' she added. 'That's to be understood.'

'Oh, Ellen!' he said. 'You are so independent.' But he was smiling. 'We'll have a really good time.'

That evening, Ellen burst into the kitchen as Lily was setting the table. 'I've had the most wonderful chance!' she exclaimed.

Lily smiled. It was good to see Ellen so enthusiastic about something. She often felt her youngest girl worked too hard.

'Colin's asked me to the Empire Exhibition at Wembley, next month – he's going with his cousin, Lizbeth. Please say I can go!' Ellen told her mother all about the trip organised by the Merchants' Association.

'You're grown up now,' Lily said. 'And I know you'll come to no harm with Colin.'

'And I've been saving – I can pay my own fare,' Ellen went on.

'Well, now,' Lily said. 'I think the pirlie pig could help out there. That's what it's for, after all.'

'Oh, thank you.' Ellen glowed. 'I can hardly wait.'

Lily smiled. Ellen was so easy to please, so

sunny and even-tempered. She thought things over carefully, and faced life's problems calmly and sensibly.

If only, Lily thought, Meg could solve *her* problems as easily.

'You don't have to decide now,' Lucille told Meg. 'There's no hurry.'

But Meg knew she couldn't hesitate much longer. She would have to give Lucille a definite answer before she returned to the States.

Lucille had arranged to visit Pennyglen the following Sunday.

After all, she said in her note to Lily, *I do want to see you, Lily – and it's been so long.*

Lily sighed as she put down the letter. She couldn't help feeling that Lucille had been avoiding the visit. But then, she chided herself, it had been a long time. People grow apart.

She made up her mind that she would make Lucille as welcome as she could, and try to avoid any awkwardness.

There was a small knot of children in the street when the hired car drew up. Lucille smiled kindly at the small boys who clustered round, gazing at the shining headlamps and the leather upholstery.

She stepped out of the car, elegant in a suit with a long, loosely belted jacket. She wore a little cloche hat with the fashionable pheasant's tail trim, and carried the softest of doeskin gloves.

'You'll wait?' she asked the chauffeur.

'He can come in,' Matt said, appearing at the door with Lily and Meg. 'Come away in and get a cup of tea.'

'I'll just take the car a run round if it's all the same to you, sir,' the chauffeur said.

Matt was a little disconcerted at being addressed as 'sir'.

'Right you are.' He nodded.

'Let's go inside,' he said to Lucille.

'I'm early,' she apologised. 'I hope I'm not putting you out.'

'Not us,' Matt assured her. 'Come in.'

Lucille hesitated for a moment.

Inside, Lily wouldn't allow any awkwardness.

'I was just making scones for the tea,' she said. 'It's all ready in the parlour.'

Lucille drew out a chair.

'I'll sit here while you finish the baking – I'd hate the scones to be spoiled just because I'm early.'

Lily pushed the cat off the chair and plumped up the cushions.

'So tell me about the family,' Lucille said.

Lily needed no second bidding to talk about Janet and Rab – and little Alice, who looked just like Janet at that age. And now there was another baby on the way...

Suddenly, the door opened and Meg came

in from outside.

'There you are!' Lily turned round and smiled at her.

Flushed with the heat of the oven, she took the newly baked scones and lifted them on to a wire tray.

It was such a familiar sight – one Meg had seen countless times before. Mother at the oven; Father in his chair, lighting his pipe; the cat banished to the window-sill, sunning itself and washing its paws.

And yet, there was something out of place. She knew right away what it was.

Although Lucille seemed perfectly at ease and was chatting happily to Lily, she looked like a visitor, Meg thought.

And that was just what she was.

'What about going through to the parlour?' Meg said, to cover the awkwardness she felt.

How small it looked, she thought, seeing it from Lucille's viewpoint. And yet, as a child, she had thought it the most beautiful room in the world.

There was the armchair that had been a golden wedding gift from the family to Lily's parents; the faded sepia photographs; the piano – one of Lily's most treasured possessions.

Lucille moved over to the piano and glanced at the sheet music.

'Do you play?' she asked.

Meg shook her head.

'Mother's the pianist.' It slipped out so easily, yet it lay between them – that word, 'Mother'.

Lucille told herself she had no right to expect anything else. But one day, given time...

'I'm sure Lily plays beautifully,' she said.

After tea, Lucille glanced at her watch.

'I don't want to rush things,' she began nervously, 'but I'm going back in a week's time. I really can't leave Elmer any longer. I know it's hard...' She broke off.

'I'm putting this so badly. Of course, my dear,' she turned to Meg, 'you mustn't decide anything in a hurry. After all, it's your life. But Elmer and I would love to have you make your home with us.'

There was a long silence.

'Well?' Matt said. They were all waiting for Meg to speak.

'I don't know what to do!' she burst out. 'I've thought and thought and oh, you're so kind and it's such a wonderful offer. Don't think I'm ungrateful – I'm not, but I just can't decide. It's not like me, but–'

'I know, my dear.' Lucille rose and put her hand on the girl's arm.

'I understand. And no-one's pushing you. Just take your time. I'll be in touch before I go back.'

When the chauffeur-driven car had glided

away, Matt pulled on his old gardening boots.

'I'm away up the garden,' he said. He smiled at Meg. 'We'll miss you if you go, but don't let that sway you.'

'Oh, it's so hard,' Meg complained.

'You take your time, like she said,' Matt told her. 'We only want what's best for you. We'll not stand in your way.'

A few days later, Meg and Alec were walking in the park.

'You know I told you about this friend of mine,' she began hesitantly.

Alec stopped skimming stones over the pond and turned to her.

'The one who was adopted?'

She nodded.

'It's me. I mean, I was really talking about myself...'

'I thought you were.'

'Did you?' Meg was surprised.

'Oh, Alec, I can't decide what to do. It would be a wonderful life in the States! A few years ago I'd have given anything for the chance, but now – I can't think what's holding me back.'

And then, as she spoke, she suddenly knew. If she went to America, she'd never see Alec again. The thought was unbearable.

As he looked at her with that slightly crooked smile of his, she knew without any doubt that he was the reason she had hesitated.

'I can't make up my mind,' she said lamely. She longed for him to beg her to stay, to tell her he needed her...

But he didn't. Instead, he picked up another pebble and tossed it from one hand to another.

'Well, if you're in any doubt, I think you should stay,' he said.

'Really?' Meg's heart lurched.

'I know you're fond of your family. I think you're anxious about leaving them,' he went on calmly, as if they were discussing someone else.

Oh, Alec, Meg thought. I don't want to go away from *you*. I never meant to fall in love, but I have...

'You may be right,' she murmured.

Still he said nothing, just smiled at her.

'It's up to you – no-one else can make the decision. They're offering you a wonderful life,' he pointed out.

'Yes,' Meg burst out suddenly. 'I've had enough of scraping and working away for other people. I want to enjoy life.'

'If you go,' he said, his eyes fixed on the ground, 'you can't come back to the old life, you know.'

'Well,' Meg retorted, in a high, brittle voice, 'why should I want to? Maybe I'll meet some rich American and marry him and live in style and comfort for the rest of my life.'

'If that's what you want,' Alec said in an off-hand way, 'why hesitate? Accept the offer with thanks.'

'Oh, you don't understand!' Meg burst out, her face flushed.

'No,' Alec said, and his voice was distant. 'No, I don't really. If luxury and wealth are what you want, I can't see what's keeping you here.

'Isn't it time we went home?'

They walked home in silence and he left her at the door of her digs.

'Good night, Meg. See you at work.'

'Good night,' Meg said in a small voice. She went indoors without looking back.

That night she cried herself to sleep as if she were a child again.

Alec would never care for her, she told herself. She would have to try to forget him...

But she didn't want to. She wanted to stay near him...

Oh, what am I to do? she asked herself, as she watched the dawn come up.

Chapter Ten

Meg hardly noticed that the days were growing longer, and the trees were bursting into bud; or even that the smell of spring was in the air at last.

She still felt unsettled, and anxious about the future. Oh, what's wrong with me, she asked herself, frustrated. She had so much to be contented about.

She had a good, responsible job, which she enjoyed. And, though she sometimes had regrets about her friendship with Philip – she still blushed when she remembered how close she'd come to making a fool of herself – she'd put that behind her now. She was no longer under any illusions where Philip was concerned...

And Alec? Well, he was only a good friend – not even that, she thought a little sadly.

Their previous easy friendship had been strained lately, as if it had lost all its sparkle. Alec didn't even seem to mind whether she went to the States with Lucille or not.

Meg had her pride – she wasn't going to beg Alec to try to care for her as she cared for him. But his indifference hurt. If only he'd tried to persuade her not to go to

America – but he hadn't. He hadn't said a word.

Meg sighed. It was warm for the time of year and the office seemed suddenly stuffy.

She rose from her desk and looked out of the window. Soon she could be looking at quite a different view, if she decided to go to the States with Lucille. If...

'Have you finished those letters, Miss Barclay?' Mr Baillie appeared at the door of his office.

'Yes, almost,' she said, startled. 'I'll bring them in shortly.'

Meg roused herself from her daydreams and sat down at the typewriter again.

Keep your mind on the job, she told herself firmly. If she decided to stay, she would need it.

But what was she to do? Try as she might, she couldn't make up her mind whether to stay or go.

Her kindly landlady, Mrs Maclean, noticed that Meg wasn't eating. Often, in the evenings, the girl would toy listlessly with a piece of embroidery, whereas before she would have been playing rowdy games with Mrs Maclean's youngest child, or helping the older ones with their homework.

Lizzie, the eldest, came in from school one day with great news.

'We're doing a play,' she announced, eyes shining, 'and I've got a part. There's an awful lot to learn. You'll help me, won't you, Miss Barclay – you'll hear my lines?'

'I … oh, don't bother me now!' Meg snapped at the child, who looked astonished.

This wasn't the friendly, helpful Miss Barclay, who would always join in a game or tell a story...

Then, suddenly, Meg burst into tears.

'Off you go, Lizzie, and don't trouble Miss Barclay just now,' Mrs Maclean said. She sat down beside Meg, and stretched out a hand to the girl.

'Can you tell me what's wrong?' she asked quietly. 'I've noticed you've not been yourself lately, and you're looking a bit peaky. Is something the matter?'

Meg mopped her eyes.

'I'm sorry for snapping at Lizzie like that. It was so unkind...'

'Never you worry about that,' Mrs Maclean told her.

Suddenly, Meg felt ashamed. Her kindly landlady had known so much heartache. Mrs Maclean had lost her husband in an accident, and was bringing up three children on very little money, yet she always had a smile and a kind word for others.

'It's so selfish of me,' Meg blurted out. 'I've been brooding about my own problems, and you – you never complain, or say that life's been hard...'

Mrs Maclean smiled.

'Well, I won't say it's been easy – but you just have to keep going and do the best you can.' She paused.

'Sometimes it helps to talk about a problem. If you wanted to tell me what's been worrying you…'

Suddenly, Meg knew she could tell Mrs Maclean anything, and would be heard with kindness, and given wise advice.

'I was adopted,' she began slowly. She told Mrs Maclean all about Lucille and how she'd come back into her life, and about the wonderful offer of visiting the States. As she talked, she gazed into the flames dancing in the grate.

'It's such a marvellous chance – a whole new future…' she faltered.

There was a silence.

'But you don't really want to go, do you?' Mrs Maclean said.

'No,' Meg admitted. The relief was enormous. 'No, you're absolutely right. I don't.

'It's funny – it's what I've hoped for all my life, to live in luxury and want for nothing. I thought if ever such a chance came, I'd jump at it. But now…' She gazed thoughtfully into the fire.

'It's not that I don't want to see America – I do. But it's partly that I feel I belong here with Mother and Father and the family, but more–' she suddenly knew that she was right '–I want to make my own way, not have things decided for me.

'I'll tell Lucille the answer's no. I know, if I go, even for a short time, it wouldn't work. I hope she'll understand...'

Mrs Maclean knelt down and lifted a cinder from the hearth with the tongs. She smiled at the girl, and the tension was eased.

'Thank you for listening to me,' Meg said, standing up.

'Will you tell Lizzie I'm sorry? Of course I'll help her learn her words.'

There was no point in delaying any longer, Meg told herself firmly. So, after work the next day, she dressed carefully for her visit to Lucille.

A glance in the mirror showed glossy dark hair, high cheek bones and bright eyes. She looked very like Lucille, Meg realised now.

All the way to Broughty Ferry on the tram, she planned what she would say.

'It's such a wonderful offer, and I've thought it over carefully. Please don't think I'm not grateful...'

What would she say if Lucille tried to persuade her to change her mind? It would be hard to refuse. Could she play for time, ask if she could think about it?

But then she *had* thought about it. In fact, she'd thought of nothing else for several weeks.

Lucille's parlour maid answered the door and showed Meg into a small sitting-room.

'Come in, my dear,' Lucille greeted Meg warmly, gesturing to the boxes that littered the floor. 'I'm trying to pack – you can see what it's like. I've bought so many things to take back, wonderful knitted jumpers and tweeds...'

She chattered on, but Meg was not deceived. She knew that Lucille was trying to cover the awkward moment, to help Meg to compose herself.

'Do sit down,' Lucille said suddenly. 'If you can find a space, that is.

'You've decided, haven't you?' she added quietly. 'And your answer is no.'

'How did you know?'

'I knew as soon as I saw your face. You and I are very much alike, really.' Lucille gave a rueful smile.

'I knew because you're impulsive, like me. Usually, your heart rules your head – and if you'd really wanted to come and live with us in the States, you'd have jumped at the chance. Wouldn't you?'

Meg nodded. She was finding it difficult to speak.

'This time,' Lucille went on, 'your head has ruled your heart – and that's no bad thing. You've thought it over carefully and you've decided against it.'

Meg didn't know what to say. All her carefully prepared speeches went out of her mind. She flung her arms around Lucille.

264

'I'm sorry ... I never meant to hurt you,' she mumbled into Lucille's shoulder. 'But my life is here – this is where I belong.'

'You don't have to apologise. I understand.' Lucille stroked Meg's dark hair. Then she drew away slightly, and held Meg at arms' length.

'I know you've good reasons for staying here, but one day, I hope, you'll come and visit. And you'll write, won't you – and keep in touch?'

'Oh, yes, I will,' Meg promised. 'And thank you – thank you for everything.'

When Meg returned to Pennyglen at the weekend, there was an air of excitement in the cottage.

Ellen was full of her plans for the trip to London to see the Empire Exhibition. She'd already met and liked Colin's cousin, Lizbeth, who was to go with them.

'She's so charming – beautifully dressed, and good fun, too,' Ellen told Meg, without a trace of envy.

'What does she do?' Meg asked, trying to show an interest.

'Oh, she doesn't need to work,' Ellen said.

'So she's a lady?'

'Don't sneer,' Ellen retorted. 'She's well off, but that doesn't make any difference.

'You know, you could come with us, Meg – why don't you?'

Meg shook her head.

'Thank you, but I'd just be in the way.'

'Oh. Well, if that's how you feel.' Ellen frowned, puzzled. She just couldn't make Meg out these days – she'd been so moody lately.

Later, when Ellen had gone, Meg told Matt and Lily that she'd turned down Lucille's invitation to go to America.

'Are you sure you've made the right decision?' Lily looked a little troubled.

'I thought you'd be pleased!' Meg burst out, dismayed.

'Of course I'm pleased,' Lily reassured her. 'It's just – you're giving up such a wonderful chance...'

'Am I?' Meg said. 'I don't know. Oh, it would be grand, the luxury and everything.

'But I want to make my own way, not be beholden to anyone. And,' she finished with a rush, 'I like being here at home.'

'And we like having you here.' Lily reached out a hand to Meg. 'I just want you to be happy.'

'I am, Mother.' Meg's eyes sparkled.

Later, Meg wandered out into the garden. Matt was in the vegetable plot, hoeing between the rows of beans.

He turned round and smiled when he saw her.

'Going to be a fine crop this year.'

Meg nodded. There was a pause.

'Are you sure you won't regret staying?' he asked, concerned.

Meg shook her head.

'That's all right then,' he said quietly. And with that, he smiled and turned back to the job in hand.

Colin, Ellen and Lizbeth fought their way through the crowds at the station to their train.

'We'll be in London in time for breakfast,' Colin said breezily. 'First stop Edinburgh. Then Newcastle, York, Doncaster and on to King's Cross.'

'I've never been further than Edinburgh before,' Ellen said shyly to Colin's cousin.

At first she'd been a bit in awe of Lizbeth, in her elegant summer crêpe de chine and dainty shoes. But Lizbeth was friendly, and not a bit standoffish.

'You'll enjoy London,' Lizbeth promised her. 'We'll have a chance to see the sights before we go to the Exhibition.'

With a sigh of pleasure, Ellen settled back into her seat.

The guard blew his whistle.

'We're off!' Colin said. The crowds lining the road above the station cheered and waved.

'Makes you feel like royalty,' one of the people in the compartment joked.

How lucky I am! Ellen thought. She felt

sorry for Meg, missing out on all the fun.

She could hardly sleep that night. Oh, it was so exciting, as the train puffed through the countryside towards the Border.

Darkness fell as they travelled further south, and what with the throb of the wheels and the glare of light from the foundries at Newcastle and beyond, Ellen thought she'd never be able to sleep.

But, just as she was resigned to staying awake all night, the jumble of impressions merged, and she dozed off.

'Wake up!' Lizbeth nudged her. 'We'll soon be at King's Cross. We're having breakfast at Lyons Corner House in the Strand. I hope you're hungry.'

'I'm starving!' Colin said, as he helped the girls off the train.

'I couldn't eat a thing!' Ellen put in. 'I'm far too excited.'

But for all that, she managed to do justice to the ham and eggs she ordered for breakfast.

There was a fleet of buses waiting for the travellers at Trafalgar Square.

'Oh, look at the lions!' Ellen exclaimed. All the way up Fleet Street, she craned her neck, anxious not to miss anything.

'There's St Paul's,' someone said, as they caught sight of the great dome.

They travelled on through the city, past the Tower.

'I wish we'd time to stop.' Lizbeth sighed.

There was so much to see as they crossed the Thames and gazed at the ships lying at anchor in the Docks.

The whole party fell silent as they passed the Cenotaph. It was not quite six years since the Armistice, and that November day when the guns fell silent. There was a short pause while one of the group from St Andrews laid a wreath.

Over lunch, Colin smiled at Ellen.

'Tired yet?' he asked.

'Oh, no!' Ellen beamed back. 'I'd like to stay here for ever. There's so much to see – the shops and the river and the parks...'

Colin was so kind, she thought. What trouble he was taking to make sure she and Lizbeth enjoyed the day.

And then they set off for Wembley. Ellen had read all about the wonderful Exhibition, but she still wasn't prepared for the sight. How vast it was! There seemed to be one marvel after another!

'There's the Indian pavilion, and the Australian and Canadian ones,' Colin pointed out, looking at the souvenir programme.

'Where would you like to start?'

'Well,' Lizbeth said firmly, 'I want to see the Queen's doll's-house.'

'There'll be long queues,' Colin warned her.

'Then I'll queue!'

Lizbeth was already wishing that she hadn't worn her best shoes. They might be the height of fashion, but how they pinched! Look at Ellen in her low-heeled shoes. How much more sensible!

'Listen,' Lizbeth went on, 'why don't you two go off and see the other sights while I queue?'

'All right,' Colin agreed. 'We'll meet you at the gate at five. You'll be OK on your own?'

'Don't worry,' Lizbeth assured him. One of the other girls from the coach was eager to see the doll's-house, too, so she and Lizbeth went off together.

'What will we do first?' Colin turned to Ellen. 'The pavilion? Or the rodeo, and then maybe the funfair?'

Ellen's eyes shone.

'Oh, the rodeo, please!' she said. That really would be something to tell Willie about back home!

The bareback riding and the bronco riding was just as exciting as she'd expected, and Ellen found herself quite breathless with cheering when at last the exhibition ended.

'That cowgirl was really wonderful!' she said as they left the arena.

'Time for something quieter now, I think,' Colin suggested. 'There are boats on the lake. Would you like to try that?

'Then perhaps we could go and see the

pavilions – maybe watch them cutting diamonds in the South African one, or see the fountains in the Indian pavilion?' He looked at the programme again.

'I think I'd like to go on the boats,' Ellen decided.

As the motor boat chugged round the lake, Colin put his arm around her and smiled down at the flushed, happy face turned up to him.

'Oh, I am having a good time!' she exclaimed. 'Thank you.'

'I'm glad.' He paused. 'Ellen, I mean – would you?'

'Please,' she said hastily. 'Don't spoil things. We're having such a good day.'

'And would it spoil things if I asked you...?'

'Sh...' She put a finger to her lips.

In the distance, a band was playing, 'If you were the only girl in the world...'

It was a much quieter party that left King's Cross Station, just after seven, on the homeward journey.

Now and then someone would say, 'The switchback – did you try it?' or 'I liked the displays of wild animals...'

'The water chute – that was the best...'

'The doll's-house was worth the wait,' another murmured.

Gradually, all the passengers fell silent.

Some slept, while others half-dozed, or gazed out of the window at the sleeping towns and villages as the train steamed on towards the Border.

When Colin helped Lizbeth and Ellen off the train at Cupar, they waved goodbye to their companions who were going on to Guardbridge and St Andrews.

'Well,' Lizbeth said, 'I'm exhausted! I think I'll sleep for a week.' She yawned. 'What about you, Ellen?'

'Not quite a week. I'm back on duty tonight.'

'Are you really?' Lizbeth gazed at her in astonishment. 'But won't they give you time off to recover?'

'I'm afraid Matron wouldn't see it that way.' Ellen smiled.

Colin laughed.

'Not everyone's a lady of leisure like you,' he told his cousin.

'Well, really, it is too bad. Poor you,' Lizbeth sympathised.

Suddenly, Ellen felt like Cinderella. It had been a wonderful trip, but now the party was over. It was back to old clothes and porridge, as Lily would have said.

She and Lizbeth lived in different worlds, she realised with a start. It was hard for someone from Lizbeth's kind of background to understand Ellen's way of life – to appreciate that you were lucky to have a job, and you didn't just take time off when you felt like it.

And it dawned on her, as she had slowly been coming to realise, that there was a similar gulf between her family and Colin's.

She shivered a little as they stood on Cupar station platform in the bright summer morning. Colin put his arm round her protectively.

'Tired?' There was no mistaking the tenderness in his voice.

Ellen shook her head.

'You've given me such a wonderful time. Thank you.'

'We've got the car here,' Colin said. 'At least we can drive you home.'

Colin helped her into the car, tucking the rug round her knees.

Oh, it was nice to be spoiled, Ellen thought, and wouldn't it be wonderful to lead a life of luxury.

'He's a farmer,' a voice inside her said. 'It wouldn't be luxury. He works very hard, and you would, too.'

'But,' another voice said, 'there's a big difference between his world and yours. Nothing will ever change that...'

Ellen was quite hoarse with talking by evening. She'd told her family every detail she could remember about the wonderful visit – the tour of London, and the Exhibition, with the pavilions, bands and the amusement park.

Matt smiled at her when she eventually stopped for breath.

And next weekend she'd have the fun of telling it all over again to Meg. Except that Meg was – well, a little downcast these days. She'd lost a lot of her sparkle lately.

Next Saturday, Meg tried hard to share her sister's pleasure as Ellen recounted all the exciting events.

But Ellen couldn't be sure that Meg was even listening.

'He's very kind, your Colin,' Meg said at last, after a long pause. 'To take you on such a marvellous trip, I mean.'

'He's not my Colin.' Ellen sounded a little sharp. 'And I paid for myself – or at least Mother did, from the pirlie pig.'

Meg whirled round from the window where she'd been gazing down at the street.

'I'm all for being independent,' she said, 'but…'

'But what?' Ellen was tired. It had been a busy week at the convalescent home, and she was uncertain about the future.

Of course Matron would give her a good reference, but where would she go? She'd read that nurses were desperately needed in London. But then London was a long way away. Maybe she should try for a post in Edinburgh or Dundee?

'Well,' Meg went on, rather lamely, 'I only

meant you're lucky to have Colin courting you...'

'Are you jealous?' Ellen didn't mean to speak sharply. She'd meant it to be a light-hearted sort of remark, but somehow it didn't come out that way.

'Me? Jealous? Don't be stupid!' Meg snapped back at her.

Ellen was sorry she'd spoken so sharply, but she wanted to make things clear.

'He's not "my" Colin, not at all,' she said. 'There's nothing between us – how could there be?

'We're from different backgrounds. His family are comfortably off, while we're – well, we're ordinary people.'

Her words touched Meg to the raw. She was still feeling a little sensitive about Philip, though she tried not to let her disappointment show.

The knowledge that she hadn't been good enough for Philip and his family still rankled.

She knew in her heart that Philip had never cared for her, not deeply, and she realised that his family might have raised objections to a marriage. But still...

'No-one's ordinary,' she said sharply. 'You're being a fool, Ellen. Why let Colin go? Take your chance while you can – that's what I say.'

It was all too much for Ellen. She whirled

round to face Meg.

'Leave me alone!' she said angrily. 'You haven't any right to tell me what to do.

'Why can't you let me run my own life? It's none of your business what I do with it?'

'But I only meant–' Meg stuttered, completely taken aback.

Ellen had gone. She slammed the door behind her and left Meg feeling wretched.

Oh, what have I done now! she thought. Why can't I hold my tongue?

That summer was a happy one. Years afterwards, Lily was to look back with nostalgia on the many fine days her family enjoyed.

Little Alice was growing fast, and soon Janet's second child would be born.

There was the excitement of a trip to the Trossachs in the new charabanc that Rab had bought, too. Every week now he ran tours from the garage – to Pitlochry, Crieff, Gleneagles and Milnathort.

How comfortable it was, this 'luxurious pneumatic-tyred charabanc,' as he advertised it.

'You'll be one of our first passengers,' he promised Lily, and scolded her when she reached for the pirlie pig to pay for her fare.

'This is our treat,' he told her, and she accepted happily.

The future was looking bright for young Willie. Rab had offered him a job at the garage, and he was to start in the autumn.

During the autumn and winter of that year, Meg's friendship with Alec continued, though to her disappointment they grew no closer.

Her decision not to go to the States seemed to have raised a barrier between them, Meg thought sadly, and she had no idea how to overcome it.

Her feelings for Alec hadn't changed since the evening she realised she was in love with him, but if he saw her as nothing more than a friend – well, she'd just have to be content with that.

It was an undemanding friendship. Sometimes they'd go to the Caird Hall to concerts, and one night, Alec took her to hear the Queen's Hall Orchestra.

On other evenings, they'd play piano duets at Alec's home, or Meg would play the accompaniment while Alec sang some of his mother's favourite songs.

Thanks to the matron's recommendation, Ellen was to start nursing in Edinburgh at one of the big hospitals.

'It's a great chance!' she told her family excitedly.

'Congratulations!' Meg said when she heard the news.

She was thrilled for Ellen – wasn't it what her sister had always wanted? And she and Colin wouldn't be too far apart. There would still be opportunities for them to meet.

'Thank you.' Ellen wasn't one to harbour a grudge, but though she spoke warmly, Meg was aware that there was still a coolness between them.

Hogmanay that year saw all the family gathered together to bring in the New Year.

The past year had been a good one, Lily reflected contentedly. Janet's baby, Callum, was six months old now and growing more of a character every day.

Lily had shortbread and black bun ready as midnight approached. Old Walter from down the road was always their first foot. He'd wait until he heard the church clock strike the hour, then make his way hastily up to the house.

When they were young, Meg and Janet had been a bit ashamed of having Walter as a first foot. Why couldn't they have some tall, dark, *young* man instead?

But every year, there was old Walter, shabbily dressed, sitting silently in his corner, nursing his dram, his watery old eyes taking in the scene around him.

'He's so...' Janet used to whisper.

'Shabby,' Meg finished. 'And dirty, too.'

'And when he starts to sing...' Janet put in.

But Lily would have none of it.

'Walter has brought us good luck every

year,' she told them. 'And he's an old man – don't grudge him the pleasure of first-footing us.'

But now... Maybe I'm growing up at last, Meg thought. She didn't mind old Walter as much.

He was a bit of a fixture – there every year, like black bun and shortbread. It wouldn't have been Hogmanay without Walter.

And here he was again.

'A good New Year to you, missus, and you, too, Mr Barclay, and the young ladies. I'm hearing you have a new bairn.' He pressed a silver threepenny bit into Janet's hand.

'That's for the baby.'

Janet, knowing how poor the old man was, felt deeply touched, and thanked him warmly.

Matt filled a glass for Walter and Lily heaped a plate with black bun and short-bread.

By now, other neighbours had joined the family. Matt raised his own glass, and they all fell silent as they waited for the toast – another Hogmanay tradition.

'Well,' he said, 'here's a happy New Year to each and everyone. We've had a good year and we're grateful for our health and our friends, and the blessing of two fine grand-children. So welcome to 1925 – and a good New Year to you all.'

Amid all the laughter and fun, Meg was

suddenly struck by how different it might have been.

She could have been seeing in the New Year thousands of miles away, with Lucille and her husband and family, among strangers. For the first time, she knew she had no doubts – she didn't regret her decision.

Oh, she was fond of Lucille and grateful to her, but she belonged to another world, another life. She was glad she'd chosen to stay at home.

Over the months that followed, Meg saw little of Alec. She felt rather hurt that he didn't seek her out more often.

On several occasions, she suggested to him that he join her on a theatre outing, or go with her to a concert, but he turned down her invitations.

'I'm sorry,' he said, sounding disappointed. 'But I can't. I'm – er – busy.'

'Oh.' Meg was disappointed, too. Was he telling her, as kindly as possible, that he didn't want her company any more? She hoped not.

Meg was grateful to be kept busy at work, and was taking on more responsibility.

'We're very pleased with the extra you've been doing,' old Mr Baillie said a little gruffly. 'We're going to raise your salary.'

Meg blushed and murmured a thank-you.

It was very good news, but she wished she had someone special to share it with.

Then, one summer afternoon, Alec came into the office.

'Are you free this evening?' he asked. 'I've some news – two bits of news, actually.'

Meg looked up and smiled.

'Oh, what is it?'

'It'll keep.' He smiled back. 'After work?'

She nodded.

He was waiting for her when she came down the stairs at the end of the day.

'It's a fine evening – what about a walk?' he suggested.

'Yes, that would be lovely.'

They'd reached the entrance to the park when Alec turned to her.

'I can hardly wait to tell you my news!' he blurted out. 'Jamie's got a bursary to the university.'

'That's wonderful!' Meg knew how proud Alec was of his younger brother.

He nodded, his face serious for a moment.

'Yes, he deserves it. He's worked so hard. And the money – that matters a lot. We probably couldn't have managed otherwise.'

'I know.' Meg nodded. 'And the other bit of news?'

'Well, you know I saw Mr Baillie this week?'

Meg nodded again. Alec had been in Mr Baillie's office for a long time that day.

Eventually he'd hurried out, looking preoccupied. She hoped it wasn't trouble.

'He's offered me promotion.'

'But Alec, that's wonderful!' Meg was genuinely pleased for him. Alec was clever and hard working, and he deserved promotion.

'I'm so glad for you,' she told him.

'Thank you.' He grinned at her. 'I haven't told you where I'll be working. I'm going out to India, to the office in Calcutta.'

'India!' Meg repeated, shocked. 'But that's…'

'A long way away. That's what my mother said.

'But I'll be home on leave, remember. It's a chance of a lifetime! And now that Jamie's going to university, his future's certain, so I'm free to go…'

'Free to go.' The words fell between them.

Meg felt numb. She cared so much for Alec; had hoped that, one day, he might come to return her feelings. But now, he was going away. She might never see him again…

She shivered, suddenly thankful that there had never been anything except friendship between her and Alec. She'd miss him dreadfully, of course she would, but at least she'd been spared from making a fool of herself…

'I'll miss you,' he went on. 'But you'll

write, won't you?'

'Of course I will,' she said, forcing herself to sound cheerful.

'And if, sometimes, you could call in on my mother, I'd be very grateful. She's been very good about it, but she might be a bit lonely when I've gone – especially now that Jamie's leaving, too.'

'I'll do that,' Meg told him. She liked Alec's mother, and was glad of a reason to keep in touch.

'Speaking of which, can you come to tea tomorrow? I said I'd ask you,' Alec went on.

'Oh, yes, please,' Meg accepted.

It was a cheerful evening. Jamie was full of his plans, and Alec, too, looked happier than she'd seen him for a long time.

'You've done well,' Meg told Jamie.

'Alec helped me a lot,' he said with a grin. 'Night after night, he helped me with my maths when I was all for giving up!'

So that was why Alec had been so busy lately. But why hadn't he just said?

'So, when are you leaving?' Meg asked Alec. There would be lots for him to do over the next few months, she supposed – travel arrangements to make, clothing to buy...

'You're going to have a hectic month or two,' she added.

'Weeks, more like,' he said. 'I'm going in two weeks' time. The firm's been having a bit of trouble out there – they want me to get there as soon as I can.'

'Two weeks!'

'Yes, I know it isn't long.'

Meg could hardly believe it. She couldn't imagine the office without Alec, life without Alec. And so soon...

'I expect this has all been a bit sudden,' he said, as he walked her home.

'Well, yes.' She kept her voice light, determined not to let her feelings show.

'But I'm really glad for you. It's a wonderful chance.' And that, at least, was true.

'I sail on the twenty-fourth,' he said. 'Would you come and see me off? I'd be glad if you would.'

Her heart leapt. Did she mean something to him after all? But Alec was just a good friend, she told herself firmly – nothing more.

'Please, Meg, say you will.'

'Yes, of course I will.' Meg looked up at him. 'I'll be there.'

Chapter Eleven

'You'll write won't you?' Alec had Meg's hand tightly clasped in his. They'd slowly walked the length of the station platform, and now it was time for him to board his train.

'Of course I will,' she assured him.

'It would mean a lot to me–' He hesitated. 'To have news from home, that is.'

'Then I'll write often!' Her cheerfulness sounded false, even to Meg's ears. She was determined not to let Alec see how distressed she was by his decision to leave.

'I'll tell you all about what's happening in the office, and Pennyglen, too,' she went on brightly.

'I'll look forward to that.' Alec smiled. 'You're so good at describing all the little things – everyday, amusing things, like the putting contest at the fête.'

'That was funny, wasn't it?' Meg smiled. 'Willie was so sure he'd win – he'd already decided how he would spend the prize money. Oh, how his pals teased him when he was beaten by a girl!'

Their laughter died away and they stood in silence, waiting for the train.

There seemed so little to say, Meg thought sadly. But that was because the one thing she longed to tell Alec had to be left unsaid. How could she tell him she loved him, when he was on the brink of a new life in India?

Meg wanted Alec to have cheerful memories to take away with him, but it was so difficult to choose the right words. And time was slipping away from her...

'The train won't be long now. It's signalled,' she began. 'Oh, look – here it is...' She felt so foolish, gabbling away like this.

But Alec understood.

He took her face between his hands and kissed her gently on the cheek.

'Goodbye, Meg. Look after yourself.'

Oh, why was he going so far away, a voice inside her cried. She'd miss him so much. Would she ever see him again?

She swallowed back the tears that threatened and smiled bravely.

Alec pulled down the compartment window.

'You won't forget to write, will you?' he asked anxiously.

'No.' Meg shook her head. 'I promise. I won't forget.'

The guard blew his whistle, drowning out her words. Alec waved and waved as the train pulled away.

Meg shivered a little in the early autumn chill. How quiet life was going to be without

Alec's jokes and laughter, she reflected. And how lonely…

But, in spite of her feelings for Alec, she was glad there had been nothing more than friendship between them. That would have made this parting even harder to bear.

In the few quiet moments that she was able to snatch out of her busy days, Janet found herself thinking that, while not exactly difficult, life could be a little wearisome sometimes.

She was ashamed of herself, but looking out at the rain, and wondering how on earth she would get the washing dry, she felt a little stab of self-pity.

Just sometimes, she wished … and then she paused.

What was she thinking of? Hadn't she a full enough life, looking after the house and the children, preparing Rab's meals…?

It's not that I'm discontented, she told herself. Only, sometimes, I'd enjoy doing something else, something of my own.

She took up her sewing basket and the darning mushroom, and looked ruefully at Rab's socks. How did he manage it? Such enormous holes!

She might have gone on feeling slightly sorry for herself, in a vague sort of way, if it hadn't been for a chance meeting.

She was pushing the pram along the

Bonnygate in Cupar one day, with Alice by her side, when a voice called to her.

'It's Janet – Janet Barclay, isn't it?'

'Janet Barclay that was.' She smiled in return. 'I'm married now.'

'Do you remember me?' the young woman asked.

'Of course – it's Katie,' Janet said, delighted to see her old school-friend again.

'And are these your two? Of course they are. My, they're bonnie...'

Katie was as bright and outgoing as ever, Janet thought fondly.

'I live quite near,' Katie went on. 'Come and have a cup of tea.'

'I can't manage today.' Janet shook her head. 'I've shopping to do for my mother.'

'Well, how about tomorrow? Bring the wee ones, and we'll catch up on the news,' Katie invited.

'All right,' Janet agreed. 'Thank you – that would be lovely.'

'I'm glad you could come,' Katie said, as she opened the door to Janet the next day.

'The children won't be a bother,' Janet promised her.

'Oh, don't worry about that. I'm pleased to see them.' Her friend smiled, showing them into the living-room, where a bright fire burned in the grate.

'But you're busy sewing,' Janet realised. 'I'm interrupting you.'

'Not at all. I'll just put all this to one side,' Katie assured her.

'You always were neat-fingered,' Janet remarked, interested.

'These days I have to be.' A shadow crossed Katie's face. 'I work for my living now.'

She explained, simply and without any self-pity, that her husband had returned from the war, shell-shocked.

'We'd hoped he'd recover, but he's still in and out of hospital,' she told Janet.

'So it's just as well that I enjoy sewing. I've turned to dressmaking for other people. It keeps me busy, and it brings in an income.'

'I didn't know...' Janet broke off, feeling rather ashamed of herself.

There she was, feeling miserable and out of sorts because she was busy and tied to the house with two small children.

She realised how lucky she was. Rab had recovered well from his wartime injuries, and the business was going from strength to strength. And she had two healthy children.

'That looks really lovely,' she said, pointing to a half-finished garment.

Katie lifted the filmy material.

'It's a trousseau I'm sewing, for a Miss Macrae. It's fine work and I've got to take it slowly. It's a pleasure to do, though.'

She folded the garment carefully.

'You used to sew a lot, I remember.'

'I made all my own clothes,' Janet told her. 'And I did quite a lot of work at one time for the people at Pitlady.'

'They'd have high standards, those folk,' her friend remarked. 'Your work must have been good.'

'Oh, I don't know.' Janet shrugged. 'I loved doing it – I must say I miss it.'

'Well–' Katie paused.

'I'll put the kettle on, and there's milk and biscuits for Alice. Just sit down – I won't be a minute.'

Janet gazed idly around her as she waited. It was a small room, and the furniture was old, but the brass shone, the curtains were of a pretty chintz, and the old wood of the dresser shone with polish.

The afternoon sped past as the two women reminisced over old times. At last, Janet rose reluctantly.

'Don't go just yet – I want to ask you something,' Katie said, laying a hand on her arm.

'What is it?'

'I've a lot of work at the moment. I can't turn it down, yet I don't quite know how I'm going to get through it all. I wonder – would you give me a hand?

'I'll pay you, of course,' Katie added hastily, 'but it would be great if you could help me out sometimes.'

'But...' Janet began doubtfully.

'I know you've probably enough to do, what with the wee ones,' her friend interrupted. 'You might not want to. It was just a thought.'

'Oh, it's not that,' Janet said. 'But I don't know if I'd be good enough.'

'Oh, away with you!' Katie laughed. 'Of course you would be. You were good enough for the folk at the Big House, weren't you? And I'd soon tell you if your work wasn't up to standard,' she said with mock sternness.

'Then I'll do it,' Janet agreed impulsively.

'I'd enjoy it. It would be good to be working again, and with such beautiful materials. But I don't want you to pay me,' she protested.

'I'm not a charity,' Katie said a little stiffly.

'I didn't mean that,' Janet put in hastily, afraid that she'd offended her friend.

'Well, we'll need to talk about terms.' Katie's smile returned. 'If you'd agree to help out...'

'There's nothing I'd like better!'

Janet hummed cheerfully as she walked home, happy to have so much to look forward to.

How could she have been so selfish and self-pitying before? She should be deeply thankful for her own good fortune – look at all that Katie had to endure. She couldn't wait to tell Rab about her plans.

'As long as it won't be too much for you,'

he said that evening. 'I don't want you overdoing things.'

'Too much?' she scoffed. 'It will be a pleasure.'

'Then I'm pleased for you.' He smiled.

Janet's face was serious.

'Katie's having a hard time, and yet she was so bright – she didn't complain at all. It made me realise how lucky I am.

'I'd been feeling – I don't know – a bit, not exactly bored, but, you know…' She found it hard to put into words, but Rab understood just how she felt.

'I know,' he said softly, putting his arms around her. 'But it's me that's the lucky one.' He smiled down at her, and at the glowing face turned up to him, and saw again the happy, carefree girl he'd married.

'There's a letter for you, Meg.' Mrs Maclean put her head round the door. Meg had at last persuaded her landlady to stop calling her Miss Barclay. 'After all,' she'd reasoned, 'I'm not just the lodger. We're friends, aren't we?'

'Thank you.' Meg took the letter, realising from the handwriting that it was from Alec. She put it in her pocket – she'd have time to read and enjoy it later.

Alec's letters were full of interest. He was good as describing even the most trivial things – the farmers bringing the raw jute on bullock carts, or by boat when the rains made the roads impassable; the compound and his bungalow; the bearer who looked after him; all the strange new sights – the birds and animals. He described everything so well, Meg felt she was seeing it all for herself.

And if, sometimes, she wished that his letters were a little more personal, she pushed the thought away. She and Alec were good friends, nothing more.

'You'll be late for your train if you don't hurry,' Mrs Maclean said. 'We'll see you tomorrow evening as usual, and I'll have your supper ready.'

'Thank you.' Not for the first time, Meg thought how lucky she was to have met the kindly Mrs Maclean, and to have her as a friend.

She picked up her bag and set off briskly in the direction of the station. She was well accustomed now to catching the train from Dundee to arrive home early on a Saturday afternoon.

Sometimes, it meant rushing from work, but once on the train, looking out over the Tay towards Newport and the Fife coast, she was able to relax.

'There you are!' Lily turned round from the sink, her hands covered in soap suds.

'I saved your dinner for you. I thought you wouldn't have time for a proper meal before you left. There's soup, and mince and potatoes.'

'No-one makes mince and potatoes as good as yours,' Meg said warmly, and Lily tutted with pleasure.

'Where's Father?' Meg asked.

'He's working in the garden, as usual,' Lily said with a smile.

'And how are Janet, and the children?' As Meg tucked into the broth that her mother put before her, she told Lily about a doll she'd seen in a shop in Dundee that would be just right for Alice.

But Lily didn't seem to be listening with her usual interest.

'Is there something wrong?' Meg asked after a pause.

'Oh, it's probably nothing, but I've been a bit worried lately about your father. He does too much.' Lily frowned.

Matt was always willing to help a neighbour with building a shed, or digging over a patch of garden for an old person – even lending a hand when there was a flitting. But he wasn't a young man any more...

'Still,' Lily said, trying not to fret, 'he does enjoy his garden.'

'I'll go and call him in for a cup of tea,' Meg suggested. 'That way he'll be sure to take a rest.'

'I'll put the kettle on.'

Meg went outside, shading her eyes

against the bright winter sun. Matt was coming down the path, and he waved when he saw her.

'There's a cup of tea for you,' Meg called. 'And it's getting cold – it's time you came in.'

'I'm just coming. I'll clean these tools and be with you in a moment,' he called back.

Meg went indoors and hung up her jacket, then helped Lily to set out the cups and some shortbread. There was still no sign of Matt.

'Father's taking his time,' she joked. 'I see what you mean – it's hard to get him out of his precious garden!'

Her smile faded as a shadow fell across the doorway. Both women turned to see Matt leaning heavily against the door frame, clutching his chest.

'I'm not well,' he gasped, his face grey.

Meg hurried forward to help him.

'Come and sit down,' she coaxed, trying to sound reassuring. 'Your tea's ready.'

Matt staggered towards the chair and slumped down.

'What is it?' Lily crouched down beside him. 'Tell me – are you in pain?'

He nodded, hardly able to speak.

Lily turned to Meg.

'Run next door for Nurse Macphee. She'll know what to do.'

A dreadful fear clutched hold of Meg, as if

she'd been touched by icy fingers. She hurried next door, praying that the nurse would be in.

'Oh, please,' she said breathlessly, when the door was opened, 'can you come right away? It's Father.'

She didn't need to say any more. Nurse Macphee, quietly competent, grasped the situation immediately.

Lily looked up despairingly as the nurse hurried in and took Matt's hand. Meg, in the background, watched anxiously, scarcely daring to move. Oh, please, she prayed inwardly, please let Father be all right...

Lily was silent, her eyes fixed on Matt's face.

But in a few moments, the nurse looked up, her eyes troubled.

'I'm so sorry,' she said gently. 'There was nothing I could do...'

In the days that followed, neighbours came and went, speaking softly, bringing food and flowers, and trying, as best they could, to comfort Lily. The family rallied round, too.

Janet left the children in the care of her mother-in-law, and Ellen travelled back from the hospital in Edinburgh.

Willie spoke little, but he was always running back and forth on messages, doing what he could to help, very much aware that he was now the man of the house.

'If only,' Lily said over and over again. 'If only I'd known he was ill...'

Ellen tried to comfort her, telling her there was nothing she could have done.

Janet prepared meals and gently persuaded Lily to eat.

And Meg sat with her mother when Lily found it hard to sleep, talking about Matt, remembering the kindly things he'd done.

'He was a wonderful father to us,' she said, remembering the toys he'd made for them as children, the way he'd played his fiddle and sung to them.

It all seemed so far away now, Meg thought. Her job seemed to belong to another lifetime, too.

Mr Baillie had written a letter, telling her she need not return immediately after the funeral, and that she should take another week's leave of absence, to be with her mother.

One afternoon, when Lily was sitting quietly, Meg felt she needed some fresh air.

'I'll be all right,' Lily assured her. 'I'll have a sleep. You go for a walk.'

'I won't be long,' Meg promised.

Her footsteps took her to the path alongside the burn, where she and Janet had so often played as children.

It was a walk she always enjoyed, even today, with only a few leaves clinging to the bare branches of the willow trees, and the ground muddy underfoot. She loved the peace and quiet of this spot, which held so many happy memories.

The day was chilly, with only a few weak shafts of winter sunshine breaking through the clouds. Meg shivered, and thrust her hands into the pocket of her jacket.

It was only then that she found the envelope.

In the distress and confusion of the last few days, she'd quite forgotten Alec's letter – the one that she'd tucked into her pocket as she ran for the early afternoon train.

The letter she'd planned to read and enjoy at leisure...

Her spirits rose. Alec's entertaining accounts of his new life always cheered her up. Leaning against the trunk of a tree, she opened the envelope.

My dear Meg...

She could hardly believe what she was reading. She skimmed the pages and the words seemed to leap out at her.

Till now, I've had nothing to offer you... But I would try my best to make you happy and I think I could...

Meg gazed at the letter in astonishment. This was so unlike all the other letters she'd received from Alec that, had it not been for the familiar handwriting, she'd scarcely have believed that it was from the same person. She read it again, carefully, until the truth dawned on her.

Alec loved her – and he was asking her to marry him.

I couldn't say anything before, when my future was so uncertain, he explained. *But I love you, Meg, and I can't imagine life without you. It almost broke my heart to leave you behind without telling you how I feel...*

For a few minutes, she leant against the tree trunk, bewildered and confused. Then she realised that she was shivering, and that the blink of sunlight had gone. She folded the letter and put it back in her pocket.

She'd known, for quite some time now, that she loved Alec. Since he'd gone, though, she'd become confused about her feelings. She'd always thought that he saw her as nothing more than a good friend – and his letters had confirmed that. He'd never so much as hinted that he might be in love with her, too...

It would never work, Meg told herself firmly. How could it? Alec had a new life in India, while everything she held most dear was here. She couldn't leave her family, not now.

But no matter how she tried, she couldn't blank out the memory of Alec's cheerful freckled face...

She would say nothing to anyone, she decided, walking home briskly. Alec's offer was private – between the two of them.

She knew if she mentioned it to Janet or Ellen, they would urge her to accept, and she didn't want to be influenced by anyone.

She sighed. If only things had turned out differently...

'Have you had a nice walk?' Lily greeted her. 'You do look pale – you've been indoors far too much this week. You must get out more.'

'I'm fine.' Meg gave Lily a reassuring pat on the arm. 'Don't you worry.'

Lily smiled.

'Oh, I am glad to have you here, Meg,' she said impulsively. 'I don't know how I could have managed without you.'

Meg's heart felt a little lighter. In her confusion and sadness, and the longing for what might have been, she was pleased to think that she could do something for Lily.

She couldn't help feeling glad that her mother had turned to her. All past tensions were forgotten, as the two women gave strength to each other in the midst of their sorrow.

Later, Meg sat down to write to Alec. She dipped her pen in the inkwell, but she had no idea how to begin.

'Just tell him the truth,' an inner voice reasoned. 'Alec will understand.'

So she started to write. She explained about Matt's death, and how she felt she must look after Lily, as she was the daughter nearest at hand. It was too soon to think of any plans for the future, she told him.

Re-reading the letter, she realised it seemed confused. Not, she thought a little wryly, up to the usual standards of the efficient Miss Barclay, who could write such business-like letters.

But this was a letter from the heart.

Alec, reading it under the Indian sun, sighed. He gazed into the distance. The tray of tea, brought by his bearer, lay untouched beside him.

'You have not drunk your tea, sir,' the old man said. He had a soft spot for the gentle young Scot.

'Later, later,' Alec said absently. He was many miles away, on that favourite walk beside the burn at Pennyglen. How he wished he could be there to comfort and help Meg.

He folded the letter carefully and put it away. Then he rose and went outside, his face serious.

He is not laughing today, the old man thought. Something is wrong. And he took away the tray of tea that Alec had left untouched.

Throughout the months that followed, Meg did her best to help Lily come to terms with

Matt's death. She returned home every weekend, and tried to encourage her mother to go out and visit friends.

Lucille had sent a kindly note, expressing her sympathy. She wrote to Meg, too, but there was no further invitation to join her in the States.

Meg knew in her heart that she had made the right choice, but all the same, she thought wistfully, it would have been nice to travel, to experience a little excitement.

Oh, she enjoyed her job at Baillie's – but sometimes, especially now, the world seemed a very grey sort of place.

Gradually, Lily began to pick up the pieces of her life again. She liked nothing better than a visit to Janet's house, and would come back full of the children's latest antics.

Alice was at school now, and Lily loved to show off her granddaughter's drawings.

'And that wee lad – you should see him. He's into everything you'd need eyes in the back of your head,' she said fondly.

Of course, the house was empty without Matt. Often, Meg would come across some of his possessions – one of his pipes, or his gardening tools – a favourite trowel or fork. Then she'd have a quiet weep, as she thought of the gentle man who'd raised her as his own and been such a caring father.

But Lily was Meg's main concern now. Although she was busy at work and willingly stayed late if needed, her thoughts were constantly at Pennyglen, and she spent as much time there as she could. She even persuaded Lily to travel to Dundee from time to time.

One day they went to visit Alec's mother, who greeted them warmly. 'I've told Meg time and again to bring you over to see me,' she said to Lily.

It wasn't long before Alec's mother brought out her treasured photographs and talked about her family.

Meg smiled, pleased to see the two women getting on so well.

When they said goodbye, Mrs Webster patted Lily on the shoulder.

'You're doing the right thing, my dear – it's very wise of you.'

Meg was puzzled. What was she talking about? She asked Lily, but her mother was giving nothing away.

'It was just an idea I had – nothing definite,' she said vaguely.

Meg couldn't help feeling a little hurt that Lily would confide in a stranger – someone she had only just met – but not in her daughter.

She turned up the collar of her coat, feeling a sudden chill, though it was a sunny day and spring was on the way.

Lily smiled at Meg.

'We've had a fine afternoon,' she said, and

Meg had to acknowledge that the visit had done her mother good.

Over the next few weeks, Lily seemed preoccupied, almost absent-minded. She'd put her glasses down, then forget where she'd laid them. She would go to the shop, then leave something behind. She'd walk out of church on a Sunday, forgetting her gloves or umbrella.

'I'm getting forgetful.' She smiled.

Meg was a little worried. Was Lily ill – or was it just the strain of the past months?

'It'll pass,' Janet said cheerfully one day, when Meg confided her concerns. She lifted a piece of sewing and held it up critically.

'I suppose so,' Meg conceded a little doubtfully. 'That's lovely.'

'I enjoy doing smocking,' Janet told her, as she threaded a needle. 'And it's grand working with such beautiful materials.

'Now don't you worry about Mother,' she went on. 'She's fine.'

But as the spring days lengthened and turned into the long sunny summer months, Meg was still anxious.

One warm June afternoon, she found Lily sitting in Matt's old chair, her chin resting on her hand. It was so unusual for Lily to sit down that she felt quite alarmed.

'Mother, what's wrong? Can't you tell me? You've been worrying over something, I know. It's not just losing Father.

'Are you ill? Is there something badly wrong? I wish you'd tell me. I'd like to help, I really would.'

Lily looked up and smiled at her daughter.

'There's nothing wrong. But I didn't want to say anything until I'd come to a decision.'

'Tell me, please,' Meg begged her.

'Well, I've lived here almost all my life, but it's not the same without your father. I know I'll always miss him. So I've thought about moving.

'There's a little house to rent, near Janet and Rab. I'll not be on top of them, but I'll be there to help with the wee ones. I'll feel useful.' Her voice trailed away and she looked anxiously at Meg.

'I didn't want to tell you till I'd thought about it. I wasn't keeping anything from you, but I knew you'd try to persuade me to stay here.

'You've been so good, looking after me–' she stretched out a hand '–but I want you to have your own life, not feel you need to take care of me all the time.

'Do you understand?' Lily's voice trembled a little.

'But–' Meg tried to take it in. 'Leaving here – won't it be a wrench?'

Lily nodded.

'Of course. But life goes on, and I'm not too old to make a new life.'

'Does Janet know – or Ellen?' Meg

suddenly felt rather shut out. Had it all been discussed without her?

Lily shook her head.

'Rab told me about the house – that it was available. But they left it up to me to decide.

'I really only made up my mind today,' she went on. 'It seems the right thing to do.'

Meg threw her arms around her mother.

'Then I'll help all I can,' she promised. 'I'm good at flittings...'

Lily laughed, wiping away a tear.

'You've been such a help to me already. I don't want you to feel you've been tied down. You've your whole life ahead of you.'

But, Meg thought that evening, as she boarded the train for Dundee, what good was a whole life, with no-one to share it? Janet had Rab and the children, Ellen had her job – and Colin if she wanted him...

She gazed out of the window as the shadows of the day lengthened.

What should she do now? She hated the thought of leaving Pennyglen. Oh, Mother had said there was room for Meg in the new house, a little room that she and Ellen could share.

But the Pennyglen house was home, the only one she'd ever known. And she'd grown up in the village...

That evening, the sense of loss almost became too much for her. She was still coming to terms with the loss of Matt.

Lily was being so brave, so outward-looking. She would soon settle happily in her new home.

But Meg felt rootless, alone and a little lost. Where could she go? Did anyone really need her? She thought of Alec; so many miles away, and longed to see him once again...

Chapter Twelve

Standing in the cottage in Pennyglen, Meg looked around the familiar room and realised, with a pang of regret, that soon it would be home no more.

Oh, she knew that the move was the right thing for Lily to do – already, Mother looked brighter than she had for months.

She was thrilled with her new house, which had two bedrooms, and a good-sized living-room. She liked the modern bathroom, and the little kitchen with the up-to-date gas cooker – it was so efficient, after the old range she'd been used to!

She approved of the scullery with its washing boiler, and the trim little garden which would be 'just enough to manage'.

She'd be near to Janet and Rab and the children, she told Meg happily, and she'd a number of friends in Cupar, too.

Pushing aside her own misgivings, Meg smiled and joined in all the plans for the future.

'We'll all help you with the move,' she told Lily. 'I'm pretty strong when it comes to lifting things, and so's Ellen!'

'After lifting patients, moving the odd

piece of furniture will be no bother at all,' Ellen said.

Meg was trying hard to mend the rift with Ellen. Their close, easy friendship had been strained recently, when they'd argued about Colin.

It was all my fault, Meg thought sadly. It's up to Ellen to decide whether or not to marry Colin. It's none of my business. I was trying to help, but it looked like I was meddling. Why can't I learn to hold my tongue?

Now, Meg was doing her best to repair the damage, but though Ellen was amiable enough when the two girls met, there was little of that uncomplicated companionship that Meg had once taken for granted.

She often caught Ellen looking at her warily, and her sister seldom mentioned Colin.

Meg sighed. If only things could have been different…

But thinking like that wouldn't solve anything. And besides, before the flitting, she had a week's holiday due her. How she was looking forward to it!

Over the years, Meg had become friendly with a small group of her colleagues at Baillie's. Sometimes they'd take a day's outing in a charabanc, or play tennis in the park. In winter, they'd go to the pictures, or to concerts in the Caird Hall.

Dot, one of the group of friends, had put her head round the office door several days before.

'Are you free after work? I've something to ask you.'

'What? Can't you ask me now?' Meg raised her head from her work, a finger marking the paragraph in her shorthand notebook.

Dot shook her head playfully.

'All in good time!'

'All right, I'll see you later.' Meg smiled.

When the two girls met up after work, Dot explained.

'My family have a holiday cottage in Perthshire, just beyond Blairgowrie. Would you like to come up for a week? Go on – we'd have a good time.'

Meg knew and liked Dot's family – they were warm-hearted people who always made visitors feel welcome.

'I'd love to,' she said right away.

She'd been wondering how to spend her holiday, so Dot's invitation couldn't have come at a better time. Life had seemed so quiet since Alec left.

Oh, he still wrote regularly, his chatty and amusing letters describing his life in Calcutta, but he hadn't mentioned his proposal of marriage again. They were letters he might have written to any good friend, Meg thought ruefully.

'It's just a wee cottage – nothing fancy,' Dot added hastily. 'Don't expect to be living in luxury!'

'It sounds wonderful,' Meg assured her.

'Just picking rasps and going for walks and walking to the farm for the milk – nothing thrilling.'

'Are you trying to put me off?' Meg laughed. 'I'm looking forward to it, already!'

Lily was pleased that Meg was to have a holiday, for she knew that her daughter had been rather downcast lately. Oh, if only she could meet some nice young man! But Meg's friendship with Philip had foundered, and now Alec, too, had gone away.

Lily sighed. She worried more about Meg than about any of her other children.

Janet was happily settled, and Ellen was doing well in her job. And Willie, too, who was working in Rab's garage, and staying in digs nearby, was contented. Rab was pleased with the way he was doing.

'Willie's a real asset,' he told Janet one evening. 'Full of schemes and ideas.

'His latest plan is for us to provide radio services – you know, charge people's accumulators for them, fit aerials, that kind of thing. They're already doing it at one of the St Andrews garages.'

'That sounds like a good idea,' Janet said, her head bent over her sewing.

'And he's organised the charabanc trip to

the Braemar Gathering, all by himself. That takes some arranging, but he's got it all worked out.

'One day,' Rab said thoughtfully, 'I could make him a partner.'

'Mother would be so proud.' Janet's eyes shone.

They'd all been such a help and support to her since Matt's death, Lily reflected. And now, just a week before the move, Ellen was coming over from Edinburgh to help. How good they all were!

'I'll stay,' Meg offered. 'Dot would understand.'

Lily shook her head.

'There's no need to do that. You go and enjoy your holiday – you deserve it.

'I'd be glad of a hand the weekend before, but Ellen will be here – she can manage all the heavier things. And Willie will help, too.'

But things seldom go according to plan. The weekend before Meg was due to leave for Perthshire, she returned home to Pennyglen as usual. Ellen was already there.

Meg was folding sheets indoors when she heard her sister cry out in pain. She hurried outside. Ellen, her arms full of washing that she'd just taken off the line, had slipped on a step and fallen awkwardly.

'What's wrong?' Meg knelt down beside her sister.

'It's my arm. I heard a crack...' Ellen's

face was ashen.

'Can you move it?'

'I don't think I can.' Ellen winced.

Gently, Meg helped her to her feet.

'I think I might have broken something.' Ellen tried to smile. 'What a stupid thing to do!'

'Well, you'll be out of action for a bit.' Old Dr Brown looked down at Ellen.

'How long will it take to mend?' Meg asked.

Ellen looked ruefully at the two padded splints and sling that supported her forearm.

'I'm going to be out of action for quite a few weeks,' she said.

'Quite right, Nurse,' the old doctor agreed. He'd known Ellen since she was a child.

'No lifting patients or making beds – for quite some time. In fact, I'd say no work at all for you, for at least six weeks.'

'Oh, dear!' Ellen was near to tears, though she tried to hide her distress.

'Don't worry. You'll be as good as new once it heals,' he consoled her.

'It's not that – it's the move, and everything. It couldn't have happened at a worse time!'

'Now don't you fret,' Dr Brown said kindly. 'Sit back and try not to worry about things.'

'I'll send the district nurse in to see how

you're getting on. She only lives next door, doesn't she? She'll keep a close eye on you.'

'But what about the flitting?' Ellen repeated later that evening. 'I was going to be here for a week to help Mother. And now look at me – I won't be much good. I won't be any help at all.'

'I'll be here,' Meg reassured her. 'I've–' she gave a little gulp '–I've a week's holiday due.'

'I can't let you give up your holiday,' Lily protested. 'You'd planned to go to Blair-gowrie with your friends. You mustn't put it off because of me. I won't let you.'

'Oh, it wasn't anything definite,' Meg fibbed cheerfully. 'Anyway, I told you, I'm very good a lifting things, and now I can prove it to you...'

Looking at Ellen's pale face, Lily had no choice but to agree.

During the week of the flitting, Meg had no time for regrets. If she thought about the long summer days she might have spent idling in a deckchair in the sunshine, she was soon distracted. There was so much to do!

'And I thought I was so orderly,' Lily said in despair, gazing at the overflowing dresser drawers. 'What will I do with all this?'

'I'll help you,' Ellen volunteered. 'At least I can sort the lighter things out.'

While Meg packed boxes, Ellen and Lily

cleared out the dresser drawers and cupboards.

'I'll not put this out,' Lily said firmly, holding up a pin-cushion that Janet had made at school.

'And look at this – it's a postcard you wrote, Ellen, that time you went to stay with Auntie Jean. And here's a photo taken the day we went to Limekilns...'

'Oh, Mother,' Ellen scolded her. 'You are a real hoarder.' But she said it in a kindly way, and looked out an old chocolate box to hold some of Lily's treasures.

All through the week, Meg humped boxes and cleared cupboards and washed and baked and sang cheerfully all the time.

She paused on the landing one day looking at the expensive bouquet of flowers that had arrived for Ellen. *Get well soon, Colin.* That was all the card said.

When she'd read that, Ellen had tossed her head, seemingly quite unmoved.

But late one night, when the sisters were getting ready for bed in the room they shared, Ellen turned to Meg.

'I'm sorry I snapped at you,' she said suddenly.

'Snapped at me? When?' Meg was puzzled.

'A while ago. You asked me about Colin, and I told you to mind your own business.'

'Oh, that! I'd forgotten all about it,' Meg said airily. But she hadn't really forgotten –

the coolness between herself and Ellen that the row had caused had pained her for a long time.

'And you've been so good to me since I broke my arm,' Ellen went on. 'Helping me to dress, and do my hair, and cutting up food for me – not to mention taking care of the flitting. And you've never complained.'

'Oh, it's nothing. I'm glad I'm around to help,' Meg said, though she glowed at Ellen's praise.

'You were right,' Ellen said after a pause.

Meg hesitated.

'About Colin?' she guessed.

Ellen nodded.

'I do miss him, and I wish he was here. I've been – oh, I don't know.

'I sent him away, and we're friends, but nothing more and oh, I've been so stupid.' Tears welled up and Meg put her arms round her sister.

'There, there...' she soothed.

Ellen sat up and mopped her eyes.

'Mind my splint,' she said in her usual brisk way, and the two of them laughed at each other.

But next day, Meg sat down and wrote a letter. Perhaps she *was* interfering, she said to herself, but she couldn't bear to see Ellen unhappy.

All the way to the pillarbox, she wondered if she was making a mistake. She stood in

316

front of the box, undecided, the letter in her hand.

Then she pushed the envelope through the slit in the box, before she had time to change her mind.

Two days later, on a warm summer evening, Ellen was sitting lazily in a wicker chair at the back door. She turned in astonishment when she heard a car drawing up. Colin jumped out and pushed open the gate.

'Ellen – I wanted to see you. You don't mind?' he asked anxiously.

'No–' Ellen was, for her, unusually flustered. 'Thank you for the flowers. It was kind of you.'

'Look, do you feel up to coming for a run? It's such a fine evening, and I've – well, there are things I'd like to say to you.'

Ellen stood up.

'Yes, I'll come,' she agreed.

At that moment, Meg appeared, carrying still more cardboard boxes.

'Let me.' Colin hurried forward to take them from her. 'Where do you want these?'

'Just by the door, please. That's fine.'

Colin's face was serious for a moment.

'Thank you, Meg,' he said.

'Thank you? What for?' Ellen asked suspiciously.

'I can't imagine,' Meg told her blithely. Her heart was light, and she went about her work that evening, humming cheerfully.

It was a busy summer for Meg. What with helping Lily to move, and looking out for Ellen, not to mention coping with a hectic spell at work, she hardly knew where to turn.

And that was no bad thing, she told herself firmly.

'It's a shame you missed your holiday,' her friend Dot said.

'It couldn't be helped.' Meg shrugged.

'I know.' Her friend was thoughtful. 'But you do look a bit peaky.

'Even if you've no more holidays to take, why not come to the cottage for a weekend? Say, in August – harvest time? It's a fine time of year, and if we get a good spell of weather...'

'I'd enjoy that,' Meg said warmly.

She found herself looking forward to the break. Now that Ellen was recovering and Lily was comfortably settled in her little house near Janet, there seemed nothing left for her to do.

Dot's family were welcoming and friendly. The two girls spent much of the weekend at the nearby farm, enjoying the peace of the countryside.

'There's a dance in the village hall this evening,' Dot announced on the Saturday afternoon. 'My brother Bob's coming over – he'll take us in the car.'

When Bob arrived, he proved to be as cheerful and outgoing as the rest of the family – tall and fair-haired with a pleasant, open manner.

Meg didn't know when she'd enjoyed herself so much. She danced every dance, Dot watching approvingly.

As her brother swung Meg off her feet in a reel, she could hardly recognise the brisk and efficient Miss Barclay from the office.

And as for Meg, she felt light-hearted – a different person from the girl of the past few weeks.

It was such a long time since she'd had any fun, she thought. Not since Alec – but she pushed the thought away.

Alec was a good friend, that was all. He could never be anything more...

So why didn't she feel a flutter of excitement when Bob claimed her for the last waltz, and looked down at her with admiration?

'You look lovely,' he said. 'That blue – it suits you.'

Meg smiled back but said nothing.

Later that night, lying in bed, and listening to the wind rustling in the beech trees around the cottage, she wondered why she hadn't felt attracted to Bob. He was good company – and handsome, too.

Maybe I'm growing up – or growing old, she thought. There was a time when she would have felt flattered by the attention of someone as charming as Bob.

But, though she'd enjoyed the evening, there had been nothing more to it than that. With a little sigh, she wondered if she would ever find anyone else as special as Alec...

A few weeks later, Bob wrote her a note, inviting her to go to the pictures with him.

Meg thought about accepting, but after a few minutes, she screwed the letter into a ball and tossed it into the wastepaper basket. She wrote a polite little note in reply, regretting she was busy that evening.

What are you waiting for? she chided herself. Some knight on a white charger? Someone to sweep you off your feet? Someone like Alec...?

She shrugged and turned her mind back to her work.

The letters from Alec continued to arrive, but he avoided personal topics. He described a monsoon, a visit to Darjeeling, the sight of the snow-capped mountains.

Oh, he could write such a good letter, and if Meg sometimes wished for a few words of affection – well, it was her own fault. She had told him that she couldn't accept his proposal, she reminded herself.

One evening, she paid a visit to Alec's mother, as she often did. There was now a warm friendship between the two women.

Tonight, there was an atmosphere of

excitement in the little house.

'Only two weeks and he'll be home!' Mrs Webster exclaimed.

'Alec?' Meg felt a little forlorn. He'd mentioned leave, but he hadn't given her any details. But then, she asked herself, why should he?

'He's lucky to get leave so soon,' his mother said. 'I thought it would be another year at least. But it seems they're putting in new machinery, so it suited them to let him home now.

'I can't wait to see him...'

'I didn't know he was coming back so soon.' Meg kept her tone light. 'I'll see him when he's home, I expect.'

Closing the door behind Meg at the end of the evening, Alec's mother was troubled.

There was something wrong there, she was sure. Meg would never say, and of course Alec hadn't mentioned it. But they'd been such friends before...

Don't interfere, she told herself sternly. They would just have to work it out for themselves.

The following weekend, Meg went back to Pennyglen. She'd promised to clear out a few things that had been left in the garden shed, and take them to a neighbour.

It was strange, being there all alone, without the rest of the family and all their familiar belongings. It wouldn't ever be home again, she realised.

She remembered nostalgically the many happy evenings in the old house, when they'd sung and laughed and told stories. She recalled the smell of home baking, and the rich aroma of a stew bubbling on the stove; the smell of freshly ironed sheets.

She was being silly and sentimental, she scolded herself. It was far better that Lily had moved to the new house – it was easier to look after, and would be snug in winter.

Before she returned to Lily's new house – she found it hard to think of it as home – she decided to take a stroll by the burn.

She'd always loved that walk in early autumn. Now, the days were drawing in, and there was a nip in the air in the mornings.

Soon, the dahlias in the cottage gardens would be blackened by the first frosts, and people would light their fires earlier and think of warming broth and tasty stews.

She wandered along the path by the edge of the burn, then stopped to take a pebble out of her shoe. As she leaned against the trunk of a tree, she heard footsteps.

'Meg! Hello, Meg!' a voice called.

And then he was there, in front of her.

'I've found you! I hoped you'd be here.'

'Alec!'

Meg couldn't believe her eyes. Balanced on one leg to shake the pebble from her shoe, she almost fell forward.

Alec ran towards her and caught her in his arms.

'Oh, Meg – I've missed you. You don't know how much.'

Meg's arms went round his neck.

'Oh, Alec,' she said softly, 'I've missed you, too. So very much...'

He held her close.

'Did you really? I hoped you would feel that way.

'Oh, Meg, could you possibly care for me? You know I'd do anything to make you happy. What I'm trying to say is – I love you.'

Meg looked up at him, her heart full. There was no need for words. Her eyes shone.

'So it's "yes",' he said. 'This time – is your answer "yes"?'

'Oh!' Meg was nearly speechless with happiness. 'You know it is.'

As he kissed her, Meg wondered why she'd ever had the slightest doubt. She couldn't believe that it was possible for everything to come right, just like this, in an instant.

Alec smiled down at her.

'How did you know where to find me?' she asked.

'Your mother told me you'd gone over to Pennyglen. I'd a feeling I'd find you by the burn. We used to walk here, remember?'

'There's just one thing,' Meg said, after a long pause.

'What is it?' Alec said eagerly. 'You know I'd do anything for you. You've just to say.'

'Oh, it's nothing really.' Meg's eyes were teasing, though she tried to keep her tone serious.

'Would you mind – very much – if I put my shoe back on? My foot's getting cold.'

Alec threw back his head and laughed.

'This must be the most unromantic of proposals – you with cold feet already!

'Let me...' He fitted the shoe back on to Meg's foot.

'Like Prince Charming.' Meg smiled.

'And Cinderella,' Alec added.

'And they lived happily ever after,' Meg finished softly.

In the days that followed, Meg was swept along in a whirlwind of congratulations and good wishes.

She and Alec chose her engagement ring in Dundee the following Saturday. Then there was a celebration meal at Alec's home, with Jamie coming home specially, and Alec's mother, rosy-faced with pride and happiness.

'You've picked a fine girl,' she told Alec with mock seriousness.

'Now you see and look after her!'

At the office, Meg's friends clustered round to see her ring, and wondered how they could ever have thought her stiff and standoffish, this dark-eyed girl who was aglow with happiness.

And there were plans to make.

'Lots of people take months to arrange a wedding,' Janet teased. 'But not you!'

Meg, sitting on the floor, surrounded by boxes and tissue paper, looked up and laughed.

'We just wanted to be married quietly,' she said. 'And it was a bit of luck, being able to book our passage so soon. Anyway, I wouldn't want a big wedding.'

Janet smiled.

'Mother would like it,' she said.

'There's still one to go – and it won't be very long, either,' Meg said cryptically.

'Ellen?' Janet was astonished.

'I'm almost certain,' Meg told her happily.

Old Mr Baillie had pretended to be cross when Meg broke the news and handed in her resignation, but the twinkle in his eye gave him away.

'It isn't very much notice,' she said apologetically. 'I'd have liked to give more, but...'

'That young man!' he roared. 'Wait till I have a word with him.

'He takes the best secretary I ever had, and whisks her off to India without a by-your-leave...' Then his face softened and he shook her warmly by the hand.

'I'm pleased for you. I hope you'll be happy.'

On the day that Meg left, she looked around the office where she'd spent so many days. What a lot had happened since she'd started working here.

She was gathering her things together, when Mr Baillie's bell rang.

With a little sigh, she laid down her bag and gloves. She did hope that he wouldn't want to dictate a final letter – not at this late stage. She was anxious to leave promptly tonight to meet Alec – there were things they still had to discuss.

'You wanted me?' She put her head round the door and smiled at her employer.

'It's all right,' he said. 'I don't want to keep you from that young man of yours.' He picked up an envelope from the desk.

'That's for you, from the firm. I wish you all the best and every happiness.'

'May I open it?'

'If you wish.'

The size of the cheque astounded Meg, and she was touched by the little note with its heartfelt good wishes.

'I don't deserve this,' she said, feeling near to tears. 'Thank you.'

'Nonsense,' he roared at her and they smiled at each other, understanding perfectly.

The day of Meg's wedding was fine. 'But it wouldn't really matter if it was pouring with rain,' she said happily, as she drove up to the manse with Willie, smart in his Sunday suit for the occasion.

Meg, dressed in cream lace over georgette, with a matching lace hat, looked wonderfully elegant.

'Like something out of a fashion magazine,' her friend, Dot, said with a sigh.

But Alec, waiting with the minister, hardly noticed how she looked. He saw only Meg's dark eyes, glowing with happiness, and her tender expression.

The ceremony over, everyone gathered in the village hall at Pennyglen. Lily had insisted on that.

'Pennyglen is still home,' she said.

'It always has been,' Meg added softly.

'Besides,' Lily went on, ever practical, 'there'll be lots of people there wanting to wish you well.'

For Meg, the day passed in a whirl, until it was time to go, and she and Alec left for the station in a scatter of confetti.

She looked around her at them all. How she would miss her family!

Janet, Rab by her side, and the two little ones; Ellen, standing by Colin, and shining with a special happiness all her own; Willie, a young man now, with a new confidence he had gained since Rab had taken him into the business.

And Lily, smiling bravely, though Meg knew what it cost her. She knew, only too well, that her mother longed for Matt and wished he had been here to share in the day.

Meg hugged Lily fiercely.

'We'll see you next week,' she promised. She and Alec were spending a few days' honeymoon in the Borders before they sailed for India the following week.

Lily put her arms round Meg. All her girls were dear to her, but Meg – wayward, impetuous, generous, loving Meg – had a special place in her heart.

In the months ahead, whenever Meg sat on the verandah and fanned herself against India's sultry heat, she would remember that day and look at her precious possessions.

There was the beautiful string of pearls, sent by Lucille. Even more precious was the letter Lucille had written.

Meg read it again and again, cherishing the loving words, the good wishes, and the ending: *You will forgive me if I sign myself, on this day of all days, your loving mother, Lucille.*

But still more dear to her was the gift that Lily had given her the night before the wedding.

'But I can't take it, Mother! It belongs to you!' she protested.

'No,' Lily had insisted. 'It's yours now.'

And she'd lifted the pirlie pig from the mantelpiece and handed it to Meg.

'I'd like to think of it belonging to you. I hope you'll never want for anything. Alec's a fine lad and a good provider, as Matt was to me.

'But sometimes, a woman needs to be that little bit independent, to have a few shillings of her own put by, for a little luxury, or to help out where there's need.'

Meg had recalled, then, the way Lily had saved up over the years. The pirlie pig had provided, not for her own wants, but for those of her family.

It had bought new boots for an interview; a length of dress material for a Sunday outfit; even a special outing or two.

Meg knew that Lily had spent very little on herself, and realised that, for her mother, the pirlie pig had been a way of giving. It wasn't just a token of independence – it was a symbol of Lily's loving nature, her un-selfishness.

She'd tried to say something of this to Lily, but her mother had just smiled.

'Take it. It belongs to you now,' she'd said. 'And maybe, one day, you'll hand it on to *your* daughter.'

Meg could hardly speak. She held the pirlie pig in her hands, realising that, in giving this precious gift to her, rather than to Janet or Ellen, Lily was saying plainly,

'You are one of my family.'

'There's a sixpence in it for luck,' Lily said.

'I'll treasure this always,' Meg told her, choking back tears.

'I wanted you to have it,' Lily explained, 'because Matt and I – well, I'm proud of you, and I know he was. You are our daughter.'

'Thank you, Mother,' Meg said, and the words came from an overflowing heart.

The publishers hope that this book has given you enjoyable reading. Large Print Books are especially designed to be as easy to see and hold as possible. If you wish a complete list of our books please ask at your local library or write directly to:

Magna Large Print Books
Magna House, Long Preston,
Skipton, North Yorkshire.
BD23 4ND

This Large Print Book, for people
who cannot read normal print,
is published under the auspices of

THE ULVERSCROFT FOUNDATION

... we hope you have enjoyed this book.
Please think for a moment about those
who have worse eyesight than you ...
and are unable to even read or enjoy
Large Print without great difficulty.

You can help them by sending a
donation, large or small, to:

**The Ulverscroft Foundation,
1, The Green, Bradgate Road,
Anstey, Leicestershire, LE7 7FU,
England.**
or request a copy of our brochure for
more details.

The Foundation will use all donations
to assist those people who are visually
impaired and need special attention
with medical research, diagnosis
and treatment.

Thank you very much for your help.

**Other MAGNA titles
In Large Print**

LYN ANDREWS
A Mother's Love

ANNE BAKER
Keep The Home Fires Burning

ROBERT BARNARD
The Graveyard Position

JOAN JONKER
The Girl From Number 22

DENIS LAW WITH BOB HARRIS
The King

KEN MCCOY
Jacky Boy

NORA ROBERTS
Homeport